ANOTHER DAY, ANOTHER BULLET

ALSO BY NICHOLAS OSBORN

Bullets Trilogy

A Day Late and a Bullet Short

Three Bullets to the Wind

ANOTHER DAY, ANOTHER BULLET

BULLETS TRILOGY BOOK THREE

NICHOLAS OSBORN

WOLFPACK
PUBLISHING
— EST 2013 —

Another Day, Another Bullet
Paperback Edition
Copyright © 2025 by Nicholas Osborn

Wolfpack Publishing
1707 E. Diana Street
Tampa, Florida 33610

www.wolfpackpublishing.com

Paperback ISBN 979-8-89567-071-2
Ebook ISBN 979-8-89567-070-5
LCCN 2025931254

ANOTHER DAY, ANOTHER BULLET

CHAPTER 1

The glorious west Texas sun above was shining down on yet another day in the desert.

It was an insatiable, undeniable force of nature which cast doubt on even the most stoic of souls within such a barren patch of land. A heat that had been endured for generations, inescapable yet somehow admirably unrelenting, caused beads of sweat to pop up one by one until the face of Thomas Hunter was drenched with the only liquid to be seen for miles.

Thomas Hunter was a man who knew to stand upright, look another dead in the eye, and grip a handshake like he was strangling a rattlesnake. Thomas was also a man you could never turn your back on—not even in church. He'd rambled his way through life, bolstered by the wealth of a family legacy unearned by his hands, but he remained ultimately only a man who sought his own best interests.

This afternoon was not unlike any other. Thomas

was completing the only task of the day worth doing, the only reason for stepping outside beneath the brutality cast down onto his skin. Everything he had was built on the interest of who came before him, of what they handed to him. The only thing he'd ever had to do was collect it. Each step forward brought him closer to his livelihood, delivered by hand to his address each and every week.

It was mailbox money.

Thomas was a mere fifty paces beyond his front door, covered in sweat and dreading the walk ahead already. Although it had to be done, he never looked forward to putting even one foot out in the West Texas desert. Dust coated his two thousand dollar full-quill ostrich leather boots with every unwilling step, and if it weren't for the hundreds of dollars worth of shades and beaver fur silverbelly cowboy hat covering his face, that same dust would be floating right on up into his eyes.

The driveway leading to the fifth-wheel camper he called home felt like it went on for miles in such a place. The dually pickup that had towed him out to the middle of nowhere of Sierra Blanca, Texas—less than an hour's drive from the border of Mexico—had taken off the day before on what was supposed to be a grocery run. People couldn't be trusted in this place, or at least not the ones his money could hire. Thomas didn't need to trust anyone. That wasn't his problem, his only real problem was the godforsaken walk to the mailbox that threatened his very existence once a week, on Tuesdays, at around three thirty p.m. to be exact.

Why couldn't they deliver mail in the morning? Thomas allowed the angry thought to wash over him as a distraction from the chore of walking. *Why does it gotta be the hottest damn time of the day?*

It wouldn't do any good to vent to himself, but there wasn't much else he could do other than complain. Thomas put one boot in front of the other, keeping his eyes down as he walked. The driveway, if you could call the winding trail of packed dirt such a thing, snaked its way through swirling sand and around an occasional saguaro cactus jutting into the air. It was a worn path with treasure waiting at its end, promising Thomas a new adventure each week.

The only problem with never lifting your eyes to what's to come is the simple fact of missing out on what's about to happen. People like Thomas were never the kind to be bothered by what would happen to them. Too much money, not enough responsibility, and a self-imposed sense of security were more often than not a cocktail too few could ever order for themselves. Luckily for Thomas, he'd drowned in it all ever since leaving the confines of the other side of the state in deep East Texas.

Maybe it was a bad decision to double up on the six packs the night before, or maybe it was just a lifetime of bad decisions which made him so careless, but Thomas never stood a chance at seeing who was waiting for him at the end of the driveway. As he wiped the sweat from his brow, nudging his aviators to the side to reach his soaked, bushy black eyebrows, he caught sight of a silhouette perched against his mailbox in the distance.

What... he started in his head before the words escaped his tongue. "...the fuck?"

His cursing took only a few seconds to spur the silhouette into action. Thomas watched as the mysterious figure stood up from the mailbox, moved into a wide stance with hands at their hips, then stared right at him. The person was certainly a sight to see, though Thomas couldn't help but think to himself that even the pose had been rehearsed.

"Who the hell are you?" Thomas called out.

Silence was all that came back.

Thomas took a step forward, this time pulling his half-tucked pearl snap shirt up from his waist just high enough to reveal a silver six-shooter with handles to match the snaps of his button-down. Its polished finish made the pistol look like it had never fired a single shot in its lifetime. That didn't stop Thomas from hovering his right hand above his hip like he knew exactly what to do, though.

"Ain't gonna ask again, just gonna get to shooting," Thomas yelled out again. "This is private property, so just know I'm bein' damn nice about this whole thing already."

"It's your fault," a man's booming voice finally answered. "It's all your fault."

"Wouldn't be the first time. You're gonna have to be more specific than that."

The mysterious man took a step forward and Thomas didn't think twice when he followed suit. They weren't close enough to tell one another apart beneath the blinding West Texas sun, but that time would be upon them soon enough.

"My family owned that land for seven generations. My great-great-grandparents on down were buried there. I was supposed to join them in a hole of my own when my time came. Ain't nothing left if it now."

The stranger took another step. Thomas did the same.

"You always blame everyone else for your own damn misfortune?" Thomas knew better than to put up with any kind of tongue-lashing from a man who couldn't even say his own name.

"Just you, is all."

"You know who I am?"

"Don't know your name, but I know you. My whole family knows who you are. You are the one who brought this on us all."

This time, Thomas had heard enough. He took a step forward and watched as the mysterious man in front of him answered in kind. It was a dance that had been done many times before—from high noon in the middle of town to midnight in the middle of an inter-section—and it could only lead to one inevitable ending.

"All I do is point. Those other places, they do all the dirty work. They're the ones who bring in the trucks, the equipment, and as pissed off as you are about it, they're also the ones who write all those checks."

This time, the man standing across from him didn't have anything to say. Thomas knew all too well about the money that circulated his line of work. Once you get caught up in that many zeros, you don't ever tend to look back, or at least not if you know what's best for you. This guy clearly didn't.

"You did cash that check, didn't you?"

"You know I had no choice. They took everything from me."

"And you know they *paid* for what they took. Fair and square. Ain't my fault you accepted a shitty deal."

With the next steps taken by each man in unison, they stood closer than ever before. Just twenty paces away, Thomas stared down the man blocking his path to the mailbox that held his livelihood inside. He was a gangly man, red cheeks hidden behind a bushy beard with dark eyes covered by a greasy baseball cap. His thick denim jeans did little to hide a bow-legged posture, the kind that most develop after a few decades of working harder than their body could take for too many years. Thomas could see in an instant that he was facing down a man who had no problem never walking away from the fight ahead.

"You sicced a group of men on my home when you lifted that rotten, crooked finger of yours. You sit up here alone, telling evil men where to dig on good men's land, pretending you don't go around ruining people's lives. I'm gonna change all that." The man refused to waste so much as a single breath in his explanation. "I'm gonna make sure you don't ever forget what you've caused."

"They were coming for you no matter what. If you can't see that, then you're stupider than most who get the idea to yank that pistol out and point it at me."

"Well, I ain't done it yet."

Thomas took another step to challenge the stranger

in front of him, but the man with no name stayed still. This time, the two had nothing left to say. There was only one thing left to do.

Thomas wasn't surprised at the situation he'd found himself in. It wasn't the first time he'd been forced to stare down the consequences of his work. The work he did for his money was far from difficult. It could bring both riches and despair, all depending on your point of view. Whoever it was standing across from him clearly saw it as the latter rather than the former.

Some call it an exploration company, but Coyote Crude was more than that. It started off as a shell of a business. With an original purpose of funneling money from thousands of acres of his own land through the mineral rights owned by his family, it became something else entirely when more money than he knew what to do with came pouring in. The only idea that made sense was to use it all as a means to make more. It didn't take long before Thomas became the boots on the ground with a mission to leverage tax-delinquent land to grow his empire.

Turns out, not everyone found it amiable to have their land confiscated by some unknown oil baron. Thomas did his best to have empathy for those he affected. Despite his slacking posture, careless demeanor, and smart-ass mouth, he really did feel something deep down for those who couldn't control their own lives.

That didn't stop him from waking up every day and strapping an S&W.44 magnum adorned with pearl handles and a hellish attitude to his hip. Some men just didn't understand what was happening to them, some men could only understand an age-old language only the six-shooter he carried could speak.

The man standing across from Thomas—the one sweating and cussing and aching for a fight—was one of those men.

Thomas removed the aviators from his face and nudged his silver belly down a little lower over his eyes to block the glare. When he finally got bored of the silence that had fallen between them, he decided to get the show started himself.

"I'm gonna get what's inside that mailbox," he started. "One way or another."

The man still didn't say anything. Thomas had no qualms with carrying on.

"I can go through you and get on with my day, or we can walk back together, and I can help you and your family get through these hard times. I don't care much either way."

"You think I'd trust you to help us?" This time, the man found the nerve to do a hell of a lot more than just talk. "The only thing I trust you to do is bleed out into that godforsaken dirt you probably stole just like you did mine, you no good son of a bitch."

Thomas knew what was coming. He squinted his eyes and watched the man hurl off about every obscenity he could think of in his direction. It was as volatile of a countdown as anyone could imagine, but eventually, the man would run out of cuss words and go for his gun.

The West Texas heat sent waves off of both revolvers soon to be called into action. It was hot enough to make a man cowboy-load his gun out of fear for the worst popping off out of nowhere. Thomas and the stranger were in a standoff not seen since the clock struck high noon over the O.K. Corral. Before any hot lead would be fired off, leaving one life snuffed out, the two shared a stare-down that was befitting of the meanest rattlesnakes around.

As each stood waiting for a sign to urge them to draw and gun their opponent down, Thomas watched the man's hand tremble while his own remained frozen in place. It was right then he knew exactly what was about to happen. Before taking a man's life, most would shudder to think what would happen to them. Not just legally, but psychologically, through some innate expectation to be forever changed by the action. To put it simply, Thomas was already a changed man.

The sign that would bring with it the demise of one man's life took the shape of a Chihuahuan raven overhead. Its flapping wings, indistinguishable to the human ear from up in the sky, carried the bird through the heat effortlessly, leaving only a shadow gliding across the sand and rocks below.

Once it had arrived directly above Thomas and the man who'd confronted him, the silhouette raven let out a cry that ushered in a flurry of violence.

Bam.

Thomas was standing still, his hand now gripping the six-shooter at his hip pointed straight ahead. A thin trail of smoke lifted from the end of the barrel, rising in a perfect twisting motion until it passed by Thomas's squinted eyes. He stared without blinking. There was no regret, no pain, not even the depravity that one would expect to push a man to such actions to be found inside him.

The stranger was now perched up on the mailbox he had stopped Thomas from reaching. He leaned heavily to his right, putting all the weight he could on the wooden post of the mailbox driven haphazardly into the sand. Thomas watched as the man's strength continued to fade and his knees grew weaker with every passing second.

There was nothing left to say. Thomas holstered his pistol and allowed himself to slowly walk toward the mailbox, his route still no different than when he'd first left the fifth-wheel. The raven continued its path every bit as unchanged overhead. Forces of nature no different than the dwindling breeze were impossible to change, they could only be dealt with, no matter the outcome.

Thomas finally stopped his stride once he'd reached the mailbox. He stared down at the man clutching his gut, rolling in the dirt, fighting against the throes of death.

"You're gonna die," Thomas said.

Against the grunts coming from below, a ragged voice broke through. "So are you."

A wicked smile stretched across Thomas's face. He lifted his right boot, now covered in a thin layer of dust broken only by the cuff of his pants, and nudged the dying man onto his back. Without hesitation, Thomas placed one boot over his body and stepped across to continue his walk to the mailbox.

There was never any doubt as to how that confrontation would play out. Even then, it didn't make Thomas feel righteous by any means. What sustained him was inside the mailbox, waiting for his own hand to take it once more. No matter the carnage that was left in its wake, it was always there to carry him onward. Thomas wasn't the type to look back. He was more concerned with the path ahead, and it was a path that had taken him far from home.

The steel of the mailbox damn near seared his fingertips when he released the latch on the door to let it fall open. It was a reminder of the toll West Texas took on everything under its sun. When Thomas reached inside, there was an unfamiliar feeling that made him turn his head to the side in confusion. As sweat ran down his brow, just barely missing his eyes, he pulled out the check that brought him out into the heat, but he also pulled out something else.

"What the…" His voice trailed off as he read the second letter in his hand to the tune of the man's dying groans fading away in the background filled with the cries of ravens and swirling dust devils.

My dear Thomas,

We are under attack. The life you've been chasing has taken you too far from where you belong, from those who love you most, and from what you were born to do. Even though you won't admit it to yourself, we both know it's true. We've stood aside as you sought yourself in every manner of dealings. We've heard the rumors of your line of work. We know what you've gotten into and where it's taken you. I bet you didn't expect to even be reading this, ain't that right? I am finally reaching out to tell you it's time to put a stop to it. You are needed here. There are forces gathering outside our doorstep and they want to lay claim to what isn't theirs. We've been fighting them in our own way, as we always have, but it's no longer enough. More are arriving every day it seems, and I fear we might not with-stand much more. If you are reading this, you should know that there isn't much time left. It's time to put aside our disagreements and show that we can still be a family when it matters most. There is too much at stake. If you don't come home, there will be nothing left to come home to.

Love,
Mom

CHAPTER 2

I n the face of oppression and backed by those who stand in its way, it can be easy to believe the impossible is anything but. It's a feeling that can be hard to overcome and even harder to channel, but when the cause is just and the stars align, there are those few who will see each and every struggle through to the end.

Kaya Hunter was one of those few.

She stood up with a straight back and a clenched fist where others knew only to cower down. She stared down all the unfairness in the world that dared show itself in her presence. She had enough fight in her to spare, and she never had a problem showing others what exactly that looked like. Kaya was a warrior like her mother and grandmother before her, but she also took after her ancestors in other ways as well. For better or worse, Kaya was a loner.

The world around her had shown its true colors, and she refused to look the other direction.

Surrounded by chants, posters, and the powerful steps of a thousand others just like her, Kaya marched through the streets of downtown Austin, Texas. A proposed pipeline running through what little of the Reservation they had left in upper East Texas and into Oklahoma brought Kaya and those around her to face down the state capitol, but the fight for what was rightfully theirs had started long ago.

"Justice!" the crowd chanted. "Now! Justice! Now!"

Kaya joined in with her own voice, adding it to what felt like a crowd of thousands swarming through the streets. "JUSTICE!" she screamed as loud as she could. "NOW!"

Their yells came in unison and she felt more empowered with each person who arrived to join in. It wasn't long before Kaya strong-armed her way to the front of the crowd and assumed the position of leading the protest through the streets. She knew the route around the capitol building, and she knew the plan to be sure they were not just seen but heard as well. The United Native Justice nonprofit organization had rallied behind Kaya and put real resources behind her efforts to stop the pipeline legislation being debated inside the doors of the capitol. All that remained was to carry it out.

"Justice!" She continued the chant, this time all by herself, allowing her own holler to echo off the walls around her.

"NOW!" The crowd completed the call with a roar behind her.

This continued for what felt like hours. Kaya led

the protestors through three laps around the route that had been established. Some of the protestors broke off at random to return to their lives, but others joined in when they realized what was happening. By the time the sun had started to fall in the west, Kaya was ready to call the day a success. She'd even started to look forward to a bit of scrolling oh her phone to see just how often their efforts would pop up on her timeline.

Kaya stood tall with long black hair running the length of her back. Her sharp eyes had a way of piercing anything she focused her gaze on, punctuated by broad cheekbones which put an edge to her stare. She wore a worn brown leather jacket fraying from age with fringe that draped down from her elbows. She was youthful but showing signs of experience as she grew closer to the big number thirty. Kaya was a woman who'd seen more of the world than most, and she carried herself as such.

As a golden light of the sinking sun danced across the rooftops in Austin all around them, the protest had started to wind down at a predictably natural pace. Kaya never really did know the word quit, though. She pushed on. They had attracted the attention of more than the passerby's cameras or the local reporters looking for a story. Word had spread of what they were trying to do.

Because people are the way they are, when word spread far enough, that meant some who showed up had their own disagreements with the protestors. They were burly, bearded, and walked like they had a stick jammed right up their ass. Kaya knew their type. She had organized and led more than a dozen similar events and such antagonists almost always found a way to put a damper on everything one way or another.

"Justice!" she continued as the men began to pour into the downtown area, waving indecipherable flags of their own and staring her down behind black sunglasses. Before the crowd at her back could answer her call, the men arriving at the capitol mocked it in a way only they could.

"Law!" a lone man shouted.

"ORDER!" the rest of the men shouted.

"Law!" the first one called again before being met with the same response.

"ORDER!"

Kaya did what she could to ignore them. They were so close to finishing for the day, and dealing with the likes of those men was damn close to the last thing on her list of things she wanted to do. One foot in front of the other, and one fist raised into the air, Kaya pushed on. She watched as her supporters dwindled even faster now that there was opposition to their march gathering around.

"Justice!" she called again, but this time was met with only laughs from the puff-chested men who had shown up simply to give them all a hard time.

"You wouldn't know about law and order if it smashed into your face and broke that big ass squaw nose, would you?"

Kaya turned to her right to see a bald man trying his best to rock a handlebar mustache and way-too-small sunglasses perched on top of his nose. He was in his fifties, donned a leather vest, and had sausages for fingers that were already balled into a fist in both hands. It didn't take long to see that the man was looking for a fight, too. Luckily for him, he'd met his match, even if he hadn't realized it yet.

Kaya wasn't a stranger to fighting for what she believed in. Whether it was the schoolyard bully who'd given her brother a shiner on the playground when they were kids, or the mustachioed man who didn't deserve the air he sucked into his lungs coming at her, she never knew what it was like to back down.

Her broad shoulders squared up with the latest man who'd set out to test her. She widened her stance and braced herself for what surely was to come. Chants came and went around her, but the man kept approaching. A circle was forming around them. Her only focus was the adrenaline surging through her chest and into her right arm, all the way down to her fingertips. She'd be damned if she was going to allow him to utter one more word without consequence.

The antagonizer pushed his way into Kaya's personal space on purpose, doing his best to set her on edge. She smiled instead. With a furrowed brow, the man let loose what he really felt about their demonstration without a single word. The look in his eye said everything.

"You—"

Pop.

Kaya's fist slammed into his nose, sending a splatter of blood in every direction. The man stumbled back, smeared the dripping red blood from his nose into his mustache, and gritted his teeth. Before he could make another move, Kaya was directly on top of him.

"Justice!" The chants cried out all around as Kaya reared back her fist while on top of the man.

Pop.

"Now!" They continued after her first strike landed right on his nose again, effectively snapping it to the side and leaving the man dumbfounded.

Kaya rained down her fists on the man in a flurry of punches that were almost too fast to see with the naked eye. She screamed louder with each landing blow until her voice was broken only by sporadic inhales she didn't want to take.

"Justice!"

Pop.

"Now!"

Pop.

Kaya let out a shrill cry that pierced the ears of everyone in downtown Austin. The protestors watched on in shock as one of their own organizers lost control and beat the man senseless. Those who had arrived with him had other ideas, though. Unwilling to draw the ruthless attention of the woman perched on top of the stupidest among them, the other antagonists began to pretend they didn't even know a protest was underway.

Crimson spots dotted Kaya's face as she stared with wild eyes at the results of her own rage. Every law enforcement entity in Austin would say it wasn't warranted, but she knew he'd damn sure earned every hit that found its mark. She straddled the man who gasped for air between blows. Her knees squeezed into his ribs, making it that much harder to breathe. As her fists rained down, Kaya no longer considered when or even if she should stop what she was doing. What was set in motion had become who she was. There was no stopping it.

Red was all she could see. It was blood and fury, swirling inside the tunnel vision that had set in. The color was calming, despite her burning muscles and split knuckles cracking against the cheekbones of the man who'd dared insult her. Maybe on any other day, she would've been able to find the patience, or at least the restraint, to not bash his head in. Today was different though.

The protest she'd helped lead was about more than just the generations-old fight to reclaim what belonged to her people. It was the anniversary of when she'd been kicked out of her own family's household. Her anti-authoritarian perspective had extended to her own mother just a little too far one day, and when one regretful remark led to another, she'd found herself shoving everything she could call hers into a bag and never looking back. She hadn't spoken to anyone since, and it was on her mind more than she cared to admit.

"Stop!" A cry came out from behind Kaya, and just like that, she snapped out of her violence-induced trance. "You're gonna kill the guy!"

"What the..." she whispered to herself before realizing what she just did.

The man below her gurgled and gasped for oxygen, spitting out thick blood and white chunks of teeth as his eyes rolled around in his head. There wasn't much recognizable on him other than the red-stained mustache. Kaya stared with a blank expression and allowed the pain coursing through her fists and forearms to bring her back to reality.

Before she could bring herself to stand up, a protestor leaped headfirst into her and tackled Kaya from the man. They rolled into the pavement together until landing hard against the concrete curb with a grunt.

"What were you thinking?"

"I wasn't," she said to whoever had shoved her from the jerk she'd faced down. "I don't know what happened."

"Well, they do." The man's voice was discerning, almost like he cared for Kaya more than the protest he was trying to save.

When she saw what the man was talking about, her stomach sank and a lump formed in her throat. No longer was she worrying about the pain in her knuckles, nor the life of the one she had just beaten senseless, she was worried about the dozens of cell phones that were trained on her every move.

"Shit," she muttered.

"Half of those are already live."

"That isn't helping any," Kaya said as she turned her attention toward the man who had stopped her before there was no coming back from her own actions. "Who are you?"

"Adam," he answered. "And I'm your guardian angel."

With those words, he stood up from the pavement and held his arms out to his side. "This is what happens when you stand on the side of history with oppressors, thieves, and tyrants. You want content for your followers? You want your socials to be worthwhile? Then look no further than the men inside that building," he shouted with a finger directed right at the capitol. "The House bill being voted on right now will force the South Central Pipeline through lands they do not own. They need to hear what they are doing is wrong. If they cannot hear us in the street, they will hear us online."

He turned to Kaya and gave her a wink. "If you got people watching, maybe they could at least hear the message you were fighting for."

"Thank you," Kaya mouthed, unable to bring herself to speak aloud.

She picked herself up off the ground and watched in dismay at what the protest had turned into. It was chaos. Despite Adam's best efforts, she knew the message that brought them all into the streets would be lost in the flurry of her own fists. Legislators would write them off for it as they always did, and she shuddered to think of the comment section of every video that was undoubtedly flooding every social media platform. Kaya allowed her head to fall in shame.

She stood in silence, surrounded by both those who had her back and those who wanted nothing more than her to fail. She wanted to escape. She wanted to run in the other direction, but she knew that wasn't an option.

Austin returned to its natural state all around her. Cars full of impatient drivers, pedestrians hurrying back and forth, and sirens blaring through every red light showed the city's true colors. As the shuffle of people scattering the area continued, Kaya felt a sense of loneliness wash over her. She thought of Adam, and of how her people would be impacted by yet another government overreach through the South Central Pipeline. It was almost more than she could handle.

Almost.

Kaya didn't know how to quit. The fight itself was who she was. With the protest all but dissolved against a backdrop of the setting sun casting an orange glow along the hedges lining the way to the capitol building, Kaya swallowed her pride. Just as she lifted her head to push forward again, a hand grasped her shoulder. When she turned to see who it was, she was face-to-face with something she would have never expected. It was a letter.

The envelope was pushed into her chest by a faceless protestor she didn't recognize, who disappeared as quickly as they had arrived. Before she knew it, she was left alone again, this time staring at something that cut deeper than anything she had just experienced. It wasn't the words that were scratched on the front of the envelope, or even its untimely delivery, it was the handwriting. She would know it anywhere.

With a gentle tear of the envelope, she pulled out a handwritten note that had been addressed directly to her. Amid the bustling swarm of Austinites buzzing in every direction she looked, Kaya stared at the note and felt more lonely than ever.

My dear Kaya,

We are under attack. Your heart has taken you from us, in search of a better life not for yourself, but for those who look like you. You've always been the honorable one, the one who made the world in your own image instead of succumbing to its worst ways. The world has reached our doorstep, however, and it has brought with it our own destruction. You know I have always been on your side, even when no one else was. I still am. It's time that you returned to stand by our side, though. We've been doing our best to withstand those who are after us, as we always have. More are coming as I write this. We are running out of time. I have no other choice but to beg that you put aside the differences that drove us all apart and help us with our own fight. It's time for you to come home. If you don't, there will no longer be a home to come to.

Love,
Dad

CHAPTER 3

"They're dead! My whole damn herd gone overnight. My grandad's dad started that bloodline. Don't you understand? Those cattle have carried my family for generations and they ain't coming back. They ain't ever coming back!"

The man's booming voice echoed through the makeshift courthouse located at the Transportation Center in downtown Jefferson. He wore a sweat-stained mesh back cap and overalls tucked into muddy boots. His gray stubble looked as white as snow beneath a cowboy's manure-covered boot pressed against his beet-red face as he yelled at no one in particular.

"I tried to be nice about it," the man continued. "Prayed on it even. What's attacking my poor cows ain't anything that listens to God, though. At least not the one I'm prayin' to."

The development organization sat quietly in each of the seven seats across the folding plastic table, holding outdated microphones and notepads filled with scratch and doodles. Each one showed a face of concern, but behind their glossed-over eyes, they were each a hundred miles away in their own world.

The man speaking was one known all through town to have a particular brand of imagination. He was not stupid. He was well read, and he was unwilling to back down from anyone. The only problem, as was so often the case, was the scent of liquor that escaped on the breath of the man named Bill *Billy* Boyd.

"I ain't never seen bites like that outta any flesh, and I've seen firsthand what a gator from south of Slidell, Louisiana, can do to a man. Whatever is left of their bodies is so torn to shreds you can't make hide nor hair out of it," continued Billy. "I won't even let my dogs out at night. They're too damn scared!"

"Thirty more seconds, Billy," interjected the development organization's senior member, Mark Anderson, the longtime local feed store owner who sat hunched over on the lefternmost seat at the table. "Two minutes of public comment is all we're allowed to give."

"I've tried the city council and the sheriff's department. If you all don't see how this is gonna impact the local businesses in the area, there ain't much else I can do. We're too small of a community, I'm telling you, this is all of our problem. There's something out in those godforsaken woods."

"That's time, Billy, I'm sorry," the attending Mayor Walker cut in with a gentleness to his voice that had not been found in Mark's. Mayor Walker was a heavyset man with a bald head and sports coat with sleeves just a few inches too short. His posture alone showed that this was most likely the most exciting part of his day. "Moving on to our consent agenda."

"Actually, there was one other person who signed up for public comment," said one of the board members for the development organization, Tonya Whitehouse, one of the newest members and the sole woman at the table.

"There was?"

"Cassidy," announced Tonya to the crowd of five people sitting at the other side of the room in chairs, most likely pulled from the waiting area in the next room over. "I don't have a last name."

"Well, actually," a voice came from the back row of chairs. "That is my last name. I am the last known living descendant of the infamous outlaw Butch Cassidy. What I lack in his penchant for criminality, I more than make up for with his undeniably revolutionary vision."

Silence fell over the temporary boardroom. Cassidy stood up from his seat with black pointed leather cowboy boots, skin-tight black denim jeans pulled down neatly to cover each finely stitched boot shaft, and a striped pearl snap tucked neatly behind an ostrich leather belt. Two long, perfectly positioned braids draped down his chest, punctuating the black eyes that Cassidy used to stare down every individual board member at the regularly held meeting.

Cassidy took a step forward through the rows of mostly empty seating.

"Let me take a step back. Good evening to each of

you. My sincerest gratitude goes out to you all for your dedication, for spending your valuable time working tirelessly to improve this beloved community," Cassidy laid the charm on thick. "It is with great pleasure and humility that I stand before y'all today."

"Two minutes, Cassidy," said Mark. "Just like everyone else."

"Consider this an introduction," continued Cassidy without missing a beat. "As you'll see, later in this very meeting, there is an action item I will be presenting that will require all of you to step up in ways you have never imagined before."

Cassidy took another step forward.

"What you consider tonight will be the most important initiative to ever find its way within the city limits of Jefferson. I can promise you that."

Then another.

"It will change all our lives for the better. It will place our community here at the forefront of the minds of Texans, of Americans, all over."

And another.

"It will be a game changer, through and through."

An awkward silence followed. Each of the board members turned their heads and tried to steal a glance at one another. Mayor Walker caught a sigh from Mark and his eyebrow raised before he could stop it. Mark was dead-faced like he hadn't heard a single sentence of what Cassidy had just said. Tonya was scanning every face in the room, hoping to find a reaction worth seeing.

Daniel Coleman, the young man to the right of Mayor Walker, was the only one who seemed to welcome Cassidy's introduction with apparent excitement. Daniel had leaned forward in his seat, smiling from ear to ear. His eyes were locked on Cassidy. Eyes that held wonder to their core. A heart that had searched for every single word that had been spoken to him.

Cassidy was no fool. He knew what to say for those who believed him, and for those who never would. He opened his arms wide and showcased the slightest of bows to admonish his time and allow the proceedings to continue.

"It's...uh...good to have you here with us." Mayor Walker tried his best to catch up. "I'm sure we are all eager for what you have to say."

"Consent agenda," Mark chimed in.

"Right," Mayor Walker said.

Cassidy would not allow his presence, however strange, to go unnoticed. Instead of returning to his seat, he simply stayed right where he was. He stood in front of the few people who decided to mosey in and find an empty seat in the audience, facing the board members without breaking eye contact. The economic development organization carried on with their routine meeting. They cast votes beneath their fluorescent lighting and engaged in halfhearted discussions, knowing they could do nothing more than encourage those with real money to bring it to their town. Cassidy stood motionless, watching without fail, the entire time.

It was about ninety minutes of mundane business as usual before action item number seven came up for discussion. Without missing a beat, Cassidy let his arms fall to his side and smiled once again.

"Up for discussion, the approval of a contract with Longabaugh Builders in the amount of..." Mayor Walker's voice trailed off as he stared at the agenda in his hands. "I'm sorry. Is this right, Tonya?"

"Yes sir," her response came immediately.

"In the amount of fifty million five hundred thousand dollars, presented by—"

"—Cassidy, my good sir." The man in black spoke up once again. "As I was saying, what I bring is more than just some contract. What I am here to present is a future for the community, and it is I alone who can make it happen. Well, alongside my longtime business associates Longabaugh Builders, of course."

Cassidy lifted a boot and began pacing from side to side as he unleashed his speech to the board members. "What do you think about when you think of a better future? Do you think of money? Do you think of growth? What I offer is so much more than that. Some may try to sell you on the wealth of luxury rooms, as if your community has the disposable income for such expenses. Some may try to sell you on the excitement of theme parks, as if your community has the time to spare. All while others promise riches for industry investments, from coal to gas and everything in between, as if you don't have work as it is."

Cassidy stopped in front of Mayor Walker and held eye contact with him. "The contract that is offered tonight will solve every single problem you have discussed tonight, and every other night as well. It will bring real estate, entertainment, and industry to your doorstep. With those in your back pocket, the community will once again know success not seen since the city's port was among the most popular in the state in the mid-1800s."

"What exactly are you talking about, Mr. Cassidy?"

"Just Cassidy, please," the man answered Mayor Walker with a gentle expression. "I'm talking about economic expansion, sir."

"With this Longabaugh Builders company? You're gonna need to give the board here a little more information to go on. Do they want to build a building, open up some jobs?"

Cassidy produced an aging, yellow parchment from a place on his body that no one truly got a good enough glimpse of. He waved it in the air briefly before speaking up.

"This is a deed to land no further than a few miles away. Not just a few acres, but hundreds. Enough land to build each of those industries five times over. What I ask for tonight—what I am willing to beg for—is a chance to save each and every one of you. You need only to give a thumbs up to the economic plan provided in the one hundred and fifty-page document included in my proposal, tailored specifically to your community alongside Longabaugh Builders."

Mayor Walker quickly thumbed the pages of the proposal. As each page turned, his eyes got bigger and the page flipping got slower. The look on his face told Cassidy he didn't believe what he was looking at. It was just the reaction he was hoping for.

"This is too good to be true," Mayor Walker finally said.

"Do you not deserve a shot at success? A shot at building the city of Jefferson back to what it once was?" Cassidy asked with genuine sincerity laced in his voice. "I know this great city once stood as the sixth largest in the state. The port was your lifeblood, delivering a legacy to your doorstep that is still felt to this very day. It is our duty to uphold this legacy. Is it not?"

"What the hell do you know about legacy, boy?" the old man Mark shot back with upturned lips. "I ain't never met you in my life. Now you prance in here and try to tell us you're some kind of savior? I only know one savior, and that's the man upstairs. It sure ain't you."

"Would you just give him a damn chance?" Daniel said.

"For that matter, what do you even know? I been on this board longer than you been alive, little Danny."

"It's Daniel. You call me that again, and you won't be sitting there much longer, old man."

"Simmer down now, you two," Mayor Walker cut them off.

"This right here is what we cannot afford to do any longer," said Cassidy. "Mark represents the empty historic downtown, the bank accounts dangerously close to zero, and the population dwindling to nothing. His way of thinking has put us here. What I am offering is a solution. It won't be pretty. It won't be easy. But it will work."

One awkward minute turned to ten before anyone else dared to say a word. Each of the board members scrolled through the packet of papers thrust into their lap—except for Mark. The feed store owner had seen more than his share of swindlers in the day, and he refused to be sold on a lie.

The rattling HVAC of the old building served as the backdrop to their reading, broken up only by the occasional cough of those waiting patiently. It was a mundane building to a momentous decision.

The only problem—Cassidy was not standing in front of dreamers. He was standing in front of defeatists. Backing down was who they were.

"We thank you for your time, Cassidy." Mayor Walker finally spoke up. "I'm going to make a motion to table the item until a further meeting so that we can all get out of here at a decent hour. Do I have a motion?"

Cassidy watched helplessly as a thick-bearded man who never looked up from his packet wasted no time in raising his right hand into the air.

"I have a motion by Mr. Jones. Second?"

This was the moment Mark had been waiting for. His right hand was raised before the mayor could even finish his sentence. His face unchanged from the very moment Cassidy had first introduced himself.

"You know what? He's right." Daniel was trembling with rage from his fingertips pushed firmly into the plastic folding table, to his tapping boots against the tile floor. "This kind of thing always happens. We won't talk about it at some other meeting. We never do!"

"You sit there and shut your mouth," Mark shot back.

"You know it's true. If I didn't know any better, I'd say you wanted this town to go broke."

"I been here since you wasn't nothing but a twinkle in your daddy's nutsack, Daniel. I ain't gonna hear another word outta you."

"You're going to hear a hell of a lot more than a word, you son of a bitch."

The boiling point had come much quicker than Cassidy had anticipated, but he was never one to miss out on a perfectly opportune moment. He knew just what to do. All it would take was the slightest nudge. Even the most unstable of men could find their footing if the situation was outrageous enough.

"I have heard good things about Marshall, or even Karnack, you know. Maybe one of those cities would be a little more open to what I have to offer," Cassidy spoke up without turning to leave. Instead, he allowed his gaze to drift to the tops of his eyes and inspected the uproar that was sure to come.

"You see that? We ain't got time for another meeting. It's tens of millions of dollars. What is there to say no to?" This time Daniel turned to the crowd. "Do y'all really want another year going broke? Or do you want a chance to make some real money for once? This could be just what Jefferson needs to get put back on the map."

"I'll be sure it is *exactly* what Jefferson needs, my dear boy," Cassidy chimed in. "Cross my heart."

"If I have to sit here and listen to one more lie slither outta that spoiled silver tongue of yours," Mark pointed his finger at Cassidy.

Without hesitation, Cassidy's lips turned up into a shit-eating grin.

"You'll what?" Daniel answered for him.

The room fell silent once again. Not a single person attending the meeting took so much as a breath of oxygen from the room as they waited for what was going to happen next. It was at this moment that Cassidy did the most unusual thing yet—he took a bow.

Just as he allowed his upper half to tilt over, Mark jumped to his feet and shoved his folding chair backward with a loud screech. In the blink of an eye, there was an old stainless S&W revolver in Mark's hand, but he wasn't alone. Refusing to react the same, Daniel had stayed right where he was seated, but holding a black polymer Glock 19, aimed right at Mark's forehead. The standoff had simply blinked into existence. Before anyone knew any better, the room was staring down a shootout.

Cassidy released his bow and stood upright again. He threw his arms out, like an aging grandfather waiting to embrace his first grandchild and let out an overwhelming sigh of relief.

"It does my heart good to see this town willing to fight for what they believe in," Cassidy said. "Throw out my business proposal, or keep it as it is, all I really ask is for you to put that fight you got inside you to better use. My partners and I are willing to put $50.5 million where our mouth is. You just need to go ahead and accept that. The sooner you do, the sooner we can all figure out how to spend it."

Mayor Walker clapped his hands and sat upright in

the folding chair he was spilling over either side of. "Instead of shootin', let's try votin'," he told both Mark and Daniel.

"Do I have a motion to approve as presented?"

There was no movement or words given for a few fateful seconds. The gun in Mark's hand began to tremble slightly, while Daniel's remained steady. Cassidy darted his eyes back and forth to each side of the room with every ticking second. One of the men would back down eventually. It was only a matter of when. The tremble in Mark's veiny, paper-thin-skinned hand grew stronger, and the barrel of the revolver soon fell.

Cassidy watched as two things happened in rather rapid succession. Mark tossed the revolver down onto the plastic table and slammed his butt back down into the seat without another word. Daniel did no such thing. Instead, he lifted his right hand, keeping the barrel of the Glock in his hand trained on Mark the entire time.

"I have a motion to approve as presented by Daniel," Mayor Walker said before glancing to each side of the table. Much to his surprise, he and everyone in attendance reacted with a drop of a jaw as Tonya lifted her hand.

"I second." She spoke with a seriousness that had never found its way into her voice before.

"I have a second," said Mayor Walker, sounding more surprised by the second. "All in favor?"

Cassidy watched with glee lighting up in his black eyes as six hands rose into the air. Mayor Walker followed with a quick scribble on a piece of paper in front of him before calling out into the room again.

"Oppose?"

This time, Cassidy stood still and focused his gaze on the old man. Although Mark had given up on the fight against Daniel, a fight he would've been more than glad to take on thirty years ago, he still didn't know what the word quit was. He raised his hand, never lifting his eyes from the chipped tile floor at his feet.

"Six to one," Mayor Walker acknowledged. "The motion passes. At our next meeting, we will allocate the approved funding of $50.5 million for economic development under the direction of Longabaugh Builders and one Mr. Cassidy."

Daniel's face lit up like the Fourth. Cassidy watched him approach the board members' table like he was starstruck. There was some shuffling by the handful of people sitting in the room as they leaned in to whisper halfhearted gossip at the vote. But most importantly, the man who'd come to position himself as their city's savior watched as the two pistols that had been drawn in during the meeting found their way back to their holster.

Cassidy's walk to the table with an outstretched arm to shake the hands of each of the six voting members was cut short, though. A cord stretched across the room to power the microphones that we never needed to begin with, hooked itself on the right black leather cowboy boot of Cassidy's. He went down hard, but popped up just as quickly, brushing himself off as he did.

"Sorry about that," he said while nudging his boot against the tile as if the entire room didn't just see him bust his ass. "Need to get that looked at. Mayor, take a note."

Cassidy completed his handshakes to each other six members who'd approved, conveniently passing by Mark, the sole vote in opposition of him. He walked back to the center of the room with calculated steps and direct eye contact. Nothing was ever too far out of place for his own conniving ways. It was just a matter of how hard he'd work to make what he wanted a reality.

Without another word, he backed his way to the edge of the room, spun around in place, and walked out of the meeting.

CHAPTER 4

The Cowboy Corral wasn't just a bar. It was a cigarette smoke-stained, pink and blue neon-lit, rundown hole-in-the-wall place called home to the same crowd just about every night. Nestled at the end of a winding dirt driveway in the middle of the piney woods at the edge of Marion County, the joint had a reputation for not actually being open to the public despite the open sign hung on the door. It was all about who you knew.

Thomas Hunter didn't know anyone.

He wore the most expensive pair of boots the bar had ever seen with a beaver pelt cowboy hat that didn't match the beat-up straw hats everyone else seemed to prefer. Nonetheless, he was perched on a stool at the end of the bar like he belonged there.

He'd nursed a handful of beers over the last couple hours in a halfhearted attempt to brace himself for what was sure to come. The letter that roped him back into a mess of a situation with his family was tucked neatly inside a denim jacket he didn't need to be wearing, considering the humidity outside. It wasn't the weather that made him wear the jacket, though, it was what else was tucked beneath its cover. His trusted six-shooter was pushed firmly against his hip, just in case.

"Can you believe they wanted to kill our chance at finally getting some steady work around this place?"

"That's all those people in Austin care about, making sure we can't support ourselves."

"All we're tryna do is feed our family. Why can't they see that?"

Thomas took another sip of lukewarm beer as the conversation bounced back and forth between four visibly disparaged men crowding a stand-up table wedged into a corner behind him. The clatter of balls from the pool tables served as a backdrop in the one bar in Texas that didn't play any sad country songs to accompany all the drinking going on.

"That pipeline would have given us work for years. Now they're talking about shuttin' it back down until they get it figured out."

"You know what that means."

"It means we ain't getting shit."

"We shoulda went down there and showed 'em what was comin' their way."

"I heard some fellas did," one of the men answered with a drop in his voice. "I heard one guy got his face caved in by some crazy broad out there."

Thomas didn't set out to eavesdrop, but the opportunity sure as heck presented itself regardless. He thought about the pipeline they were discussing and knew he had two cents of his own to chime in. After another sip, he decided against it.

"It's all over online, some guy went live when it was happening. That bitch was out of her mind. All the guy did was try to talk to her and she just lost it."

"I wonder if the cops got her yet?"

"They need to put a bullet in her, teach those assholes a lesson they won't forget."

Thomas let out a sigh. Whatever they were describing sounded a little too familiar to him. This time, he couldn't help himself. With a gentle kick from his boot to spin himself around in the stool, Thomas turned to see the burly men clutching half-empty bottles of beer with red faces and disheveled clothes. They weren't the kind of men any sane person would try to pick a fight with.

Thomas shouldered his way into their huddle without so much as a passing smile. He lifted his beer up to check how much was left before pushing it to his lips and polishing it off. Before any of the men could ask what was happening, Thomas went ahead and saved them the effort.

"Wanna show me that video? I just need to check something real quick," Thomas said.

The man on his right wasted no time in whipping out his phone with a big smile washing over his face. It took just a few seconds before the bright light from the screen was shoved into Thomas's face. A video was playing of a woman straddling a man in the middle of a street in downtown Austin, raining down punches amid a splatter of red. There were screams and chants in the background, letting Thomas know it was some kind of protest without a doubt. When the camera angle moved, Thomas squinted his eyes to get a better look.

"I thought so," he said to no one in particular.

He took the empty bottle of beer in his right hand and smashed it against the cheekbone of the man holding the phone in the blink of an eye.

The first man went down like a fly. He landed hard on the shattered glass of the bottle, adding a few more scrapes and cuts to his face. As blood rushed out onto the floorboard of the Cowboy Corral, a frenzy was just getting started.

Thomas was holding the one piece of glass that was still intact from his bottle. He quickly turned his attention to the man on his left and launched the razor-sharp chunk of bottle at his face as hard as he could possibly muster. The shards cut into his face but did nothing to stop the man's charge right into Thomas's stomach. He lifted Thomas up into the air, tossing both of their cowboy hats to the ground in unison, before the crack in his back rang out from being thrown to the ground. Thomas rolled to his side and tried to catch his breath but was met only with the hard wooden soles of leather cowboy boots stomping down everywhere he turned.

One boot took a little too long to pull back, however, giving Thomas just the chance he needed to grab hold of it. With a single yank, one of the men went tumbling over. Thomas popped back up in a heartbeat, lifted his fists, and braced for an onslaught he knew was coming.

"I don't take kindly to that kind of talk," he said

through a bloody mouth and watery eyes from the fight already. "Ain't very becoming of a man."

"The hell do you know!" A cry came that was followed up immediately with a fist aimed at Thomas's face.

A quick duck and a hook to the gut put a stop to that would-be attacker. Thomas spat out a bit of blood and returned to his stance, fists up and feet wide, ready to take on the next one. His chest heaved frantically, but his focus stayed razor sharp. It wasn't his first bar fight by any means.

Boom.

A shotgun blasted out inside the bar, and everyone inside turned to see where it came from with far less panic than they were rightfully owed. The three-hundred-pound man who had been serving drinks with a half-assed smile was now holding a pump 12-gauge shotgun aimed at a conveniently placed hole in the ceiling just overhead. What Thomas saw was the look of a man whose livelihood was being messed with, and he knew they were all in trouble. The neons flickered and hummed in the silence that followed until the groans of men picking themself up off the floor broke through.

There wasn't much of a fight left to be had, but Thomas wasn't done with them still. He dropped his fists and lifted his finger to point at those who ran their mouths just a little too much this time. Sometimes, afterall, an education was the best thing you could give a man.

"Next time you want to talk that dumb shit again, maybe you'll think of me. Hell, maybe I'll be standing behind you again and we can go through this whole mess all over," he explained, wagging his finger through it all. "There are people in this world who are trying to help others, and just because they ain't helpin' *you*, don't make them bad people."

"You can take that preachin' outside with the rest of this mess, you hear me?" The bartender had already had enough. He wasn't interested in any lessons that Thomas was keen on giving.

"I usually don't do this." Thomas turned his attention to the owner of the establishment he had just caused a ruckus in. He reached inside his jacket and pulled out a wad of rolled-up cash. He took a second to cut it in half and dropped it on the bar next to a batch of empty bottles. The hundred-dollar bills spread out across the wooden top, soaking up spilled beer as they fell. "For the hassle."

The bartender stared at him and squinted. After a few seconds, he slowly pulled down on the pump of the shotgun and shoved it forward to chamber a new round. He didn't say anything.

Thomas took the hint and groaned. He dropped the other half of the cash down on the same spot and watched as the bartender lowered the shotgun in response. "For your discretion," said Thomas with a wink.

As he nudged aside a flipped-over barstool with his boot and stepped over a long-haired, bearded man in his forties still trying to stop the bleeding from a gash in his cheek, Thomas surveyed the damage. Sometimes, he felt bad for causing a scene. It was admittedly something he was prone to do from time to time. This time, he didn't. There was no backing down from that fight, not after what he saw on that man's phone.

There was undoubtedly another fight ahead of him, but that would have to wait. The trip from West Texas wasn't an easy one. It had taken hours to make it as far as he did, and even though he'd make it to where he needed to be within the hour, he couldn't help but wish he had more time.

The letter written by his mom had guilt-tripped him just enough to make the long drive. If he was being honest with himself, even he didn't know what good it would do. Whoever was going after them didn't seem to have any problems with him. He could've just as easily tossed the letter into the trash and continued on with his life. Something deep down was tugging at him though, telling him he shouldn't ignore the calls for help from his own mom. If it was bad enough for her to reach back out to him after what they had gone through, it had to be serious.

Thomas exited the Cowboy Corral on foot and with all of his teeth in his head, which was a lot more than some of the other guys he'd left behind could say. Although he wouldn't admit it to anyone, his bones were sore after the fight. His rough and rowdy ways had started to catch up to him. More often than not, he'd relied on the pistol at his hip to do all the fighting. It had been too long since his knuckles felt that familiar sting of striking bone and flesh.

When he was out of sight, Thomas limped to the three-quarter ton pickup that had carried him across the state of Texas. He climbed in with a grunt and allowed himself a few seconds to let the burning in his face and fists dissipate. As the air conditioning blasted his skin, a sad country song from Hank Thompson came through the speakers, and Thomas sank back into the leather seat.

There were always regrets in life, paths you wish you didn't take, but returning home could never become one of them. Thomas took comfort in that fact.

His boot hit the gas pedal, and his right hand gripped the steering wheel before he really even knew what he was doing. The way home was ingrained into his very existence. It was a drive he didn't have to think about, no matter where he was in the county.

When he pulled out of the bar and onto TX-49, memories of his upbringing in the area and what it had given him flooded back into his mind. It was something that had gotten worse with every mile he drew closer to walking through the front door of their family home. He couldn't shake a rather desperate feeling that was sinking in, like it was all about to be taken from him. He couldn't even explain to himself why, but he knew he had to find out what was happening to his family and put a stop to it—after he got something to eat.

The last thing he wanted to do was pull up half-drunk after being gone for so long, and he knew just the diner to stop by before facing down the pit in his stomach and the look his mom was certainly waiting to give him the moment he walked in the door.

CHAPTER 5

The roads of Texas are a living and breathing network carrying any willing soul from the coast to the desert to the towering pines. Every day, they transport the lifeblood of the state at upward to eighty miles per hour. It's an intricate process, but when it takes more than fifteen hours to drive across Texas, it truly ought to be one. For some, the highways are the only way to reach what they care about most in life.

For Kaya, those same roads were taking her right into the throes of hell.

Leaving the protest and abandoning a cause she had championed for more than a year now was difficult enough, but to be doing all that only to return to her childhood home was something else entirely. Her fingers were curled around the steering wheel in the same spot they were when she climbed into the car. The sweat beading at her brows had been there since she turned onto US-290 on her way out of Austin.

There was a sinking feeling in the pit of her stomach that hadn't left since she opened the letter from her dad.

The three-seater SUV was awfully lonely at a time like this. She did her best to keep the feeling away through the radio, but all she received were the stations surrounding Bryan, which meant it was one lonesome country song after another. She tried to focus on literally anything other than the confrontation looming ahead. Her mind had a way of replaying every situation that hadn't come to pass over and over, though. It was helpful when contingencies needed to be accounted for, less so when nothing could be done about what was going to happen.

Her drive dragged on through Madisonville and on into Crockett, giving her more time than she needed to let her thoughts wander. The letter from her dad was folded and stashed away inside the pocket of her denim jeans. It was impossible not to think about what it meant. She hadn't heard from her family since she slammed the door in a storm of fury and disgust years ago. They let her walk out, didn't even try to find out where she went and refused to contact her.

Why did her dad suddenly care so much?

The answer had driven her madder than when she left them. So much so that she couldn't resist returning to check on them. No matter where they were in their lives, she could never wish anything as terrible as what her dad had described in the letter. Their land, the family home, and their lives in East Texas didn't come easy, and she knew what it meant to them.

She knew deep down her family was disappointed

in her decision to fight for strangers throughout the state, and even the country, instead of fighting for the ones who raised her. It was a calling she couldn't explain, one that she could only act on and hope everyone else could come to understand. She took pride in not being some armchair activist. She took to the streets. She fought for what she came to simply call her people. Even though she didn't know who they were, she could feel their pain and their loss. Her ancestors carried it and gave it to her, she knew exactly what it was. There was a coordinated effort to continue taking from Natives by just about every institution and governmental agency she could think of, and if she didn't bring the fight to them, what they could still call their own would be lost with the rest. This fight took her from her home, and there was no time to stop.

She had to, though. Kaya didn't have it in her to ignore the calls for help from her family. Whatever was happening was dire, and as awkward as her return would be, it was necessary.

When she reached the Davy Crockett National Forest, just a few hours away from the family home in East Texas, a ding in the SUV and a light on the dashboard forced her to stop for gas at a small convenience store tucked in the woods. She slapped her blinker on, pretending to not be grateful for even the most minor distraction, and pulled up to a pump.

The pines of the Davy Crockett National Forest were a majestic view to witness, even if momentarily. They blotted out the sun and stretched out as far as the eye could see. They reached high into the air and invited anyone nearby to enter another world. There was a cool breeze that whistled through the limbs above and only an occasional crunch of pine needles beneath the gentle walking of the creatures that were fortunate enough to call the place home.

Kaya took a moment to breathe it all in. It was a far cry from the concrete and red tape she had been surrounded by. Instead of sirens and angry shouting, there were birds and a serene stillness that could never be recreated anywhere else. For the first time since she unfolded that letter, her mind felt calm. There was something in the wind that made her feel right at home.

Kaya wasn't lucky enough to have any plastic to swipe at the pump. That was just one of the many sacrifices she made when she walked out on the family and never looked back. The spare change she had left was meant to purchase a bite to eat to last until she could scrounge something for dinner, but it would instead be dumped into the gas tank to finish the drive and another Coke to fight off the hunger pains. It just didn't matter that her stomach was grumbling so hard. She sighed gently as she walked into the one-room convenience store packed full with candy, chips, jerky, soda, energy drinks, and beer. It was the kind of place born of necessity in the area, and one not so readily available where she had been in downtown Austin. She'd be lying to herself if she even thought she didn't want one of everything on the shelf.

"Howdy," a woman called out from behind the counter as she was bent down, grabbing packs of cigarettes for the trucker standing at the register. "I'll be right with you."

"Thank you, ma'am." Kaya spoke in a voice of her own that she didn't recognize anymore. She cleared her throat and walked to the wall of fridges that lined the back of the building.

Just as she reached inside for a can, the front door to the convenience store swung open, and a man wearing a bandanna across his mouth, no different than an old West outlaw, walked in. This one didn't carry a Colt though, he carried a steel-framed Sig P226 with fifteen plus one 9mm rounds gripped in his outstretched arm.

Pop.

The thief fired a round into the wall just a few feet from the woman running the register. She fell to her knees and let out a scream that Kaya would hear in her nightmares for years to come.

"Everyone on the ground! I swear to God, I'll kill you right here."

Kaya gently lowered herself to the ground before being spotted by the gun-wielding asshole who was threatening everyone he could lay eyes on. She listened to him bark orders, demanding everyone's money and forcing the crying woman at the register to empty the cash tray. The criminal's gaunt face, pale complexion, and dilated pupils told an all-too-familiar story.

Kaya kneeled down and moved up the aisle of candy bars and chips out of the peripherals of the thief. As she moved delicate enough to not make a sound and give away her position, she reached behind her waist with her right hand and pulled out a pocket .380 pistol with five rounds in the mag and one already chambered. Hopefully, it would be the only one she'd need. It wasn't much, and resorting to using a gun was never what she wanted. If only she could get her hands on him, she knew she could take him down with ease.

Adrenaline surged through her extremities as she got closer to the front door. She was approaching the back of the thief who couldn't be bothered by anything other than handfuls of dollar bills being shoved into the plastic bag he brought in. Kaya's hands were steady, her vision clear, and her focus undivided. She knew what she had to do.

The mundane items at her right, junk food and snacks disguised to be healthy, were a sharp contrast to the immediate danger that had just appeared. Kaya could hear the whimpers of the trucker quite literally shaking in his boots. She couldn't see him or the woman at the register, but she knew their time was running out. If someone was going to get hurt, it would be when all the money was in the thief's hand. If the trucker summoned the courage to make a move, or if the thief needed a getaway victim, she'd lose any advantage she hoped to exploit.

Kaya watched as the man raised his pistol into the air and screamed obscenities without any reason. She knew the situation was bound to unravel any second. The adrenaline slowed, and her muscle memory set in. Kaya gripped the undersized pistol in both hands, squared her shoulders, and braced herself to make a move.

As fate would so often have it, the worst-case scenario for everyone unfolded in front of their eyes. Kaya popped out from behind the aisle and pushed the pistol forward to enter a shooting stance, but as she did, the gunman turned at just the right time to watch her every move. Two pistols moved simultaneously to face one another inside the convenience store, each with deadly intent. Kaya let out a scream of her own, shrill and fear-inducing, before squeezing evenly on the trigger to let loose the 88-grain .380 hollow point round.

The gunman wasted no time in firing his own bullet before meeting his fate. The 9mm round slammed into the exterior facing window, shattering it into a million pieces with a crashing sound that covered up the shocked grunt escaping from the gunman.

Kaya was lying on her shoulder, waiting patiently for the burning sensation of the bullet she didn't know missed her. She watched as the man's eyes changed from anger to alarm as he realized what was happening to him. The man clutched at his gut, but his eyes were locked on Kaya. She stared at him as he came to terms with the hole in his stomach.

To everyone's surprise in the convenience store, the gunman didn't open fire, he didn't collapse to the floor, and he didn't even say a word. He looked down at the blood on his hand, his eyes got big and his knees started to get a bit more wobbly.

"Is he about to die?" The trucker was suddenly no longer shaking with fear.

"Why do we care?"

"Well, we don't want anyone to just die."

"He was gonna kill us. Only reason he didn't is because she showed up," The woman at the counter raised her finger to point out Kaya.

Never taking her eyes off the pistol in the thief's hand, Kaya watched him claw at the black bandanna turning red from his own blood. He yanked it down and hacked up another mouthful to spit out. Kaya knew what was happening to him, even if he didn't. On the verge of losing his ability to stand, the trucker, woman behind the counter, and Kaya watched in bewilderment as the gunman stumbled out of the building and out of sight.

"You need to call the police," Kaya told the woman. "I can't be here when they show up, though."

"You saved our lives."

"You sure did."

Kaya didn't know how to respond. She was only thinking about how she could get away without showing her face to any authorities. "Y'all understand what I'm saying?"

"There are cameras."

"Is there a tape?"

The woman considered Kaya's question, and a lightbulb turned on above her head in an instant. "You know what? They just broke this morning, I even called my manager about it."

"Go on," the trucker said with a flick of his hand.

The crunching of glass beneath her boots was the first signal to the others that she was getting out of Dodge. Considering the video that had gone viral of her wailing on some guy in downtown Austin, Kaya had a feeling she wasn't going to be welcome to do as she pleases with the cops for a while. This whole thing sure as shit wouldn't help her case at all.

"Wait," the woman called out before Kaya could get out of the door.

She stopped walking, but didn't turn around.

"Thank you."

The walk across the parking lot and through the pumps to her SUV was a surreal one. The trail of blood from the gunman turned right out of the convenience store. Kaya turned left. She swore she'd never go back to the life of being in gunfights, not after she left her family. It took less than a day into her return trip to find herself back in the same position. Her heart was still adjusting to the adrenaline that had coursed through her only minutes ago, but that didn't stop it from sinking when she realized nothing at all had changed. She was still the same person deep down that she was so scared to be.

It didn't matter that she saved those people's lives. It didn't matter that she walked away from being held at gunpoint unscathed. The only thing that mattered in her mind was the fact that she was no different than those she had tried to escape.

When she slid into the SUV parked at the pump and closed the car door, Kaya allowed herself to break down. The tears flowed freely down her cheeks, and she refused to wipe even a single one away. The ball of anger in her stomach grew even as she cried. Her eyes went cold and her lips tightened. The fight she'd taken on in her activism had hardened her, but it had not changed her.

With only a couple hours left until she'd be pulling into the driveway of her family home, Kaya couldn't help herself but to hope for some kind of distraction. She needed to get her mind right after everything she'd been through.

A sudden grumble in her stomach reminded her there was one other thing—she never did get anything to eat.

CHAPTER 6

" heard they secretly agreed to more than ten million," a whiny man's voice broke through the night air. "Every one of those city officials are millionaires now. They sold us out for hush money. I saw it on Fact Social. It's actually way better than all those other social media platforms. They actually let you say what's really happening."

"Didn't you ever hear the saying, don't believe everything you see on the internet, Ben?"

"I'm siding with Ernie on this one," another man chimed in.

"Y'all do know I'm right here, right? I am on that city board. I didn't take any money. This man is different, I'm telling you."

"Yeah right, Daniel. Like you would tell us if you were suddenly handed a million dollars," Ben shot back at Daniel.

"You'll see for yourself tonight," Daniel said.

"What does this guy want with us anyway?"

"He didn't say, Ernie. He only said to be at the old railroad bridge when it got dark."

"Well, it got dark an hour ago," Ernie smarted off. "I don't see what he needs that can't be done during the daytime."

"Sometimes there just ain't enough time in the day," Daniel tried to sway the sentiment. "This guy is a visionary, I'm telling all of you. Talk to him for just a few seconds and you'll see what I'm talking about."

"A few seconds is all I'm giving him anyway," said Ed.

The railroad bridge that was a staple of scenic structures in the historic downtown Jefferson wasn't a place that typically welcomed visitors. It was the kind of remnant of history that served as the perfect backdrop for selfies from an occasional tourist, not necessarily suspicious meetings of a bunch of grown men. It was put in Jefferson in 1907 at a time when the hustle and bustle of the city made it the Houston equivalent of its time. Known for the port that served as a hub throughout the area, the railroad bridge signified progress in an entirely different way. Through the rise and decline of the city, the railroad bridge stood as a testament to what had been accomplished, and a reminder for the residents to always keep their eye on opportunities of the future.

The Howe Truss Train Trestle, as it came to be known as, would at least for one night, serve as the location for a shady meeting between an investor, a city official, and his up-to-no-good buddies. They were a carefully selected group of men, chosen by Daniel for their ability to look the other direction for what they all agreed was the ultimate good. None of them knew what was about to be asked of them. They showed up knowing only what had been told to them.

"Y'all see this?"

"See what?"

Ernie and Ed bent over and squinted their eyes in unison, trying their best to make out anything in the dark without their glasses to ward off the effects of being in their fifties. Right when one pointed his hairy index finger at the ground, the other yelped.

"Coyotes? This close to town?"

"That don't make much sense."

"Y'all sound like that loony old Billy Boyd, rambling on about some monster in the woods like a bunch of scared little teenagers. Could be a dog for all we know." Daniel tried to calm the group. "Even if it is a coyote, they're more afraid of us than we are of them. As long as we don't sneak up on anything, we'll be fine."

"They lead right to the bridge, though," said Ben, always the curious mind.

"Think we should holler or throw something?"

"Are you *always* such a pussy?"

"Only when it comes to gettin' mauled by a coyote," said Ed.

"Come on y'all," Daniel cut them all off. "He's probably waiting on us."

All four of the men scrambled up the loose rock to reach the train track running across the red iron bridge, standing like a monument in the night. They were surprised to find the silhouette of a man wearing a cowboy hat pulled low, waiting patiently, waiting for them. He was leaned up against an iron beam and had his arms crossed casually.

"That him?"

"Shut up," Daniel hissed.

"It's one thing to be fashionably late," the silhouette's voice rang out. "It's another to be downright rude. Where I come from, showing up on time means you're late. Showing up early is the only thing to do."

"You'll have to forgive—"

"Now, now." The silhouette raised a hand. "I don't have to do a damn thing." The figure walked closer to the group of men huddled at the front of the bridge, standing out in the open for any passerby to see. Within a few seconds, the shadows lifted and revealed Cassidy standing before them in his black jeans and wide-brimmed cowboy hat pulled low, adorned with two braids draped over his shoulders and down his chest.

His cowboy hat lifted gently with a tilt of his head to show his two black eyes trained on each of the men. He smirked, opened his hands to reveal his palms and took a gentle bow without losing eye contact.

"I assume Daniel has told you all about my investment into the city of Jefferson. What he did not tell you is that those meager millions will only be the beginning of what I can offer for the fine people of this age-old community. I will be the savior if they will have me."

"The hell is this guy talking about?"

"Ed, not now," Daniel cut him off.

"I'm talking about giving you all exactly what you want. I'm talking about making everyone in Jefferson rich beyond their comprehension. I'm talking about doing something no one dreamed possible—reviving small-town America."

"And we just got lucky that you decided to start here?" Ben couldn't help but ask.

"Not quite," Cassidy answered without hesitating. "I'd say you are lucky to still be breathing after talking to me in such a tone."

"Was that a threat, you son of a bitch?"

"Guys, bring it down a notch—" Daniel tried to stop the meeting from unraveling.

"No, no," Daniel cut him off. "I like where this is going. You see, if I'm to become the savior this city needs, if I'm to build it from scratch the way I see fit, I'm gonna need to take advantage of a little chaos."

There was only silence that filled the cooling night air at the old railroad bridge. Cassidy waited with bated breath on at least one of them to get the gist of where he was going with such a comment. Not a single one did.

"You bunch are going to cause that chaos." He led them on. "One incident at a time."

"What do you mean?" Daniel wanted to follow along, he really did, but he was as lost as the other guys standing beside him.

"You might not know that my namesake isn't something that I chose for myself. It was thrust onto me by the actions of people long before me. My name is Cassidy, and I am the real-life descendant of the belligerent Butch Cassidy. You ever hear of the Wild Bunch gang? They robbed trains and stagecoaches, they wreaked havoc, and although they agreed to never kill, they made a hell of a lot of money doing what they did."

"So, is that all you're after?" Ernie asked, confusion washing over his face. "Because if you haven't noticed already, I don't think there's much money to be made in a place like this."

"You leave the thinking to me," said Cassidy. "I am the product of what is taken by force. No different than what Butch did to the woman who would lay the foundation for who I am today, I will make what I want of anything. You can either help me to make it happen, or have it happen to you."

"We wouldn't be here if we didn't want to help," Daniel said.

The night air tickled the back of their throats and put an unsettling chill in every breath. Moonlight mixed with stars to cast shadows where there should be none. Cicadas screeched into the void. There was an unmistakable dread that had crept up, brought on not only by what was being demanded of them.

The East Texas night had a certain way of abandoning you. When those bright constellations appeared overhead, everything else seemed to disappear. The company of the sun was far from welcome when its heat bore down but sorely missed when forced to stand beneath the black pines shrouded in an inescapable darkness.

Cassidy was made whole by this feeling. He was visibly comfortable in such a place, untouched by any rays of light that were not reflected from the moon itself. The two singular braids that fell on either side of his chest soaked in what little light there was, taking it all away from the black holes for eyes he used to peer at the group of men in front of him. His black attire, born of southwestern culture yet adorned in all black, did no favors for the look on his face.

"Then here's what we're going to do," Cassidy finally answered. "I'm sure you are caught up on the investment my partners and I are to make. We plan to deliver on every single promise that was made, alongside many that have never been uttered. Over fifty million dollars will be poured into the community with the flip of a switch. It will be a waterfall flowing unto the destitute."

"This is getting too weird for me," Ed commented. "Where are you going with all this?"

"Just spit it out," said Ben.

"You all will be the ones to flip the switch."

"Tell us what you need us to do," Daniel answered without waiting.

"My Wild Bunch will expose this place for what it is. When hard times are falling on the people, they will look to the one who is already saving them from what they themselves have created. You will not kill. Understand? But you will rob, and you will steal, and you will create terror wherever you go."

"Why in the hell would we do that?" Ernie asked with a slack jaw.

"To create urgency."

Cassidy watched as the lightbulb clicked first above Daniel's head, then Ben, then Ed. A few seconds ticked by, but Ernie never did pick his chin up or remove the confused tilt in his head. It didn't take much to spot the one in the group who wouldn't be able to make the cut. Even though Cassidy knew right then and there who wouldn't be walking away from the old railroad bridge in Jefferson tonight, he allowed the men a chance to make that decision for themselves.

"We're gonna have us a little lesson on urgency tonight," he told them before reaching behind his back with his right hand. What he pulled out sent a shiver down each of the spines of the men watching. The blade glinted in the moonlight. Its razor-sharp point reflected a violent intent in the eyes of the men. Although it was only a few inches in length, the leather handle and double edge made it an all too easy weapon to take a life. "This is not to cut our initials into a tree, nor to perform any childish ritual. No, this knife can do only one thing, and it is rather magnificent at doing that one thing. You see, this knife proves loyalty."

Cassidy took the knife in his hand and wiped either side of the blade as he let his eyes fall down to become lost in its shine. He held it up to eye level before turning his attention on the men and dropping the knife to the ground. When he spoke, it was a sinister tone that his voice had not carried until this point.

"Three of you will become millionaires tonight and will serve as my eyes, my ears, and my fist," he stated. "One of you will not live to see the sunrise."

"The fu—"

"Before you try to fight it," Cassidy cut Ernie off in a heartbeat.

The men watched in horror as Cassidy gently gripped the black wooden handled .357 magnum Colt six-shooter that seemed to smile in the same moon-light as the knife lying on the tracks between them. The barrel was aimed at the men and would not waver. Cassidy trained it with deadly accuracy, daring one of the men to make an escape.

None of the men could even take a deep breath, much less make a run for it.

Cassidy allowed each of the men to begin creating distance between one another as mistrust immediately ran rampant between them. At the end of the day, they would show who they were deep down. Cassidy did not trust any of the men before him, but he did trust their nature. If they were deprived of a choice, they would lash out. Men like that always would. It was more effective to root them out and force them to make the choice firsthand.

The choice that was before the men now was a simple one. It was only a matter of who would act first. For a passing moment, a thought crossed each of their minds. If they could only turn on the man in front of them, four could easily overpower one, but would they? Uncertainty crept into each of the minds almost simultaneously. Cassidy relished watching the realization wash over them that fighting each other was the only sure way to live.

It was Daniel who made the first move. He lunged for the knife, catching them all off guard. With the blade in his hand, the rest of the men showed who they really were deep down. Ben and Ed made their move, each one grabbing an arm to pin Daniel as best they could.

Ernie turned and ran.

The struggle between the three men put all three on their asses in a violent scuffle for their lives. Cassidy looked on as his Wild Bunch made themselves evident. He also watched the coward flee for his life. Ernie put one foot in front of the other, holding the back of his jeans to stop his gut from pushing them down to his ankles as he ran until he was down the gravel bank leading up to the railroad and making a break for the parking lot in the distance.

Always one to nudge things along, Cassidy let out a sharp whistle that stopped the three men from wrestling like deer in the headlights of an eighteen-wheeler charging toward them. With a glance and a quick nod, Daniel was the first to catch the hint.

"Where the hell is Ernie?"

"That little son of a—"

"Get him!"

Just like that, Cassidy stood proud as his Wild Bunch scrambled off toward their first target—their own people. Sometimes, the forces of nature were mysterious and unpredictable, blowing back and forth in the wind like the sweetgums and oaks overhead. Sometimes, they were as transparent as the wind itself, exploitable and inevitable. Cassidy had a knack for understanding the direction the wind was blowing, no matter the circumstance, and an even greater one for making sure it blew in his direction.

As Cassidy's gaze lingered on, his Wild Bunch, led by the city official Daniel Coleman, carried out exactly what had been told of them. In the trees at the edge of the old railroad, carnage ensued. All Cassidy could see from his vantage point perched on top of the bridge was Ernie collapse to the ground under the weight of three men he didn't know half as well as he thought he did. Daniel's hand clasped the knife high over his head for only a single second, torn from the horror movies of old, until the blade fell. Red was all that came up when the blade returned above Daniel's head. It fell again, and again, and again.

Daniel continued bringing the knife down until both Ben and Ed had seen enough and started to step back. They were no doubt realizing what they had just been roped into, as well as who they followed into such madness.

Daniel stood from the body that was once Ernie. He turned and walked back to where Cassidy was standing, leaving a bloody trail dripping from the blade all the way back to the bridge. He stood alone for a few seconds before he was joined by both Ben and Ed who dragged themselves to either side of him.

"It's done," Daniel finally said, shoulders still heaving from catching his breath and eyes never lifting from the black leather boots Cassidy wore.

"The Wild Bunch is alive and well," Cassidy said with a smirk. This time, he was holding a feather twice the length of his own hand. It was brown and white and perfectly preserved, except for the red stain at its tip. No different than the blade that had taken Ernie's life only seconds ago, the feather in Cassidy's hand seeped crimson drops onto the steel rails. When Cassidy spoke, his voice was a cold whisper in the night.

"Now, here's what you're gonna do next."

CHAPTER 7

The American diner is one of the last living testaments to a culture of beautiful necessity rather than needless decadence. It is the home of the vagabonds and derelicts, but also the lovesick, the successful, and more important than all— the hungry.

The latter is where Kaya found herself as she pulled her vehicle into the pothole-filled gravel driveway of the Huddle Around Diner just off TX-49 on the other side of Jefferson. It was ten thirty p.m. and the stars above had more than made their light known across the horizon. The Huddle Around Diner sign that Kaya drove beneath was lined in red buzzing neon and featured faded, vintage writing as if it was pulled from a 1950s commercial. It wasn't the kind of place that Kaya would typically stop at, but given the fact that it was one of the only open places in the area, and that she was still ready to welcome anything that delayed her arrival to the family home, it was the perfect place to pull in for a bit.

The diner welcomed Kaya as most do, without so much as a glance from anyone inside and an endless clatter of coffee mugs being refilled. It was a place where she could escape the world and the troubles that followed her. It was a grease-filled refuge, and although she had never even stepped foot inside before, the Huddle Around Diner felt like a home away from home.

"What'll ya have, hun." A woman's harsh voice came from the other side of the diner.

"A booth and whatever this will get me," said Kaya, opening her hand to reveal three quarters, a dime, and a nickel.

"Sit wherever ya want, we'll take care of the rest, sweetheart."

"Thanks."

Kaya had forgotten the language of the area and the niceties that were so commonplace in small talk. Austin had lost any sense of such charm. Small talk was mostly cussing or rage-honking at the next car in line. To say these conversations were a nice change of pace would certainly be an understatement. By the time Kaya sat down in a corner booth with her back against the wall, there was a stained white mug in front of her and a steaming pot of coffee filling it up.

"You like pancakes?"

"Depends. You got whipped cream?"

"Sure do," the waitress said with a gentle smile.

Kaya lifted the mug to her face and blew into the mug not knowing whether it was too hot to drink or not. The first person to catch her attention was a middle-aged Native man, dressed in all black, topped off with a black felt cowboy hat and black leather boots. His two braids were neatly kempt and rested perfectly still on his chest, reaching almost to his belt. Kaya didn't pay much attention to him. It didn't take long to see he was a man who liked to hear himself talk. His voice echoed through the diner louder with every sentence.

"It's an eagle feather," the man explained. "The Caddo say it played a crucial role in the permanent state of death. A bloody eagle feather foretold loss at a time when it could be undone. It was a sign from above."

"Is that right?" The only waitress on duty nodded and smiled as she continued her work to the sound-track of the man's rambling.

"Does this look like it has blood on it to you, ma'am? You can be honest with me," the man said.

"I honestly couldn't say either way, Cassidy."

Kaya took a mental note of his name and sipped her coffee again. She wanted so badly to roll her eyes. Although she couldn't quite articulate exactly why she wanted to beg the man to stop speaking on something he knew nothing about, it ached her to remain quiet. She did so anyway.

She watched as the waitress continued her duties despite the rattling from Cassidy. Lucky for her, this time, the plate that hit the serving window from the kitchen, accompanied by the ringing of a bell, was a short stack of pancakes with extra whipped cream. There was so much, in fact, that Kaya could see the white cloud towering above anything else on the plate. Her mouth was already salivating before the plate was pushed in front of her with a smile. While the pancakes looked good enough to dig in, it was the words imparted by the waitress that made it worthwhile.

"On the house."

"Must be my lucky night."

"For one of us at least," the woman told Kaya with a quick flash of her eyes toward Cassidy.

"You got this," Kaya assured her.

It took only a few steps away from the table before Cassidy settled right back in. This time, with more questions involved.

"Do you know much about the Caddo people?"

"No sir," the waitress responded kindly.

"It isn't easy information to find. I only know what's been told to me. The Caddo have a lot of stories that have survived because of exactly what you and I are doing at this very moment—talking."

"That's nice, hun."

Kaya watched the situation continue to unfold with admittedly increased interest. She cocked her head sideways as Cassidy twirled the eagle feather in his fingertips. He leaned over the only wall separating the kitchen from the preparation area. The waitress toiled away at assembling a breakfast plate as the man continued to intrude on any sense of privacy she once had in her little nook at work. The diner was, after all, a place for vagabonds and derelicts.

From across the diner, it was difficult for Kaya to make out whether or not the eagle feather actually had any blood on it. The question alone was enough to make her wonder about the well-being of the man who'd asked about it. He wasn't trying to be flirtatious, this was something different.

The next question from Cassidy spurred the immediate focus from three people in the diner, for three entirely separate reasons as well.

"Did you know this thing can predict when someone will die?"

The waitress turned around to make eye contact with a shocked look already written plain as day across her face. Kaya looked up from shoveling a bite of her late-night supper—a bite that was more sugar topping than fluffy pancake—and her eyes got big. The man sitting in the other corner of the diner, trying to look for who asked such an outlandish question, reacted the same way.

"Kaya?" the man mouthed quietly while locking eyes with her.

"Thomas?" she mouthed back with her brows scrunching in surprise.

Kaya was dumbfounded. Seeing her brother in this little hole-in-the-wall diner outside Jefferson was about the last thing she'd ever expected. From the look on his face, he felt the same way. There was no time to react, however, because Cassidy had already taken his questionable antics to another level.

Kaya and Thomas both watched as Cassidy lifted the eagle feather up above his head and watched as a tiny streak of thick blood ran down the quill, soaking it deep red, before trickling onto his wrist. As the blood ran down his arm, Cassidy turned his attention to the waitress.

"I was going to ask how you thought it might do any predicting, as it is just a feather, but little did I know it was up for a demonstration tonight," Cassidy said, trying to be coy.

"What do you mean?"

"I mean, it might be somebody's unlucky day here in this diner. It's impossible to say one way or another, and maybe I don't have a clue what I'm talking about, but when this feather turns red—someone is getting hurt."

No more than a few moments after the final words left Cassidy's mouth, the door to the diner burst open and three more men shoved their way inside. They walked as upright as someone who just won the lottery and swayed like someone with enough money to not worry about the price of a drink.

Kaya knew in an instant these men were only looking for trouble. The way Thomas stood up in a hurry told her he was dialed into the same feeling, too. Nothing good was about to happen, especially to that nice old waitress who gave Kaya the pancakes served with extra whipped cream.

The three men made their presence known the way most men like them did. They were loud. They were boisterous. They were annoying. It took only seconds before they had knocked over someone's mug, screamed several obscenities, and even got in the face of a man who dared stand up to stare them down.

"Settle down now, boys," Cassidy called to them, breaking up the fight that was one wrong flinch away from breaking out. "I was just telling dear..." He looked over at the waitress and tried to find a nametag on her chest.

"Macy."

"You look like a Savannah, or maybe Samantha," Cassidy said. "Something with an *S*."

Kaya was listening, holding herself from getting up and slapping the men who'd interrupted her distraction from where she was going. If she did that, she'd have to just go on ahead and slap Thomas also, though. She chose to just sip her coffee and do her best to put the men's nonsense out of mind. Unfortunately, they were impossible to ignore.

Macy did her best to get away from the confrontation. When she made eye contact with Kaya, she grabbed another hot pot of coffee and snaked her way through the tables to top off her mug that was only half empty. It was a kind enough gesture, but Kaya got the hint and offered what little she could.

"They bothering you?"

"No, it's all right," she said, still holding the pot above her mug. "Happens from time to time. It's just part of the job."

The smile that Macy gave her said something else entirely. It was heartbreaking, born of years of abuse, hidden behind the familiar curl of lips and disappointed eyes. There was so much that Kaya wanted to do to help her, but she also knew that the smile Macy gave her also said to just let her get through the night. Instead of making a scene and punching some teeth in, she decided to force some small talk and pass just a few moments of her time in peace.

"This the best coffee in Texas?"

"The best you'll find in a three-hour drive, at least," said Macy.

"I believe it. Thanks again for the pancakes. You have no idea how much I needed that."

"S'alright. We gotta keep the cook busy on nights like this. He has a tendency to wander."

The two shared a brief laugh together, drawing the focus of Cassidy and the three men who had barged in, unable to keep their mouths shut for even a second. Their gaze was drawn to Kaya, one by one, and she took notice.

"How long has he been here?" Kaya asked with a nod of her head in the direction of Thomas in the other corner of the diner.

"About an hour. Nice enough guy."

"I don't know about all that. He order anything?"

"Just coffee."

"Well, be sure you double his ticket to cover mine too."

"You got it." A different smile came from Macy this time.

"What time do you get off?"

"A couple of hours."

"Almost there. You got this."

"Thanks, hun."

With that, the waitress turned and walked back toward the men still huddled around where she needed to work. She gripped the coffee pot tight enough for Kaya to see her knuckles turn red and then white.

There are few who ever walk with the knowledge

of their own impending death. Most would prefer to never experience such a way of existence. If given the choice, people will always choose to keep themselves in the dark, even if only because it is more familiar to them. The unknown is something much more terrifying. Some things are just better not known.

Kaya wondered if Macy carried such a weight on her mind as she approached the men. The Huddle Around Diner seemed different than it did before. It felt different. It even smelled different. There was a change in the air.

"How the hell do you open this thing?"

"I think you just smack the shit out of it. That's how they do it in all the movies."

"Just shut up already, you jackass."

The three men were hunched over the cash register not too far from Cassidy. They each bickered over who should be the one to look inside, not trying to hide their intentions or shy away from anyone who thought to stand in their way.

Cassidy simply twirled the eagle feather in his hand. His eyes were transfixed on it, unable to look away. As the men continued their tirade, Kaya kept her focus on the mysterious man in black.

"Please," was all Macy could let out.

"Open it up," the apparent leader of the men demanded.

"There ain't anything worth taking in there. You do know most people pay with plastic these days, right?"

The first escalation came when one of the men decided to get less than a few inches away from Macy's face, barking insults with veins coming out of his face as he screamed louder and louder. It wasn't just some highway robbery, these men were after something else. Macy caved almost immediately and went to work opening the register to defuse the situation.

The tray popped open with a *thud* that could be heard throughout the diner. It was all the men needed to push the envelope a little further, all while Cassidy lingered in the background, still watching his feather spin in his fingers.

Kaya set her coffee mug down and took a deep breath.

"Get everything out," one of the men shouted.

"There's like fifty bucks in here. Is this real?"

"I told you, people don't use cash anymore, you assholes," Macy said.

The man who'd gotten in her face took a step back for his buddy to escalate the confrontation even further. When the frantic, unexpected shove put Macy on her ass in the middle of the diner, Kaya stood up from her seat. She wasn't the kind to sit by and let this happen to someone as innocent as the poor waitress just trying to get through her shift.

As she stood, she couldn't help but notice Thomas across the diner doing the exact same thing. They rose in unison, at the calls for help by the waitress still trying to pick herself off the grease-stained tile floor.

Before either could make their move to help, the men in the diner did something no one could ever come back from. It was unprovoked and cruel. Depravity had set into the three in a way that seemed unnaturally spurred on. One man shoved his hand into the register as the waitress finally returned to her feet, then tossed the twenties, fives, and ones to the floor with a twisted grin.

"Find a bag," the other man said, standing over her.

Macy grabbed a to-go bag from the counter next to where she was standing and started to get down on one knee, knowing she was about to be told to pick up all of the money that had fallen to the floor.

Kaya was already walking toward them, beating Thomas by a few paces and getting angrier by the second at what was unfolding. She had just been thrown into a fight earlier on her drive, forced to enact justice by her own hand, yet here she was again. Her shoulders stiffened and her fists tightened at her side.

"Hurry the fuck up!"

Macy had just leaned forward to grab a handful of money when an ear-ringing blast pierced the diner.

Pop.

It was like someone had thrown a blood-filled water balloon on the floor. A splatter of red immediately spilled everywhere at the men's feet. Macy fell lifeless to the floor. She was face down in the puddle of red.

"No!" Kaya cried out instinctively.

A round of laughter burst out from the men, contrasting the horror in front of them. It was senseless violence. Macy had died for a few seconds of entertainment by some brutes. Kaya could do nothing about what had just happened. All she could care about now was making all of them pay for what they'd done.

Kaya toppled a couple of chairs, tossing another to the side and knocking over an entire table of dishes as she charged the laughing men. In her blindness, she didn't notice the fact that Cassidy was nowhere to be seen. She saw only the faces of those three men, burned into her memory alongside the look on Macy's face when she brought her pancakes. She didn't deserve what happened to her, but Kaya knew those men damn sure deserved what was coming to them. She finally made it just a few feet from where they were standing and raised a fist almost at her eye level.

Kaya threw herself forward, only to be stopped dead in her tracks by Thomas.

He grabbed her fist, shoved her backward with his shoulder and walked against her in the other direction, almost dragging her with him. As much as she forced herself forward, trying to lunge at the murderers in the diner, Thomas wouldn't allow it. They blended into the handful of people doing their best to get out of the building as quickly as possible before becoming a victim themselves.

"Come on," he finally told her. "We're getting out of here."

CHAPTER 8

"If it isn't my weasel of a little brother."

"You are like two minutes older than me. And if you're having a hard time remembering, you are the one that ran out on us. What's that make you?"

"You know why I couldn't stay. If you're having a hard time remembering why I left, just take a look around."

Thomas and Kaya were doing their best not to draw attention through their bickering as they walked away from the Huddle Around Diner. There were red and blue flashing lights dancing in every direction, illuminating the small crowd beginning to form in the parking lot.

The death of the waitress inside the diner had brought out the local police department, sheriff's office, and volunteer fire department. Jefferson wasn't the kind of town that had to deal with such tragedy regularly. When something like this happened, it impacted the entire community, both tearing them down and riling them up all the same.

The brother and sister duo had spoken to a cop about what happened and detailed their perspective as a bystander and witness. After jotting down some scribblings in an unused notepad, the buzz-cut-wearing, broad-shouldered cop let them go on their way without asking for any way to follow up with them. It was likely a rookie mistake, a side effect from being so raw to such levels of depravity. Thomas and Kaya both had learned the world was a random, uncaring place to exist, but the young cop was still too naive and purpose-driven to accept such a fate.

The only part that lingered in the back of Kaya's mind was the unwillingness to believe these men were capable of such actions. The cop acted like he knew who was responsible for Macy's death personally. The young man seemed disinterested in accepting what had so obviously happened, unable to comprehend that someone could just snap like that. Kaya did her best to not think about it. Her trip to the diner was supposed to be a distraction from her anxiety about walking through the front door of her childhood home and confronting her past actions. The more she thought of what the waitress looked like lying on the floor of the diner, the more she welcomed the thought of being around her family again.

"I'd ask what the heck you're doing in town, but I have a feeling it's the same reason I'm back," said Kaya.

"The letter?" Thomas asked.

"The damn letter."

"You think Mom and Dad are serious?"

"When are they not? Dad seemed pretty concerned about what was happening."

"I don't doubt that they are fighting someone," answered Thomas. "That's all they've ever done, ever since we were kids."

"The fight is all they know, Thomas. We've talked about it. That doesn't mean it has to be all we know," Kaya said.

"You don't have to lecture me about that. You are the one who's still fighting, even if it's not with Mom and Dad."

They were in the parking lot of the Huddle Around Diner, walking toward Kaya's SUV, keeping their distance from one another but not so far as to make the police think differently of them.

Kaya shrugged the comment off and did her best not to exacerbate the rift that was already between them. She was tired. Of course from the exhaustion of the last few days, but she was also tired of the same old fights resurfacing yet again. She thought she'd escaped him when she left home, but here they were again driving her mad as they always did.

Thomas never did make eye contact with Kaya. His sister had burned more than one bridge when she left home. He hadn't forgotten about that. His concerns for what happened to the waitress weren't the same as Kaya's though. Her thoughts may have been with the waitress who gave her an endearing smile and a stack of pancakes. Thomas couldn't think about anything other than the man who went by Cassidy. The eagle feather was a sign. The blood that ran its length when nothing else happened set him on edge. His chest felt heavier with every step.

"What did Mom say?" Kaya asked, stopping his spiral into conspiracy.

"Do you really want to know?"

"Only if she mentioned me."

"Kaya," Thomas started.

"I know she didn't. She never does."

"It's not like that. When you left, she changed. She had to. There were too many frontlines and not enough people. Dad tried to quit his job about a dozen times. Mom wouldn't let him. She kept bringing in new people, but none of them ever worked out."

"And you were just an innocent victim forced to carry the family on your back?"

"I didn't say that. I've got my own skeletons to deal with. You think I want to be back here dealing with this shit?"

Kaya let silence fall between them as they reached her SUV. Neither were sure of what to do next. As the red and blue lights flashed behind them, they both turned to see only one man in handcuffs being brought out of the diner. He was the one who pulled the trigger, but he wasn't the one who led them inside. The man dragged both feet and screamed indistinguishable obscenities through a beet-red face.

Cassidy was nowhere to be found, nor were the other two men that had been involved in the incident. The solemn quiet that had fallen over them was broken only by the screams of the scapegoat, echoing into the night, excessive and vain despite its fury. The cops had found someone to place the blame on, to satisfy the local newspaper's inquiry, and to quench the thirst of justice from the community. They had not put a stop to the problem, however.

Thomas had a sinking feeling in his gut, one that matched the feeling Kaya took with her just about everywhere she went. Together, they stared at the diner, each one refusing to acknowledge the impact their experience would have on what was to come.

"I know you don't want to be here," Kaya said, unable to break her concentration from the authorities shoving the man into the back of the cop car. "I don't either."

"I know," was all he could say back.

With the flashing lights reflecting in their face, they once again returned to their normal silence. All of the commotion was at the front of the diner, with ambulances and fire trucks still trying to fill the parking lot as the crime scene was being taped off from the handful of people who had nothing better to do than stand around and spectate.

The chaos unfolding seemed to happen without end. Before long, what had to be the family of Macy, the waitress, showed up. There was an old man in a t-shirt and shorts bawling in the arms of an officer and a younger woman in a baseball cap lugging a car seat in the crook of her elbow doing her best to hold it together. Their cries were unmistakable. Grief only knew how to sucker punch, and those poor people were feeling its unwelcome sting.

"What the..." Thomas's voice trailed off as his focus shifted to the back of the building.

Kaya followed his watchful eye to a strange silhouette exiting the diner out of the back door used for grocery deliveries and staff. A lanky figure topped with a distinctive cowboy hat strolled out of the diner without a care in the world.

"That's that Cassidy son of a bitch," said Kaya.

"Where the hell is he going?"

Thomas might have well been talking to himself, as his sister had already started off toward the direction of the diner, sneaking through the cars separating them from the turmoil happening at the front door. Thomas followed as best he could, unsure of what was happening but remembering all too well the feeling of chasing off after his sister to a place they shouldn't be going.

The diner was tucked back off the road against a backdrop of trees that formed a wall of blackness when the sun was no longer hanging above. The bright stars of Texas didn't stand a chance of shining down their light, and the neon of the diner sign was lost in the distance. There were no red and blue police lights where Kaya was leading Thomas, only shadows and dread.

They chased after Cassidy for reasons only Kaya knew. She wasted no time in picking up her pace, planting one boot in the mud after another, keeping her eyes locked on the man still meandering his way into the woods. He walked with knees lifted high, a straight back, and never turned his head to look around as he moved.

Kaya and Thomas tracked him down like hounds in the night. They left everything behind them, from the body of the waitress to the conflict that had kept them apart for years. They focused only on the strange man in the distance, fading into the tree line.

"Don't lose him!" Kaya shouted back at Thomas.

"I'm going, dammit, hold on!"

"He can't get away. Those men listened to him. They were following him."

"We can't prove that, Kaya!"

No response came. Kaya picked her pace up, hurrying after Cassidy before she lost sight of him in the pines and oaks looming high overhead. Within seconds, she had disappeared into the woods right behind Cassidy.

Thomas followed only seconds after. Without even realizing it, he had started running as fast as his overpriced cowboy boots would allow. His calves started to burn, and his chest heaved as he gulped as much oxygen as he could. He couldn't catch up, no matter how hard he pushed himself.

Kaya was right on the trail of Cassidy, both at a dead sprint now. He ran like a madman, legs and arms flailing in every direction. His gait struck a bizarre contradiction between humorous and horrific. If Kaya didn't know any better, she would've said that Cassidy looked clumsy as he ran.

"We're just getting started, you asshole!"

The chase through the woods continued. Kaya's cries did nothing to slow him down. Sweat started to bead at her forehead, and everything from her shoulders to her toes began to feel the familiar burn of lactic acid in her muscles.

Thomas had no chance of catching up. He gave it his all, but watched both the silhouette of the strange man and the back of his sister move further and further ahead of him, darting their way through the trees.

"I'm coming!" he called out to Kaya more than anyone.

The pursuit left any sign of civilization behind them. Neither Kaya nor Thomas were sure just how far the trees extended behind the diner, but they were finding out firsthand in a hurry. Cicadas screeched against a symphony of branches, vines, and weeds slapping against the legs of all three people rushing through the woods. An unending stomping of boots into the dirt was the rhythm to their race. Their effort seemed futile, however.

Kaya could've sworn she was closing the distance. She could feel herself getting closer to Cassidy as if she could leap with each next step to take the man to the ground. She was on his heels. She could feel the draft at his back. She needed only to make one final lunge to catch him and find out what his role in the death of the waitress really was.

So, she leaped.

Her vision went black, and she could taste the earth itself. It wasn't until she was spitting out dirt and feeling Thomas tug on her back to stand her up that she realized Cassidy had stayed just out of reach.

"Why aren't you chasing him, you dumbass?"

"He's already gone," Thomas answered. "Did you trip or something?"

Kaya thought twice about the question. "You didn't see him? He was right there. I don't know how I didn't hit him."

"He disappeared way back, Kaya. You weren't chasing anyone when you face-planted into the mud."

"Huh?"

"We need to split up, see if we can find anything."

Kaya shook her head and stood up, trying to get her bearings again. After a brief stumble and a reassurance from Thomas, they both walked in opposite directions. Kaya would've sworn she was inches away from Cassidy, she didn't know anything about what Thomas was saying. She did her best to scan the woods overcast in darkness and shadow, but her mind scrambled to piece together what had just happened.

Thomas had gone in the opposite direction. Uncertainty about the health of his sister had already begun to make itself known. Whether she hit her head too hard, or was just turned around in the pitch-black woods, he was already worried. He kept his head down as he walked. His thoughts swirled around, trying to process seeing his sister again after so long and what their parents were going to put them through. He didn't understand why they were combing through the woods at first, but the more he thought about what was still ahead, the more it made sense.

An hour went by, and nothing had been found. After another twenty minutes were wasted, Thomas had enough. He turned to call for his sister. She was nowhere to be seen.

"Kaya!"

There was no response.

"Kaya! Where the hell did you go?"

Silence.

Thomas felt a tinge of panic flare up in his gut. He considered leaving it all, including his sister, behind in the woods. He tried to look in every direction but saw no sign of Kaya. There were no sticks cracking beneath her heavy step, or breathing still heavy from the chase, or even a flickering shadow in a sea of darkness to give her away. She simply was no longer there.

"I'm right here." Her voice came from inches behind Thomas.

"Don't do that again."

"You did miss me, didn't you?"

"Let's just go."

The path out of the woods was dreary and quiet. Their unexpected sibling reunion had taken a turn for the worst because of the killing at the diner. Whoever they had chased into the dark was long gone, but the chill that ran down both Thomas and Kaya's spine lingered. Neither could escape the feeling that something was happening to the historic town of Jefferson.

CHAPTER 9

S mall-town America needed saving. It needed a figurehead with a vision, with resources, and with the tenacity to see it through. East Texas could be where it all began, where change could turn the tide of decay and revive communities in need. When the sun eventually comes to set in the West, it could be setting the stage for a new dawn of destined prosperity.

These were lofty ideas, born of even more extravagant goals, but they had to be done, and Cassidy knew he was the only one who could do it. What he brought to the people was the chance to find hope in his plan to save them. Millions of dollars, economic development, new businesses, houses, and opportunities, all laid at their feet for next to nothing in return. How could they not throw themselves at his will?

The refusal to accept his offer was most surprising for Cassidy. His proposal to the city of Jefferson was met with disdain and stonewalling in a way that he had never anticipated. There were those few who did the reasonable thing, but not enough.

With one more twirl of his fingertips, the eagle feather kept his gaze longer than it should have. He wasn't watching where he was walking, and he wasn't paying attention to anyone or anything in his way. He knew exactly where he was going, though.

Downtown Jefferson was not an impossible maze to navigate. Since its founding in 1841, the city had risen and fallen with the tides of an economy far too dependent on local stock competing with national interests. Although the downtown buildings boasted a walkway reminiscent of the streets of New Orleans, there were no tourists or families strolling here and there. It was yet to become a ghost town, but it was surely on its way.

Sometime during the rise of the information age, healthcare became a number one concern. This was a problem that Cassidy was well aware of. He'd heard the county itself referred to as a healthcare desert, and in his brief experience, it was unequivocally true. There were no doctors, no hospitals, and no emergency rooms. For some, this lack of service was a nightmare with no end. For Cassidy, as most circumstances tended to be, it was just another opportunity.

If someone were to wake up a bit under the weather, it might be easy to drive to the next county to see a doctor. Some in town were even lucky enough to have telehealthcare from the newfangled phones. Cassidy wasn't out to make someone sick, though. The black wooden handled .357 magnum Colt six-shooter strapped to his hip had a determination all its own.

As Cassidy moved alone through the downtown area, the wood heels of his boots clicked on the brick pathway, and his black cowboy hat shielded his eyes from the glare of the street lighting. He watched for people inside the general stores and antique shops that attracted the elderly to pace the sidewalks on the weekends, yet found only silence in from every alleyway and building he passed.

His walk took him by the Excelsior House Hotel, and beside the historical museum, a path typically tread by the haunted ghost tours that had become popular in recent years. Bateman Alley would soon dead end into Market Street, but before that happened, there was a house that had earned itself a visit from Cassidy.

The house had stood in the city's center since 1890 and was visited by dignitaries and politicians, even entertainers and investors, as a hallmark of what it was like to live in Jefferson. Now, it was the home of none other than the infamous Mayor Walker. Two pillars of brilliant white stood like beacons in the night, upholding a symbol for the way of life that both revered the nostalgia of what once was and eyed a future brighter than any have ever seen. A porchlight glowing next to the nine foot door adorned with an oversized brass handle called for Cassidy to simply walk right in.

A black sedan parked out front told him nothing would ever be so easy, however. There were men inside who were on payroll for one reason—to put a stop to the exact kind of intentions that Cassidy held. Right on cue, two men with suits barely covering their muscles climbed out of the sedan with their attention focused solely on Cassidy.

"Evenin' boys," he told them both.

"Can we help you find your way, sir?"

Cassidy allowed an enigmatic smirk to cross his face. "I seem to be turned around. I knew where I was going, until I realized that I actually had no idea where I was. Has that ever happened to you?

"Where you headed?"

"I seek an audience with the infamous Mayor Walker this evening. We have much to discuss, he and I. Maybe you could point me in the right direction," Cassidy said, pointing into the air at random several times in several directions.

"The mayor isn't taking any visitors. You'll have to try again in the morning."

"Does that mean this is his home? I had no idea," said Cassidy. "However, in that case, I think it is prudent for me to go on in."

Both of the security guards moved carefully in front of the oversized door to the mayor's home.

"Not tonight, you won't."

The porchlight cast down an uneasy yellow glow on the men, but Cassidy thought nothing of it. He approached them on the sidewalk, ignoring whatever the guards were telling him, and noticing the neatly trimmed lawn and perfectly sculpted hedges that conveyed a sense of importance around the home. When he came to a stop only a few feet from where the men stood, he sized them up and squared his shoulders.

That's when the men noticed the .44 magnum

slung across his hip. They shifted their stance slightly. To an untrained eye, their shift would have been considered mundane, but Cassidy knew they were already doing whatever they could to make drawing their own firearm that much easier. Tension settled in as thick as the East Texas humidity between them.

"I'd say you don't have to do this, but we all know that's a damn lie," said Cassidy.

"We don't want no trouble, mister," the other guard finally figured it was time to speak up.

"You just can't be here," his partner clarified. "Not right now."

"I know."

Although they were both identical in size, the guard on the left was clean-shaven with slumped shoulders and eyes that betrayed every worry running through his head. The guard on the right was all false confidence. He was upright, broad-shouldered, bearded, and stood ready to pounce at a moment's notice. They made an awkward duo.

Cassidy moved fast, too fast for the guards to notice what was happening to them. They had been trained in pristine conditions and never experienced the fight-or-flight sensations of duress. When they saw the end of the Colt in Cassidy's hand aimed at them, both learned just about all there is to know about the panic of being under duress.

The first blast took out the confident one. His shoulders slumped just like his partner's when the bullet tore through his abdomen and exited out of his lower back. For just a few fleeting seconds, the second guard watched in horror as the man next to him slid down the wooden door, staring in shock at the hole in his stomach. When the man's ass hit the ground, he was dead.

"Holy—" was all the last guard alive could get out before realizing he should be going for his gun.

Cassidy stood waiting, almost feeling bad for the poor man doing his best to defend himself against such a ruthless, unprovoked attack. The cicadas blaring in the distance were a startling soundtrack to die to. The clicking of the hammer on Cassidy's six-shooter sent another wave of fear through the guard, causing his hands and knees to tremble uncon-trollably.

Keeping his eyes locked on the gun trained on his every move, the guard caught a glimpse of hope that he couldn't believe. The barrel wagged to the side, motioning him to take off. The guard wasted no time in taking advantage of the opportunity, forcing one leg in front of the other as quickly as his body would allow him. He ran with a waddle, immediately starting to cough as his chest tightened from the adrenaline surge.

Cassidy turned his head to watch the man attempt to flee for his life. The braids that draped across his chest reflected the yellow light of the porch just like his eyes, making him look like a demon waiting in the night. His glare was cold and unfeeling. His pistol moved gently in front of his hip, turning to aim at the man's back.

Pop.

The gunshot rang out alongside a scream of fire from the barrel and a recoil through the handle that would put a mule on its back. Cassidy never flinched.

He stepped up to the door, nudging one of the men to slump over with his leather boot. When the door creaked open, Cassidy let himself in with a single step, holding onto the door handle as he entered. He didn't account for the blood that had been puddling under the door, though. As soon as the slick sole of his boot touched the laminate floor inside the home, down he went.

The crash sent Cassidy tumbling into the home, arms and legs flailing to get a grip and his cowboy hat flying off his head. He was on his back in just a second, yet popped right back up in half that time. He only hoped no one had seen what happened. He brushed his clothes off, inadvertently running his hands into the blood soaked into his black denim jeans. With his hands stained red, he took a moment to look around.

"Stop horsing around down there," a shrewd voice came through the house. "Get up here already if you're gonna do it."

Cassidy didn't say anything. His eyes scanned the inside of the dated home, cluttered with every antique imaginable, sometimes stacked haphazardly on top of one another. It smelled of old dirt and whatever decades of humidity-ridden boxes accumulated through the years. There were dozens of paintings on every wall, doilies on every table, and splotches on every piece of furniture.

"Well, you comin' or what?"

Cassidy moved toward the staircase tucked away

in the corner. Every step up resulted in a creaking board loud enough to wake the neighbors, in case the gunfight just outside didn't do the trick. He winced with every movement, sending another annoying squeak through the house. It was only seconds before he was approaching the final step to peek his head around the room of the second floor.

What came up the staircase was not what began the climb on the first floor. Eyes glinting in the candle-light and too many teeth for any man to have drooling on the hardwood planks with audible drops in the silence. The sight alone of what had appeared in his home sent Mayor Walker into an immediate frenzy.

Pop. Pop. Pop.

The .22 pistol he had cried out in yelps that matched the old man who was pulling the trigger without so much as aiming. The bullets splintered the wall around whatever it was that had made its way up the staircase, shrouded in darkness and slowly walking toward him on all fours. It moved unnaturally, and Mayor Walker wasted no time in getting to his feet to prepare for a fight.

"What the fu—"

He was swallowed by shadows before he could finish the expletive. When the mayor opened his eyes, he saw not some evil creature of the night with fangs bearing down on him, nor the hideous eyes of fire and brimstone that had sent chills down his spine. He saw two braids falling on either side of his face. He was staring into the eyes of Cassidy, the man who he had just met at the city meeting only days ago.

Cassidy didn't say anything. He didn't blink or

even move. He just watched as the look on Mayor Walker's face turned from fearing for his life to wild bewilderment with each passing second.

"I knew you were nothing but trouble," the mayor said. "I knew it from the moment you stood up in that room to interrupt our meeting."

Cassidy stared ahead, looking through Mayor Walker, never relinquishing the weight of his body pinning the elected official to the floor. More awkward seconds passed. Slowly, a careful smile began to form on Cassidy's face, pushing his cheeks back to reveal small dimples on either side of a grin that was worse than all the teeth Mayor Walker had just thought he saw on top of the staircase.

"Why do you think I paid for security? I know who was behind the death of that waitress at the diner," Mayor Walker continued to speak. "I know that was you. I knew the moment I was informed of what happened. You don't bring prosperity to our community, you bring chaos—and death."

"You don't have a clue what I bring," Cassidy finally spoke up. The braids lifted up above Mayor Walker's face and the weight of Cassidy was gone in an instant. "I have a feeling you are about to, though."

Cassidy turned to pace back and forth in the sitting room the two were in. He had an inquisitive look on his face and motioned with his hands as if he was speaking, but no words came out. He was working his way through the speech that was about to come in his head.

Mayor Walker took the opportunity to bring himself to his feet. He was wearing a striped robe to cover the boxer shorts and worn-out white tank top underneath. His hair was thinning and messy from being tumbled over. His slippers were laid out where he'd been standing before he was tackled. The stained cotton socks he stood in now were less than ideal.

Cassidy made several laps to either side of the room, lost in his own thoughts and rambling under his breath before he finally turned to face the mayor. With a raise of one finger and a twisted look in his eye, he explained himself.

"I wasn't lying about what I offer this town you love so much. Neither of us wants to see such a magnificent, historic city turn to dust and fade into distant memory. But only one of us has the money to make sure that happens."

"We already told you we'd take your damn money."

"It's just not enough. There is simply too much work to be done. So, believe it or not, I actually shot my way inside your home tonight to offer you a choice."

Mayor Walker's own mortality suddenly became his biggest worry in life. Cassidy could see it, plain as day, and he knew the overweight and mildly popular mayor took his word to heart. It was enough, for now.

"Despite what you might think, I am not some mysterious man. I am actually quite straightforward. Would you believe that?"

"What the hell do you want."

"I want just a little more than you do, that's all," Cassidy answered. "I want this city, and all of those who have suffered just the same to feel vengeance at their doorstep in a way rarely felt today. I want the land that was taken so long ago, forced from our hands in the name of progress then destroyed all the same."

"You don't make any sense," said the mayor. "Would you believe that?"

"Let me say this in a way you'll understand, then."

Cassidy took a step forward, inching closer to Mayor Walker's face.

"I need your job."

Try as he might, Mayor Walker just couldn't hold in his laugh. The outburst didn't surprise Cassidy, but the hearty chuckle and misty eyes of the mayor didn't do much to help his mood either.

"Are you interested in hearing the choice I have for you?"

"Sure, buddy, you go on ahead," said Mayor Walker.

"In order to do what needs to be done, as I said, I will need to be the next mayor of Jefferson. I will take that position by use of nitroglycerin if I must. It's a mundane role, I know as much, but it's a necessary one. And honestly, what have you actually done since earning the few hundred votes to hold the position?"

"Is that a rhetorical—"

"It's just the truth, honestly. We all know what you've done, and it ain't worth squat."

Cassidy took another step closer toward the mayor.

"You can step down, announce your sudden and understandably shocking retirement, and name me as the interim mayor without any consequences. There will be no harm that falls on you, I give you my word, man to man."

"You are no man. And there is no real power with that title. Do you even hear yourself?"

"Now, now," said Cassidy. "Just hear me out."

Mayor Walker gestured for Cassidy to continue, refusing to make eye contact as he did. Cassidy obliged him, but not before taking another step closer.

"If you refuse to step down, or if you otherwise subvert my becoming the new mayor of Jefferson, you will unfortunately become yet another statistic for rural suicide awareness and prevention."

"You *must* be high. I ain't gonna kill myself over this stupid bullshit."

"So, you will step down, effective immediately?"

"I didn't say that at all."

"Then it seems we got ourselves a problem."

The mayor shifted his stance. "Seems so."

"There are no other choices to be had, Mayor Walker. As much as I hate to be the bearer of bad news, this is your life now. You can either have it, or you can't."

The standoff between the two had already been tense, but it had reached a new level at this point. Cassidy and the mayor refused to move a muscle, seemingly assuming the next move would be taken by the man standing across from him. The creaky old house held a sour odor, one that could only come from too much moisture contained for too many years. There was a foul feeling that accompanied such an odor, but the mayor was the only one bothered.

Cassidy could see it in his eyes. The decision could not be escaped.

Cassidy had all the patience in the world for the mayor. It wasn't his life on the line, but it was his future. For something like that, he would do whatever it takes. If he had to stand in front of the mayor until they could no longer stand, he would do exactly that.

For reasons impossible to explain, the mayor did the unexpected. He made his decision. He took no time at all in coming to his inevitable conclusion, as grim as it may be. Mayor Walker understood there was no way out of what was happening to him. A man willing to kill his way into his home was a man who had no problem leaving no one left alive on his way out. That much had become painfully clear.

No man could ever face down what stood in front of Mayor Walker and hope for more courage than he had. Even so, it was far from enough. The decision should've been an easy one to make—whether he wanted his life or not. It was not easy, though. In fact, it was anything but. In those final seconds, Mayor Walker was compelled to do something he would have never done before, and in that moment, he felt a loss of control, of agency, and even independence.

As ashamed as he was to admit it, he took comfort knowing he could never do such a thing in his right mind.

CHAPTER 10

Returning home sounds impossible to consider as anything other than an experience of nostalgia, joy, and reunion. It should be the warmest of welcomes, like the embrace of a loved one once thought to be lost. A home that can't provide such a feeling has lost the very fabric of what makes it a home.

For Thomas and Kaya, their return was anything but welcoming. They had each left on their own accord and using their own justification. The road home was the opposite of uplifting. Familiar roads and sights that would have most people fondly looking back on what once was only sent each of them spiraling for reasons entirely their own. They had seen the coming and going of bald cypress trees with draping moss that seemed to foretell their arrival. They had seen the signs for Caddo Lake and knew what it meant.

Kaya had gone through a thousand condescending

comments she was sure to hear from her mom. It was something that kept her up at night, even when she was hundreds of miles away. Something about knowing what was sure to be said behind her back made her feel worse about the entire situation.

Thomas, meanwhile, could already hear the disappointment in his dad's voice. It didn't matter that his work is what sustained the family business that had fallen on his shoulders. It didn't matter that the money he made was enough to continue supporting their family for generations to come. The only thing that mattered was the simple fact that he wasn't there.

The siblings exchanged a worried glance from inside the three-quarter-ton truck flying down the farm-to-market road at what felt like twice the speed limit. They were still trying to get used to the uncomfortable silences that would arise between them. So much had changed in the last few years. It was almost like they didn't even know each other. In all reality, they had no clue who one another was anymore. They lived completely different lives and not once reached out to stay in touch.

Thomas considered bringing up what made Kaya leave. It had driven a wedge between them, and even the whole family when it happened. There were questions he wanted to ask and explanations he felt were owed to not just him, but their mom and dad as well.

Kaya sat quietly, hoping Thomas would do no such thing. The last thing she wanted to do was dredge up the same old fights that stopped them from talking in the first place.

"Well, you ready to see what all this is about?"

Thomas's question came as a relief to the tension building inside the pickup.

"I'm ready to get it over with, more than anything."

"Now you're speaking my language."

The turn into the mile-long driveway revealed more than either one had ever imagined. It extended down through the trees that lined what amounted to a dirt trail before it turned to gravel closer to the house. The family home rose in the distance like a castle tucked away behind the branches, ominous yet familiar, causing both Thomas and Kaya's stomachs to twist and turn. It was made of logs as old as the woods themselves, with a stone chimney that reached into the air on the side

As the pickup caused dust to swirl around their entrance, they realized they weren't the only ones at the home. There was a caravan of trucks, sedans, and one minivan that formed a half circle around the home. People huddled around the home as if an emergency had just happened, but there were no red and blue flashing lights or officers holding reporters back from seeing too much. There was only one man, dressed in all black, standing on top of a 1980s Dodge Ram with his arms held up at his side.

"Well, shit," said Thomas. "We might be too late."

"What do you think is going on?"

"Whatever it is, it sure ain't good."

"You carrying?"

Kaya looked at her brother, knowing damn well what he meant by that question. No one worth their salt ever went looking for a gunfight, but if anyone knew the reality of how fast things could turn fast, it was Thomas. The only problem was she had fallen out of the habit of carrying her sidearm since moving to Austin. She had learned the hard way that protesting in public with a gun wasn't the smartest idea in the world.

As they pulled closer to the house, both of them knew their situation was unraveling quicker than they would have ever wanted. Their first clue was simply the amount of guns that each of the men standing in front of their family home. The second clue was the megaphone blaring from the hand of the man standing on top of the old truck and the unfolded document stretching down from his other hand.

Thomas put their truck in park about twenty feet away from where the caravan had tried their best to encircle the front of their family home. Before he could even kill the diesel motor churning in the driveway, Kaya had bailed out of the passenger seat, more ready for a fight than any unarmed person should be.

When she heard what the man yelling into a microphone was actually saying, she froze. It was Cassidy. The man from the diner, the same one they had lost in the woods after the horrible killing of the waitress with the pancakes.

"This is a deed to *your* land. In my hand, I hold what you have unrightfully called yours for generations," his voice echoed through the megaphone, mixed with static. "I have presented our plans to the city, and they have agreed unanimously to grant me permission to seize the assets described in this deed, including the very land your home rests upon."

There was a brief pause that followed. It was just long enough to give Kaya the chance to get a bit closer to the group, for Thomas to realize he shouldn't let her go alone, and for the man with the megaphone to say something stupid.

"My name is Cassidy, and by order of the city of Jefferson, I am here to tell you that all of your land now lawfully belongs to me."

The laugh that Kaya let out was booming, as if it had been contained deep in her belly for years and years. It rang out through the woods and brought the attention from every man standing in the front yard to her. As the laugh lingered on, Thomas started to realize that she was intentionally trying to annoy whoever was there, and it was working.

"Who are these two fuckwits?" One of the men interrupted her laugh with a useless question.

This time, it was Thomas's turn to step into the confrontation, something he had never been known to shy away from.

"The real question is who the hell are you," he said, brushing his right hand over his hip to rest on the pearl handle of his trusted S&W .44 magnum six-shooter.

The trespassing men caught on quick and turned to face them, pointing their firearms at one of the two siblings. Cassidy followed suit, still holding what he claimed to be a deed to the land that belonged to Thomas and Kaya's family. He had a shit-eating grin that stretched from ear to ear.

Bam.

A bullet suddenly ripped through the document

held in the man's outstretched hand, putting a hole the size of a nickel right through the middle. The bullet tore through the paper and blasted into the earth with a *thud* followed by a puff of dust no more than a few feet from where everyone was standing.

The bullet didn't come from anyone standing in front of the home. Instead, it seemed to be fired from a second-floor window, even though there was nobody to be seen inside.

Whoever fired the bullet may have thought that putting a hole through the deed would have been enough of a warning to put a stop to whatever was happening. Instead, it had the opposite effect. The gunshot set off a chain reaction that would end with too many dead.

The next gunshot came from one of the men standing in front of Thomas and Kaya. He was eager and reckless, a dangerous combination. In just a matter of seconds, the group found themselves in a deadly gunfight thanks to that one's decision. He stood hunched over in a hoodie pulled over his face, torn jeans, and boots as old as he was. He held what looked like a Beretta in his right hand, hip level and aimed right at the siblings.

"Shit," was all Thomas could get out before reaching for the pistol on his hip. He was proud that his quick draw had been nailed down to just over a single second in his years of training. This shot gave him a new record, though. It took half that time to yank out his revolver and put a bullet of his own through the chest of the man that had fired.

Thomas was ruthless. He put another bullet

through the man he'd just hit, if only for extra measure, before he could fall to the ground.

The scramble that ensued was right out of an old John Wayne classic. Every person wielding a gun broke for cover, trying to find a vehicle, tree, or at worst, a body, to hide behind. Thomas and Kaya were no different, they turned to sprint back to the pickup that had brought them into the fight. Kaya may not have been able to return fire, but Thomas sure could. He ran forward with his head turned and his revolver spewing rounds as quick as he could squeeze the trigger. By the time they slammed their backs against the other side of the truck, Thomas was already reloading his six-shooter. He reached into his back pocket and pulled out what looked like another cylinder for the revolver, and with a simple flick of his wrist, six new .44 magnum bullets dropped into the revolver. With one more flick of his wrist, the cylinder slammed shut, and Thomas was back in the fight.

"I need a damn gun over here!"

Pop. Pop. Pop.

Thomas was already halfway through the next six shots, and no one else had been taken out of the fight. They were outnumbered and outgunned.

"I'm not dying like this, you asshole!"

Pop. Pop.

Rounds ricocheted off the truck and others sunk into the metal. Gunfire seemed to surround them, raining down from every direction. One tire suddenly popped, and a hiss of air shot out.

Pop. Click. Click.

"Shit!" Thomas was already out of ammo again. He

went into the rehearsed motions to drop in a new speed load in his revolver, not paying attention to anything other than the armed men approaching their position.

"Thomas!"

Finally, he snapped out of the tunnel vision and saw his sister screaming at him. He didn't know what she wanted and struggled to make out anything she was saying. The bullets just barely missing them were too much of a distraction. There was one word that stood out to him, though. She wanted to fight, but she needed a gun.

"In the truck!" he hollered over the gunfire. "Back seat on the floor!"

Kaya went searching as fast as her body would allow, doing her best not to catch a stray bullet piercing its way through the truck. She closed her eyes and threw herself into the back seat. When she opened them, she was looking at a lever action rifle with wood furniture. Her chest fluttered when she picked it up.

Bam. Click-Clack. *Bam.* Click-Clack. *Bam.*

"That's right, you sons of bitches!"

Kaya was kneeling just behind the front end of the truck with the barrel of the lever action rifle peeking out. She was following several men with the bead on the end of the barrel and wasting no time in firing every bullet she could at them.

Thomas followed suit, reloading twice as often and firing twice as slow. Even so, he was doing every bit as much damage with the bullets as big as his thumb he was dropping into the cylinder.

Together, they put down more men than they could

keep count of. Some clutched at their guts and gave up on the fight in fear for their life, others watched what was happening and chose to take their chances fleeing into the woods. The few who remained, those who dared to face down almost certain death, were the hardest to take down. Screams of men begging not to bleed to death beneath the sunlight filtering through trees were the only thing to cut through the gunfire sporadically popping off. The scene was a sharp contrast to the beautiful landscape that Thomas and Kaya had once called home. Bullets and blood mixed with frantic shouting and followed by awkward periods of silence for reloading created a surefire nightmare for everyone involved.

"We gotta get out of this," Kaya told her brother in the middle of slamming the lever down on the rifle before jerking it back up to chamber a new round. "I'm almost out."

"I'm already out," Thomas admitted.

"Well, here goes nothing."

"Kaya! No!"

It was too late. If there was one thing Kaya knew, it was how to win a fight. She stood up from behind cover, walked in front of the truck with the lever action rifle shouldered, and went to work. Bouncing from left to right, working the lever action with only her fingers to keep the reloads as brief as possible. It was a sight to see. For Thomas, he watched his sister put on a display of courage laced with a little bit of stupidity for good measure.

Just as she broke free and assumed everyone had either been tagged or bailed on the fight, the thought of the man dressed in all black smiling back at her made her freeze. Where was Cassidy? She hadn't seen him at all in the gunfight. She didn't know where he was. Even though she had no idea who the man was, she knew he was bad news.

The quiet that had fallen over the woods around them was eerie. Kaya's eyes raced to find any trace of the man, and she was hoping with everything inside of her that Thomas was doing the same. Birds started to return in the distance, slowly calling out as if they, too, feared for their lives. The Texas sun made itself known more than ever, casting its heat through every branch and leaf overhead to cause beads of sweat to run down her face.

Thomas could only watch as Kaya dropped her guard to search the area. He had no ammunition and knew what little she had left wouldn't go far. He felt helpless and longed for a chance to hope that no one was waiting to fire one fatal shot at his sister. Unwilling to sit by and do nothing, he planted one of his expensive boots in the dirt and shoved off in a dead sprint away from the truck. The way he figured, even a distraction could buy just enough time for Kaya to get the jump on whoever was out there.

Turns out, he was right.

The next few seconds happened in a blur. One man lifted his head from behind one of the sedans before dropping the barrel of an AR-15 on the trunk of the car to take aim. The next man to make himself known was Cassidy. He popped up in the driver's seat of the same sedan and for a split second, made eye contact with Kaya.

"Kaya!"

"I got him, I got him," she hollered back, already leaning her head onto the stock of the rifle tucked at her shoulder.

Before any bullets were fired or another word spoken, the sedan spun its front wheels in the dirt. It threw up rooster tails of mud and grass and anything else the tires could grab. Unfortunately for the man still trying to hide behind the car for cover, everything that went up into the air came right back down on his head.

Bam.

Pop.

Kaya waited to chamber a new bullet, somehow knowing deep down there weren't any more waiting inside the tube.

When the tire stopped spinning, Cassidy sped off inside the car, its engine screaming in response as it struggled for traction through the woods. It honked furiously as it roared between the trees on a wild escape. Thomas and Kaya both watched in amazement for a few seconds before remembering the assault rifle that was surely aimed back at them. Unfortunately for the man willing to fight to the end, the car that raced off into the distance was his only cover. He looked down with disbelief, sinking in only to find a hole in his chest where there shouldn't be one. Blood began to rush out of him. He dropped the AR, took a woozy step backward, then collapsed.

"You see that shit?" Kaya turned around with a smile as wide as Texas itself.

"Sure did," said Thomas. "What the hell was that all about, though?"

"That was the man from the diner, the one we chased out into the damned woods. Looks like the real question is, what the hell is he up to?"

"If I had to guess, I'd say it's the reason we both got called out here."

Thomas and Kaya met up just in front of the house, still standing tall, free of any bullet holes from the fight, and basked in the fact that they were still alive. This time, the sun shining down on them didn't seem so bad.

"I wish I would've never opened that damn letter," said Thomas.

"Think of it this way. If you hadn't, you and I wouldn't have had this chance to bond again."

"If this is what you call bonding, then I *really* wish I wouldn't have opened the letter."

Side by side, the two looked up at the house in front of them. They knew who was waiting inside and after what they had just gone through, they had a better idea as to why they were told to return to such a place. Neither wanted to be the one to take the first step, though.

"After you,"

"No," said Thomas. "It should be you."

CHAPTER 11

A rude awakening was most often reserved for those who are confronted with the unexpected, for those holding the highest expectations, only to be let down, and for those who are brought back down to the earth when their head is in the sky. They are never comfortable, yet somehow, always necessary. Those who experience such a revelation should consider themselves lucky to have been afforded a chance to change, but that is never really what happens.

Thomas and Kaya weren't the kind of people in for a rude awakening because their expectations had already been appropriately set. Their heads were not in the clouds about what was coming their way, and if they were, getting shot at had a funny way of putting all of that to an end in a hurry. There was something satisfying about not being let down, even when it came to the worst situations. After what Thomas and Kaya had survived, after what they had gone through to walk in those oversized wooden front doors, the satisfaction of knowing full well what they were getting into was quickly setting in.

The home held an aroma of ash and ember mixed with leather and wood. It had lost the familial atmosphere of baked goods and the ever-present mess of children. Now, the home was one of plastic-wrapped furniture, dust-covered shelves void of any books, and windows covered in blinds with heavy curtains drawn tight. It was surreal to see and looked like something out of a television show about obsessive recluses. It was not the home that either Thomas or Kaya remembered.

When something familiar finally made itself known, it came in the form of boot steps on the second floor, approaching the steep staircase leading toward the front door where Thomas and Kaya stood. There was nowhere either of them could escape to. They had their own guesses as to who was coming to greet them first, but neither knew for certain. The floorboards creaked and squeaked incessantly with every step.

"Here we go," said Kaya.

"We'll help where we can, then we're getting the hell outta Dodge."

"This place is a trap, don't you remember?"

Before Thomas could answer his sister, a figure appeared at the top of the staircase, wearing an instantly recognizable uniform topped with a cowboy-style hat by only the most dedicated of park rangers.

"Kids!" the man shouted with palpable excitement in his voice.

Davy had aged since they last saw him. His bushy

beard was mostly gray now with random stray hairs growing longer than others. The graying continued up to the hair tucked beneath his park ranger hat as well. His waist had grown beneath his uniform and his eyes had become more tired through the years. He wasn't an entirely changed man, but time was catching up to him. Even so, his warmth, annoying positivity, and curiosity still remained just as they always had.

He carried himself down the steps with a smile on his face and his hands lifted, ready to hug both Thomas and Kaya the moment he was close enough to them. Within just a few seconds, that was exactly what he did.

Thomas knew it was coming and was just as uncomfortable as he thought he would be in the embrace. He knew his dad, he knew this was the reaction to be expected, but that didn't mean he had to enjoy it by any means. As he stood there waiting impatiently for the hug to come to an end, he couldn't help but notice his sister. Her eyes were closed and if he didn't know any better, he could've sworn he saw a tear trickle down her cheek.

Kaya would never have admitted that the hug from her dad, Davy, was exactly what she needed in that moment. She stood there, hoping it wouldn't ever come to an end, and that she would never have to confront her mom about what she put them to. She welcomed every squeeze of her dad's arm around her shoulder as a distraction from what she dreaded most. It went on long enough for her to even consider that her wish might come true.

When it came to an end, all three found themselves speechless.

As they stood only a few feet apart from each other, trying to find words worth saying in their situation, another voice cried out that didn't belong to any of them. It echoed from upstairs, faint yet urgent, and it was without a doubt, the voice of their mom.

"Davy! Get in here! I found something." Her voice came through the steps.

"You're gonna want to come downstairs, babe," he yelled back at her, trying his best to hide the laughter coming through his words. "Come see!"

"Fine."

More boot steps approached from the second floor of the home. Kaya did her best to straighten her posture, fix her face, and for the first time in years, she actually worried about what her hair looked like. She had to suppress the urge to swipe at her short hair and push it behind her ear. It was a forgettable thought, but it irked her all the same. Something had been instilled in her that she couldn't get rid of, no matter how hard she tried. Rather than dwelling on herself, she kept her gaze trained on top of the stairs.

When Rose finally made herself known, it was impossible not to notice two things. The first was how little she had changed compared to Davy, and the second, was the aged hunting rifle she had slung carefully over one shoulder. Her straight black hair draped down her back, as long as the gun itself, looking like it could brush the floor at any moment. Her eyes were every bit as sharp as the last day they had looked through Kaya on her way out of the door. Her posture was stiff, though. During her descent on the staircase, the only discernible difference was the crow's feet that had become carved next to her eyes.

She did not smile.

By the time she reached the three waiting for her at the bottom of the staircase, the tension could have been sliced with a butter knife. Davy kept his smile plastered across his face. Thomas even allowed a smirk to cross his face. Kaya could do no such thing, her slight trembles gave away her true feelings and she knew as much. There was no sense in hiding how she really felt.

Thomas was braced for criticism, but not like Kaya was. The wait for her reaction dragged on without end. The house was dead silent, with no creaks in the walls and floorboards, or background noise from a television—it was suffocating.

"Thank you for coming home." Rose finally spoke, before holding her arms wide open and grabbing her children for a hug.

Kaya finally let her tears flow down her cheeks like rain, struggling to avoid sobbing as she leaned her head on Rose's shoulder. Thomas followed suit, then Davy as well. All four of them stood embracing each other for what felt like an eternity. Any of them could have been the one to break it up, but none of them did. It was a moment which felt to be a long time coming and it was just what the family needed to heal, if only for a few minutes.

"If y'all wanted a hug, you could've just said so." Thomas broke the ice, still held by the arms of Rose, Davy, and Kaya. "Didn't have to go through all that."

For the first time, everyone in the room let out a smile, even chuckle, at Thomas's quip.

"Can you believe we're finally all back together? I kept telling your mom, this is just what we needed, not a second too soon, either," said Davy.

"Mom—" Kaya figured now was as good of a time as any.

"No," Rose cut her off. "I didn't believe your dad when he said you would answer our calls for help. I was wrong. We can deal with that later."

"We are running out of time." Davy's voice sunk along with his shoulders, his elation gone in both his demeanor and voice. "Come here, y'all need to see this for yourself."

Thomas was too impatient for that. "Does it have anything to do with the damn firefight we just went through, out in the front yard? The hell is going on here?"

"What you saw out there has been happening more and more often," Rose said. "We are under attack. They show up, they flaunt their fake papers, and they make demands they should not be making."

"They want our land."

Both Thomas and Kaya looked at each other before returning their focus to Davy, who had become as serious as either had ever seen him before. If this wasn't the first time their home had been surrounded by these gun-wielding lunatics, they really were under attack. There were no exaggerations in the letters they had received.

"Come on," Davy repeated himself.

They all followed him up the staircase, somehow

skipping all the conflict that had been brewing for years. Thomas may have been providing income when they needed it most through his work with Coyote Crude, but if what his dad said was true, he would have no company to run, there would be no more money through the mineral rights of their land. It wasn't just their birthright at stake, it was their livelihood. He didn't understand how they could come after the land they had fought so hard to have returned to their name. He didn't understand how any of this could happen. The worried glances he exchanged with his sister said that she shared the same confusion as well.

When their walk through the old family home came to an end, they found themselves standing in a bedroom that was once deemed to be for guests. Judging by what was inside, it was only right to conclude that Davy and Rose had not had any welcome visitors to the house in a long time. There were countless survey maps pinned on the walls, seemingly detailing the exact borders of every piece of land owned by the Hunter family. It was the life's work of their entire family for generations, and it was under siege. As a result, Davy and Rose had built a war room.

Piles of books and documents, printed email communications, and more laptops than there were people to use them littered the inside of the bedroom. Noticeably absent from the room was an actual bed, or any other normal amenity like food or drinks—it was simply a place of business.

"Are y'all all right?" Thomas couldn't help himself. "This looks bad."

"It really does," said Kaya.

"Just listen," Rose told them.

Davy walked to the other side of the room and tapped a random point on a map that had been pinned up. "This is where we first saw the tracks. They started crossing over fence lines onto our property about eight months ago, and we didn't think anything of it at first. Then, we saw them more and more. We started to realize that it was intentional. So, we did what anyone would do really, we started keeping track of it with these." He reached down and grabbed a folder full of pages that tumbled out when he lifted it.

"Sure, that's exactly what anyone would do," said Thomas, giving a rapid side-eye to his sister.

"The tracks came at the same time, on the same days, leading just a little bit further into the property each time."

"They were looking for something," Rose said, moving over to where Davy was standing.

"That's right. We just didn't know what they were looking for."

This time, Kaya decided to add in her two cents. "Did it have anything to do with a burial vault inside a graveyard?"

Everyone turned to look at her. Thomas's eyes got big, and he shook his head, but Davy was already answering her.

"The family graveyard was the first place we checked. Nothing ever came close to it. In fact, the tracks were going in the opposite direction every time they crossed into our property."

"Which happened about three times a week."

"Until it stopped."

Kaya cocked her head to the side. "Wait, it stopped?"

"Whoever it was found what they were looking for," Thomas answered before anyone else could.

"That's what we were afraid of," said Davy. "We mapped where the tracks had taken us for weeks on each of these you see around you, trying to figure out what we were missing. After a month of this, your mom took me to a place I had never seen before."

"There are some things you could not understand," Rose said, turning toward her husband. "I should've told you about them regardless, however."

"What are we talking about here?"

"The day she took me out onto a trail I'd never walked, through trees I'd never seen before, to see a history carved into the earth that I had no idea existed."

"Our family has been on this land for longer than we could imagine," Rose commented, turning her back to stare at one of the maps. "There are still surprises to be found, even now."

"That wasn't the only surprise we found that day, though," Davy continued. "By the time we made it home, the tracks had reappeared and led directly into our home, right through the front door. We have a storage room downstairs in the basement. We keep important findings, heirlooms, relics of the past, and whatever else we don't want to lose track of down there, all locked away behind a steel door thicker than my growing stomach. Well, that door was wide open, and only a single object was missing."

"An eagle feather," said Rose.

One more time, Thomas and Kaya exchanged troubled glances at each other. The eagle feather was an all too familiar bit of news they hadn't expected. It was the man in black, the man named Cassidy, who had just escaped their gunfight in front of the house. He had used the eagle feather in the diner, and without a doubt, had confused its purpose in spurring on the fight at their home.

"We searched the place up and down for days and we never were able to find anything about where it was." Davy picked up.

"That's because this guy named—"

"Cassidy," Rose interrupted Kaya.

"He's the guy who is starting all of this mess. Apparently, he pitched a multi-million dollar investment to the city, sweet-talked a few of the most important people in town, like everyone down at the sheriff's office, and thinks he has the right to build everything in our backyard."

"That explains the deed he was waving around earlier," said Thomas.

"So, this guy thinks he can steal everything out from under us, and he has the entire city of Jefferson in his back pocket because of a half-assed promise of millions of dollars," Kaya was thinking out loud. "Doesn't our family have ten times the money that Cassidy has? Why don't we just buy them all out, promise something bigger to get them back on our side."

"We offered fifty million first," said Davy, walking over to a laptop and typing rapidly on the keyboard as he spoke. "When they declined that, we doubled the offer."

"A hundred million?"

"No one even batted an eye. They wanted nothing to do with us, no matter how much we offered them."

"That's *really* weird," admitted Kaya. "Something is off here."

"You're right," said Rose, finally dropping the rifle from her shoulder, letting it rest against the wall. "That's why we wrote you."

"We're running out of ideas, and like I said earlier, we're also running out of time. His attacks are getting more frequent. He's bringing more and more guns every time he shows up at our doorstep. If this was fifteen years ago..." Davy's voice trailed off, and he made eye contact with Rose. They smiled warmly at each other.

"We need help," Rose admitted without looking away.

"That's why we're here," said Thomas.

"Whatever we can do," Kaya stepped closer.

Surrounded by maps and papers and existential worry for what's to come, the family waited for an idea to stop Cassidy from coming up—any idea. There was nothing. They returned to silence, this time not worried about how they felt about one another, but instead about what would happen to everything the family had ever owned. Generations of clawing, scraping, and struggling for every single thing, wiped out by the interests of a madman. Cassidy had proven already, that he would kill for what he was after. Even though they knew what he wanted from their family, they still didn't know what he was really after when it was all said and done. There was a deadly mystery hanging over their heads.

"Why did he only go for the eagle feather?" Thomas was always the one to get directly to what mattered most. He had an uncanny knack for asking the right question at just the right time.

"Before we answer that," said Davy, shifting uncomfortably in his stance as he spoke. "We owe it to you to be completely honest. The tracks we found out in the woods, the ones we tracked for weeks, the ones we found in our own home. They didn't come from any man."

"The tracks belonged to a coyote," said Rose.

CHAPTER 12

There was just something inexplicably natural about meandering through the woods on horseback with family. The birds singing their soundtrack to the beat of the hooves smacking dirt with every step was the sort of thing that could relieve any troubled mind. The rhythmic rocking of the horse finding its own way through the trees and the gentle breeze that wicked away any feelings of discomfort. It was serene. Nothing else could come close to recreating this sense of belonging. It would keep even the most stubborn notions of being an outsider at bay.

If only Thomas and Kaya had been given the opportunity to wander so aimlessly. Instead of a peaceful trail ride to put their own mind at ease, they were almost immediately thrust into a hunt for the weeks-old tracks of a coyote, straddling frantic horses who had turned on their riders as quick as a flash.

They had been riding no more than an hour before the first word was spoken. With Davy leading the group and Rose following closely behind him, both Thomas and Kaya were doing their best to keep up. It had been quite a while since either were expected to be so nimble on horseback.

"The coyote would start over there, just above that tree line," said Davy, his arm outstretched to point out a patch of clustered pines about fifty yards away. "It'd follow a trail that runs just ahead of us, same path every time, just going further and further."

Rose turned to look at the two following behind her, she didn't say anything, but her eyes had changed. Her look was one of understanding, and she cast it toward them as Davy rattled on, repeating himself and thinking out loud as they rode. Thomas had a feeling he knew what that look was about, but Kaya knew exactly what it was. They were not dealing with something that could be explained, or even understood, by the logical conclusion of rational thought. They were dealing with something else.

"We told you the coyote tracks came to a stop one day, but we didn't tell you where," said Rose. "It's better if I just show you."

"Show us what?"

Kaya agreed with her brother's question, scrunching her face and nodding.

There was a silence that followed that didn't sit well with them, but there wasn't anything they could do about it. They did the only thing they could, they kept riding along the trail that carried them further into the overgrowing property acquired by generation after generation of their ancestors. This was only one plot of a few hundred acres that belonged to them.

There were dozens just like this, thousands of acres in the Hunter family name.

That thought didn't bring Thomas any comfort. He had used the mineral rights of their land to build unimaginable wealth for their family, living off of stipends sent to his mailbox just so he didn't have to confront the weight of his own birth which placed him into such a role. In his eyes, this land wasn't any different than any other he had used for his own gain. The black gold pulled from the earth itself sold for the same price here as it did anywhere else. He'd come to think of the family homestead as nothing more than an acreage counted along with all the rest.

Kaya had forsaken herself from the land. Unlike her brother, she knew what it really meant and the charge their family had to protect it. She understood why, and this helped her to better understand what so many of her people had taken from them. This left her feeling guilty. It had driven her to fight for what her family had prospered from, even exploited, because so few had such an opportunity.

As the siblings went deeper into the woods, the time to reflect turned them inward, far from the conversation that Davy and Rose carried on ahead of them. Minutes ticked by, another hour came and went. They still rode forward. This dragged on without another word.

Thomas started to believe his parents were going to extreme measures to shame him and his sister for abandoning the family. Their reunion hadn't gone as expected, and because of this, something deep down inside him expected some sort of retribution. He knew they deserved it. Standing across from them forced him to realize that their absence had caused the family to suffer in ways he'd never intended. The money simply wasn't enough.

It wasn't until the sun began to fall in the west, dipping through the sky and casting an orange glow beneath the trees, when their ride came to an end. The sun's rays danced off of the leaves. The birds wrapped their songs and set the stage for cicadas to take over the next performance. Whatever tracks they had been following had long disappeared, leaving only a trodden dirt path that carved its way through the pines and oaks, around the yaupons and greenbriars, and taking their horses to the mouth of a cavern buried by stone and soil.

This cave threatened to swallow their entire family as they rode toward it, staring directly into the blinding sun setting in the distance. Suddenly, despite Davy having led them here all the while, he did something curious as they approached closer to the entrance. He broke off from the trail and brought his horse to a stop, saying nothing as he did, only bowing his head.

Rose took over.

She climbed off of her horse, gently looped the reigns around the branch of a sapling cedar that looked more like a bush than a tree, and stepped into the cave, her hands brushing either side of the stone piled up around the entrance as she walked. Though she never looked back, Thomas and Kaya knew they were meant to follow.

They were met first with a gust of wind that

carried itself out of the cave. It was dark inside the place, which welcomed them into the depths of the ground beneath their feet. A foothold in the rocks could be found with only a bit of struggling, forming a path that carried the three far from the reach of sunlight. After only a few steps, it was unfiltered blackness. At just this moment, a match was struck, and Rose held the flame in front of her face.

"You can come closer," she said.

The flickering glow of the match illuminated the walls of the cave more than it did their mother's face. Thomas did his best to make out any of her features, but Kaya was the first to notice the etchings on the stone next to her. They were difficult to distinguish, but in just the right light, there were rows and rows of artwork that could be seen. Although they could be easily mistaken for vines, dirt, and cobwebs filling up the cave through years of neglect, the etchings were anything but ordinary.

"What is this place?"

"There are more secrets on our land than any of us know about," Rose began before pushing the match to what looked like a handful of sticks and straw wrapped in leather at the end. A torch was instantly made, and its flame lit up the entire cavernous opening they stood inside. "Because of what made the coyote tracks that led us here, this one is no longer a secret."

"You can't be serious," said Thomas.

Kaya slapped him in the shoulder and shushed him. Rose stared without reacting, waiting for the two to settle down in front of her. When their focus returned to her, she explained why they were brought to this place.

"There have long been stories of Coyote by our people. He's been called a trickster and a buffoon, but the legend lives because Coyote is a natural force who shaped the world around us. Different iterations of the legend and its influence have been passed down for as long as we have known to tell them. Few records exist of the most important deeds of Coyote, but in this cave, our family has preserved a single story."

"We came all the way out here for a children's tale?"

Again, Kaya slapped her brother. This time in the back of the head, forcing him to turn around and widen his eyes at her. "Really, Kaya?"

"Listen."

Rose did not wait to continue her explanation. "The story that is carved onto this stone is the tale of death and of how it came to be permanent. It is the story on which grieving and sorrow, loneliness and heartache, even painful remorse, are all built upon. Death did not always exist, not as we know it. When there was a revenant, and our people knew the return of all that we loved, it was Coyote who jumped for joy at the mere thought of true loss."

Rose returned the way she came to the front of the wall of stone, pushing past Thomas and Kaya with the flame held above her head. When she pointed her index finger at the first etching, there was a faint scratching with swirls and lines that made out a wolf-life creature on its hind legs, literally jumping. The animal was surrounded by other people in what appeared to be a tribunal. Rose continued her story, dragging her finger across the stone as she spoke.

"Coyote was alone in wishing for such misery among our people. Against Coyote's wishes, a home was built of the very earth they stood on, and it was a home for those who had died to return. Death was treated as a temporary time away from this world, but this home would welcome the return of our loved ones. The home faced the east."

"On top of this house, a black and white eagle feather was placed in an upright position," Rose said. "When that feather would drip with blood and fall from its weight, one of our people would die."

Rose let her finger sit still on the four lines that made up a home on the stone wall and the scratches that made up the feather, placed exactly as Rose had described it. Just below it, was a red stain that everyone inside the cave knew in their hearts to be the blood indication of death.

The light of the flame danced off the feather and the blood it foretold, unwavering and steady as the laws of nature demanded.

"The songs that were sung to bring back the dead have long been gone from our world. But the story that was left for us says that Coyote was not happy about what was happening to our people. The first bloody eagle feather signaled death and the return of life with but a gust of wind, but it would be the only to ever happen under such rules. When the second bloody eagle feather fell, Coyote entered the home and closed the door, stopping the wind from bringing life back to the dead."

Rose stopped again, this time at a drawing of Coyote once again standing upright, staring over a dead body from within the four walls of the home. The same red stain had smeared across the dead. For a reason that neither could explain, both Thomas and Kaya felt a chill rush down their spines simultaneously.

"Death became permanent, as we now know it to be," she said. "All because of the closing of that door, all because of Coyote."

"And the eagle feather that was stolen from y'all," said Thomas. "That is supposed to be the same eagle feather from this story? The one that predicts death's arrival."

"We have never been able to tell for certain."

"It dripped with blood at the diner," said Kaya. "I watched it happen just before those assholes killed that waitress."

Rose let her eyes fall. They each knew what it meant. There wasn't much else to say about what had been taken from their family. In their own way, each one knew the responsibility that had befallen them. There was an obligation from Thomas and Kaya that did not exist before they entered the cave.

"When the wind blows and we hear its call in the trees, we know what is passing over us," Rose told them. "I brought you here not only to tell you the story our ancestors left, and to show you that what we are facing is real. I brought you here to let you both know that the wind has not stopped blowing for some time now. I am worried that it will not pass over us for much longer."

Thomas and Kaya had never heard their mom talk like this. She was always serious, always one to use fewer words than most, but she was never one to exaggerate. If there was one thing the siblings knew to be absolutely true about their mom, it was that she did not scare easily.

Silence found them again. There was nothing else to look at inside the cave and nowhere else to go. They could only exist inside and think about what had to be done next. The only problem was that none of them knew what to do next.

At that very moment, a booming holler came from just outside the mouth of the cave. "Got his ass!" A few moments later, the same voice came through the cave once again. "Rose! Kids! You're gonna want to see this," Davy shouted at them.

Rose sighed. She flipped the torch that had already started to dwindle into nothing and jammed it into the dirt at their feet. The flame was snuffed out and light they had grown accustomed to was gone in an instant, like the flipping of a switch. The cave consumed any sunlight that dared try to enter, leaving the three in pitch black to try and find their way out. Luckily for them, Davy's excited yells carried through the cave with ease. By the time they had carefully followed his voice back to the entrance, they found a man with a lasso around his belly, his face smashed into the ground, and his hands tied behind his back with the same rope that had stopped him in his tracks.

They had been followed. The man clearly didn't expect Davy to be with them, giving the park ranger a perfect opportunity to catch the trespasser off guard.

He had a knack for being in places he wasn't supposed to be. Yet again, he knew just what to do with his gift.

"He's one of them," said Davy. "That man calls them his Wild Bunch. Thought he could get away, but he ain't faster than the rope."

Rose was the first to approach the man bound and thrown onto his stomach. She wasted no time kneeling next to his face, paying no attention to him spitting dirt out of his mouth and trying to breathe. He had long, unkempt hair and wore baggy flannel clothes with torn jeans and work boots that looked to have been on his feet from the moment he could walk.

"What is your name?"

"I ain't telling you—"

The blow that landed on the back of his head was a surefire concussion, but not enough to force him to lose consciousness. Rose brushed her sleeve off and adjusted her leather jacket. She waited for the man to focus once again before asking any more questions.

"I don't need to know your name. It won't make a difference when I bury you out here. No one will ever remember who you were anyway," she told him. "Why should I?"

"Please, you can't kill me. I wasn't following you, I swear it. I didn't even know any of y'all were out here."

"You didn't? Then why were you here?"

"I was sent."

Rose just stared at him.

"Cassidy sent me. He told me to find the cave."

"And what were you supposed to do when you found it?"

Davy nudged his horse forward and lifted his hand so that Rose could see what he was holding. It looked like a bundle of dynamite from an old Western bank robbery movie. They were red sticks with fuses that jutted out of the top.

"You came here to blow it up? What a piece of—"

Rose shushed Thomas without looking at him. When she turned her attention back to the man that Davy had roped, she had just one more question.

"What does he want? Why is he doing this to us?"

The man spat a mouthful of dirt out again and tried to look up out of the corner of his eyes to meet those of Rose kneeling next to him. His face relaxed, and he ceased any struggles to catch his breath. He held the look of a possessed man as he answered her last question.

"He wants everything," the man said in a dull tone. "He is coming for everything you own and everything you love. He won't stop until you have no land, no money, and no family left to turn to. We are here to make sure he gets what he wants."

"What's in it for you?" Thomas just couldn't help himself.

"You know." Kaya figured she'd chime in before Rose cut them off again. "He's got a point. Why are all these people doing whatever this Cassidy guy says? It doesn't make any sense."

"It doesn't have to," said Rose, never breaking her eye contact with the man. "They say they want what he wants just so he doesn't take what is theirs. It is greed that keeps them by his side, one way or another."

"There are more of us," the man continued. "A lot more. Cassidy has the money to pay us and the will to make sure that none of us fail. You might have caught me, but this cave will be lost to time by my hand or another's, that much I can promise you."

Rose stood up and turned to walk back toward her family. She watched as Davy, Thomas, and Kaya each faced her, ready to do whatever was necessary to ensure the protection of what their family left them. As the man lying face first in the dirt started to scream obscenities and threats at no one in particular, letting his rage spew out without restraint, Rose knew one thing for certain.

They were ready for the fight ahead.

CHAPTER 13

A town hall can be considered to be one of the oldest meetings of the minds between a city's greatest thinkers. They are rooted in the shared well-being of the community, of the common interest of all those involved, and more often than not, spur action in the face of complacency. Industry professionals, academics, spiritual leaders, and the common man with their family in lockstep, each working together to benefit everyone, whether they attended the meeting or not. It is in a place like this where ideas can spread and forever change our way of life.

It is also a place where propaganda can do the exact same thing.

If left unchecked, one individual's ability to convince anyone of anything can turn a town hall into a sales pitch. As Cassidy looked out over the crowd of people that sat before him in the makeshift conference room inside the cafeteria of the Loblolly Place Assisted

Living Center just outside of downtown Jefferson, he knew good and well that there was a chance to seal the deal with the small town community.

"Our beloved mayor is no longer with us," he started, interrupting the ceaseless rabble of people in attendance, forcing them to turn their attention to him one by one. Cassidy stood at the front of the room and waited patiently for everyone to stop what they were doing and wait for him to continue. "As you all know, Mayor Walker's absence will create a void that can never be filled again, not by any member of our community, much less an outsider. I know this to be all too true."

The faces of those attending were blank, but every one of their eyes were locked on Cassidy as he spoke. They hung on his every word like a child begging their parents to answer just one more question. Fluorescent lighting shone down on the crowd, hiding nothing in the shadows, yet revealing even less from the transfixed people from all around town. There were secrets abound in this room, from the city officials to the business owners and even the emergency first responders. There wasn't a single important piece of the city that was not represented at this meeting.

Cassidy felt a tinge of pride swell in his throat. His Wild Bunch was growing faster than he could have ever anticipated. With the right words reaching their ears, he knew they would do anything, go to any end, likely even lay down their life, and all he had to do was ask of it. He could only do such a thing once, though. It was all about timing.

"We are here to not only remember what he did for

us all, but to figure out what we do next. Where we want to go, when we can start our work, and who will lead us all into the future we so desperately need—all of this is on our shoulders," continued Cassidy.

Everyone inside the Loblolly Place Assisted Living Center stared at him without so much as a flinch. There was nothing to say. There were no willing leaders. Mayor Walker had been around for as long as anyone could remember, there was no one else. If there had been anyone else, they would've shown themselves by now. Cassidy knew this better than anyone. It was the exact reason he was alone at the front of the crowd. They were a community in need, and he was there to put them at ease.

"Does anyone know what actually happened to Mayor—"

"We can rise up to this challenge," Cassidy cut the intruder off sitting in the back of the room before their question could be completed. "We have to."

"Who are you supposed to—"

"The decisions we make tonight will shape our future," Cassidy would not lose the moment. "I can promise you one thing, this will not be the end of us."

There were several dozen people now who hung on his every word. The few who felt it necessary to question what was going on were quick to come to terms with what was expected of them. They fell in line just like the rest.

"As your next mayor, I will take this city forward. I promise that I will not let the hard work that has been done go in vain. I will not allow any of y'all to be left behind." Cassidy adjusted the cowboy hat resting on his head, tilting it back and wiping the sweat building up on his forehead. He turned from the microphone that had been placed on a makeshift stand and started to pace back and forth in front of the crowd. His boots clicked on the tile floor, his breathing was short, and he knew if what he wanted most were to come to pass, everything would hinge on the leverage earned inside this room. There could be no failure. "I have already informed your council members of what I can offer you. If you don't know, let me provide you an opportunity to hear it straight from the horse's mouth. I am ready to put more than fifty million dollars into developing new industries, new jobs, and new opportunities for the people of Jefferson. I am prepared to donate hundreds of acres of my own land, stretching all the way from here to Caddo Lake, just to make that a reality." Cassidy produced what looked like a perfectly preserved deed of ownership from his back pocket, letting the document unfold in his hand for the crowd to see.

When the newly produced deed slipped through his fingers and gently floated to the ground only to slide on the floor into the crowd in front of him, Cassidy couldn't help himself but to chase after it. What the people saw was not a sure-footed leader but a bumbling man who was prone to busting his ass. When Cassidy's boot slipped after a hurried attempt to grab the deed lying on the floor, the man in black went face first to the cold tile only inches away from the document he was after.

The people of Jefferson watched with a collectively confused look on their faces as Cassidy did his best to return to his feet. He brushed a bit of dirt off the deed before returning it above his head and waving it from side to side like nothing ever happened.

"I will do all of this without asking anything in return," he spoke confidently, betraying what everyone in the room had just witnessed with their own eyes. "As your mayor, however, I can do so much more for you. I will save our schools, I will bring doctors to Marion County, I will preserve your homes and protect your families. I will not stop until we return Jefferson to the glory it once knew as one of the most prominent cities in the state."

"What's the catch?"

"What a meaningful question, Mr...." Cassidy paused and made eye contact with the burly, bearded man sitting next to his wife in the front row.

"Stevens."

"Mr. Stevens! The owner of Stevens Auto, right? I want you to listen closely to what I am about to tell you, and the same goes for all of you," Cassidy said, turning his attention from the man who asked the question to everyone interested enough in the answer to stick around. "This is the most important part of my proposal. It's only natural to think what I am offering will come at some kind of cost. Only a fool would imagine such an opportunity could present itself for *free*. You need to hear me loud and clear when I tell you this—there is no catch."

He gave them a moment to let his final sentence really sink in. He knew it wasn't what they expected. The dull promises of even duller men had ransacked their own propensity to dream for anything more than a pothole to be filled, a toilet to be repaired, or a fraction of a cent reduction of taxable income. This was the ultimate pinnacle of their own potential, their power, and Cassidy knew himself to be the man to break through it all.

"I already own the land to build our future on. I give it willingly. I've already secured enough funding to give your kids careers if they so choose. I also give it willingly. I only ask for the chance to bring these dreams into reality, a chance which could be afforded to me by becoming your next mayor."

He continued pacing back and forth now, the redness of embarrassment finally leaving his cheeks and a recovered sense of confidence finding its way back into every step.

"You may know about the history of Jefferson, of its rightful place in the state and what has been taken from you all. Did you know this city has been taken before, though? Did you know the city itself was stolen the very day it was built? You see, Jefferson was founded on land ceded, rather forcibly if you ask me, by the Caddo. This began a history of its people taking what they felt belonged only to them."

His speech was poised, even if rehearsed. The people listened and nodded to acknowledge his lessons, sometimes even nudging the person next to them in a generic gesture of open agreement.

"I don't know about you all, but that is who I could only hope to become. I refuse to let bygones be bygones, to let the very land beneath our feet to be strong-armed out of our own will. I will do everything in my power to reclaim this place. I will do anything necessary to return it to what it should have always been."

Cassidy stopped again to face the people in the room. He held his chin up, cleanly shaven to reveal the smooth skin of a man without hardship. His posture reflected the bravado in his voice, and he did his best to look every single person who was listening in the eyes. He was serious, and he wanted them to see every ounce of it.

"There are those who already believe themselves to be the owners of our future, the makers of our own destiny," he continued. "I call bullshit."

"Hell yeah!" a man interjected enthusiastically.

"You heard me. I call bullshit. These people don't have the stranglehold on who we are nearly as tight as they think they do. All it takes is for real people like us to stand up and push back, sometimes even push them on their ass."

"That's right!" Another came through.

"If you haven't heard, they are even planning a takeover of their own. I've personally seen plans for a protest of our investment into our own future. They want to come into our hometown, march through our streets, tell us what we can and cannot do, then leave us to our own misery.

"I will promise you this, I sure as shit won't allow it," Cassidy told them. "You shouldn't even be hearing this from me, but these people are not from here. They are traveling from the big city, places like Austin..."

The room erupted into a chorus of boos.

"Dallas."

Another round of chanting, louder than the first poured out.

"Some as far as San Antonio," Cassidy said, throwing up his hands.

The room was shaking. A sudden life had been injected into the people that seemed to come out of nowhere. They were loud, unwilling to retrain their contempt for the protest they had only just learned about moments ago. Plastic chairs scooted against the tile floor from people rising to their feet a little too quickly. The dull drum of the fluorescent lighting was drowned out by the hollers of men and women more worked up than they had any right to be. What had started out as a community meeting had transformed into something else entirely. It was a rally now.

Cassidy was doing what he'd always intended—leading the increasingly vengeful pleas to keep the protestors out of their city. No amount of convincing would quell the uprising that was brewing inside. Even if there was, Cassidy would have nothing to do with it.

"If we don't stop people like this, it won't matter who the mayor is. The only thing that will matter is who they are going to send to tell us how to live. Do you want some outsider to say what you can or can't do?"

"No!"

The single word echoing out with enough decibels to make anyone's ears ring was nothing more than the sweetest of music to Cassidy's. He scanned the room and knew deep in his bones his work was done. The glint in their eyes, the rage clawing its way out of them, it was unnatural but it was there nonetheless. It burned inside everyone who made eye contact with him, begging to be released, in need of only a reason. With even the gentlest of nudges, Cassidy could provide just what they needed.

He could've stopped there. He could have allowed the people of Jefferson to take what he said to heart and to do with it what they will. For any other person, it would have been every reason in the world to motion for approval of his term as mayor. Cassidy wasn't just anyone, though.

"You need to fight them," he told the crowd, his voice dropping low enough to force the room into silence. "You have to fight them!"

Bam!

A pistol was raised into the air, smoke lifting from the barrel, with a trembling index finger turning bright red from squeezing the trigger so tightly. The gun belonged to a man named Issac Haley, a public transit driver for a private transportation company focusing on rural areas. He stood stoic, allowing his arm to tremble, but holding every other part of his body as still as a deer in headlights.

Bam!

Another round was shot into the ceiling. This time it was fired by the same Mr. Stevens from earlier. He was far from calm, chanting and looking in every direction with a beaming smile spread across his face.

Bam.

Boom.

Bam. Bam.

The gunshots were popping off left and right,

spurring cries of excitement as the people who had just been cheering Cassidy on turned their attention to the celebration of a fight yet to come. It was as rowdy as could be expected. Debris fell around them, lights flickered in the chaos, grown men hooped and hollered like cackling hyenas, and firearms rattled off one after another.

As the commotion continued, a familiar face broke through the crowd. It was Daniel. He was dumbfounded, that much was written all over his face. He elbowed and shoved his way out of the swarms of people in an attempt to stand side by side with Cassidy at the front of the room.

"You'll be mayor by morning," he told Cassidy.

"I'm already the mayor. We have other problems to tend to now."

Daniel cocked his head to the side. Before he could bring himself to ask what Cassidy had meant, he got his answer.

"I only wish I was lying about this protest coming to our town," said Cassidy, still staring directly into the eyes of every single riled-up community member in front of him. "You are going to make sure they don't stick around. I want you to do whatever is necessary to make sure we define any headlines that come out of this."

"You have any ideas?"

"What do you not understand about doing whatever is necessary? I'd certainly be curious to know."

"I didn't mean it like that," said Daniel. "I already know just what to do."

With those words, Daniel pulled the Glock out of

his waistband and lifted it into the air. Without breaking eye contact, he joined the harmony of gunshots going off by adding his own instrument.

Bam. Bam. Bam.

"If they do show up." Daniel spoke after the third shot. "I can guarantee you it will be the last thing one of them ever does."

CHAPTER 14

"You just have to keep following me. I promise it's going to be worth it."

"What have you done?"

"I'm making a difference."

"After what we just learned, how could you possibly know that? We don't know anything about what we're up against."

"Every fight ends the same when you have numbers on your side." Kaya winked at her brother as they turned a corner in a grassy patch, leading them toward the downtown district of Jefferson.

Scuffling, screeching, and sneering were all that greeted anyone who ventured down Polk Street and across Lafayette. Buildings erected in the 1800s watched over hundreds of people lining the sidewalks, jaywalking at random, none of which were born before the year 2000. Posters, banners, chants, and angry faces spewing rehearsed lines in unison painted a picture of public outcry. It was everywhere, making it impossible to focus on anything. It wasn't just a protest. It was an organized takeover of downtown with a mission to be heard.

Their message was simple—justice. They called for justice for the death of Mayor Walker, justice for the death of Macy the waitress, and justice for the death of the process of choosing the city's next leader.

"Justice!" The chants poured out. "Now!"

Thomas was stunned. He turned to make eye contact with Kaya and held his gaze for a few seconds before speaking. "Did you do this?" he finally asked.

"Justice!"

"It wasn't just me."

"How?"

"While you were chasing money beneath our feet, I was building an army," Kaya said.

"Now!"

"No, Kaya, that is not what I mean. How could you do this after what we just learned back in that cave? It hasn't even been twenty-four hours. We don't even know what we're up against."

"It's the same thing we're always up against, don't you see?"

"Justice!"

"This is *not* the same thing. Not even close. You are going to get these people hurt."

"Now!"

The people were coordinating their chants in the midst of unfiltered madness. Somehow, they formed a single voice that could be heard all through town. It was a signal to those who called Jefferson home, beckoning them to stand up to the injustice that was happening right beneath their noses, because the crowd itself was not made up of those who lived nearby. They were not tourists. They were not concerned neighbors. They were protestors, traveling into town solely to make a point.

As the event raged on, the citizens of Jefferson were separated into two groups, neither of which was visible by the eyes of those demanding justice. The first were citizens who couldn't be bothered. They were still locked away in their homes, wasting themselves on serial television playing background to entrenched algorithms aimed at fruitless pacification. The second were those who were too heavily invested. They were followers of Cassidy's, believers in his promise, and they were all too willing to start a fight where there didn't need to be one. It was this group of people that worried Thomas, because while Kaya had remembered the waitress who was gunned down unjustly, he remembered the ones who carried out such a heinous act.

Their chants rang out over and over again as the siblings made their way deeper into the fray. Kaya had a smile from ear to ear as she saw the results of her work. Her heart beamed at the thought of what she could enact with a single phone call. It took only minutes after returning from the cave and listening to the dire situation from her parents to know that she needed to call in every favor she had. This was a case of people undermining institutions, and that was something she knew how to stop. She'd done it before with these very people at her side, and she'd damn sure do it again.

"Kaya!" A man's voice rose from the crowd between chants. "Kaya! Over here!"

Both Thomas and Kaya turned in circles, trying to find where the voice was coming from. A sea of protests flowed by them in every direction, ignoring everything but the fight at hand. It wasn't long before Kaya spotted a face she could never forget, though.

"Adam?" she mouthed, knowing there was no chance for her to be heard in all the commotion.

There he was, plain as day. The man who had tackled her in Austin and stopped her from leaving some asshole lifeless in the street had once again shown up to save her. For a split second, she truly considered the fact that maybe the man really was a guardian angel. When he came up to her and Thomas, she was at a loss for words.

"These people all showed up for you," he told her, still not making eye contact with Thomas. "One phone call turned into a dozen others, that dozen turned out to do more than any of us imagined."

"Not sure how you found enough parking, to be honest," Thomas commented, forcing the strange man and his sister to acknowledge him.

"This is my brother," Kaya said.

"I know what this is going to sound like," Thomas wasted no time. "But you need to get everyone out of here. Y'all shouldn't be doing this."

"Would you stop it already?" Kaya answered for Adam, who was almost immediately caught between the awkward confrontation between siblings.

"You don't know what that man is capable of."

"You don't know what *we're* capable of."

Kaya took a step forward to position herself at Adam's side and turned to face Thomas. She slapped her hand on the back of the man she had only met once before and vouched for him, letting her brother know that she still trusted those who showed up to fight injustice more than her own family.

As fate would have it, the turning point of the protest came when the crowd of people turned onto Austin Street, running right through the historic downtown area. Cobblestones and pavement met in a clash of eras. People marched through a town built more than two hundred years ago with problems inconceivable to those who first laid the bricks that surrounded them.

When the protestors turned onto East Austin Street, just beyond the General Store, cramped to the ceiling with antiques, they were met with a line of unyielding supporters of the man named Cassidy. They stood shoulder to shoulder with one another, making direct eye contact with every person from out of town who showed up to decry the injustice at work, refusing to move so much as an inch. It was clear to see, they would not budge. It was hundreds of people against a few dozen. The proverbial line in the sand had already been drawn.

It took several minutes for the protestors to file through the streets and come face-to-face with the citizens of Jefferson, who had already made up their minds. Thomas and Kaya may have been at the back of the crowd of protestors, but they could still barely hear one another speak from all the racket.

"You have to call these people off," he begged his sister.

"These are the people who are going to put a stop to all this. Why can't you see that?"

"Do you remember the stories Mom used to tell us as kids about Coyote? He's a trickster. We don't have a clue what game he is really playing at. We know he is willing to hurt, even kill, in order to get what he wants, though. If we risk these people's lives knowingly, their blood is on our hands."

"Do you even hear yourself anymore? When did you grow so obsessed with inaction? You used to be all about shoot first and ask questions later. Now you want to do nothing?"

"That's not what I'm saying, and you know it," said Thomas.

"I brought these people here because our family is under attack. You think we can keep this fight up much longer by ourselves? You saw what they did to our home, they surrounded it with guns and misguided men. Whatever it is we are up against, it's obvious that we don't have time for talking. We have to act."

Thomas thought for a second, trying to find the words that would always escape him in moments like this. "Do you have some sort of plan? Or is it just a bunch of yelling and arts and crafts to make posters?"

"The plan is to draw out Cassidy," she said bluntly. "We know he is behind this somehow, but if he is always hiding and making other people do his dirty work, nothing will ever catch up to him. We need this

town, and anyone else who will look, to see him for
what he really is."

"Which is what, exactly?"

"A murderin', lyin', son of a bitch!"

This time, Thomas considered something he hadn't
thought of yet. He gazed around at what was
unfolding around them, thinking about what they had
already witnessed in just a few days after returning
home, and asked the most important question yet.
"Does Mom and Dad know about this?"

"Well," she started. "About that."

"Kaya!"

"Thomas!"

It was Rose and Davy, and the guttural fury in their
shouts were palpable from a mile away. They had
caught wind of the protest, and it didn't take long for
either of them to figure out who was behind it all. For
those who know firsthand the angriest their parents
have ever been, who can recognize a particular tone
even out of a crowd of hundreds screaming at the top
of their lungs, they also know there is no getting out of
what was to come. This was the feeling shared by both
Thomas and Kaya, who stood reduced to helplessness
in the face of their parents' blistering expression and
knew their day was about to get a lot worse.

"What in the actual hell is going on here?" Davy
was heated. "Did either of you have anything to do
with this?"

Kaya looked at Thomas, only to find that he was
already throwing her under the bus.

"I was just asking her the same thing," said
Thomas.

"This has to stop," said Rose. "Now."

"All of you need to let me handle this," Kaya immediately pleaded. "This isn't my first fight. We all know who's behind all of this. Cassidy is up to the same bullshit we fight almost every day back in Austin. These are fights we *win*."

"This ain't Austin," said Davy.

"And this ain't just some career politician." Rose backed up her husband.

"Kaya, how do we get these people to leave here?"

"You can't," she admitted. "It's not like they obey every word I say. We work collectively, chasing injustice and putting a stop to it wherever we go. This is what these people do every single day. They know too much of what is going on here. They think a hostile takeover is happening and that it's only a matter of time before the media shows up with cameras and microphones to make sure the rest of the state, and hopefully the country, knows what's happening."

There wasn't even enough time to huddle before the situation turned south. While the Hunter family was lost in their bickering about what was unfolding in town, the dominoes had already started to fall. They were too late. There were too many forces at play for anyone to stop.

Everything started with something as mundane as a passing glance. A protestor crossed paths with the wrong man standing in line at the end of the road. Even though nobody arrived to smash their fist into the nose of an agitator, that's exactly where these two random individuals found themselves. With a railroad at their back and a churning sea of protestors approaching like waves pouring onto the shoreline, the first two fists flying in the air were the only spark needed to ignite a flurry of violence. It didn't matter that the citizens standing up for Cassidy were outnumbered. It didn't matter that they didn't possess a single advantage. They were up for the fight.

Thomas could only see a swarm of people swallow the brawl unfolding ahead of them. It was impossible to make out what was happening in the chaos of flailing limbs, frantic faces, and a complete breakdown of any sense of affability. The only thing left for him to do was to assume the worst.

Kaya had already come to that conclusion. She had broken from her family in a dead sprint toward the swirl of people either joining the fight or trying in vain to bring it to a swift end. The protestors flung themselves in every direction, giving away their intentions with every desperate action. Some of them were no different than Kaya, all too willing to throw their fists into the mix only to see what landed. Others couldn't get out quick enough. Their escape made for a challenging route not only for Kaya but for the inevitable chase her family would surely be forced to endure.

By the time Kaya shoved her way into the skirmish, there was only blood and carnage to be found. She was horrified to lay eyes on what the people she had come to know were truly capable of. Five men with hair to their shoulders, month-long beards, and torn shirts barely staying on their bodies were piled on top of the only citizen willing to break the line they had formed. As the protestors beat him senseless,

Kaya couldn't help but notice the trance-like stare frozen on the faces of Cassidy's supporters.

The line they held still had not been broken. Only one of them had taken on what felt like the entire protest. Kaya shuddered to think of what they would all be capable of. Instead of allowing such a thing to happen, she fought tooth and nail to pull the protestors she'd unleashed on the town off of their victim. The blood on her hands was not her own, but it made her see red, nonetheless.

When Thomas arrived, he saw the worst-case scenario playing out. His sister had thrown herself into the pile, trying to claw raging men off of one another to no avail. He hoped there were authorities on the way who could put all of this behind them, but something deep down told him the only chance they had of getting out of this unharmed was slipping through bloody fingers.

"Everyone get out of here!" It was all Thomas could think to say.

"Don't you even dare!" His begging was met with an unexpected voice carrying out across the crowd from the blast of a megaphone. It was Cassidy, standing on a makeshift lectern. His braids were parallel with his frown. His eyes seemed to overlook a dire tragedy. His posture was anything but defeated, however, with a megaphone grasped in one hand and his other resting on his hip, just above a revolver tucked inside a black leather etched holster hanging from an oversized, worn belt.

"You've come this far! Each and every one of you," Cassidy spit into the microphone. "You can't leave now, not when there is so much left for us to do!"

"Thomas, get Mom and Dad out of here!" Kaya wasted no time in trying to change the tide against her family.

"You're coming too," he hollered back at her through the riot beginning to take root in downtown Jefferson. "This is getting out of control!"

"Just go!"

Thomas turned to see if he could find Davy and Rose, scanning a distraught horizon to find the two people who were undoubtedly the oldest in the crowd. His eyes darted back and forth, and his stomach sank a little further every second. He started to contemplate the decision he was now confronted with. Was he supposed to run off and find Davy and Rose before they were trapped in the frenzy, or was he meant to save his sister before she became a victim of the riot herself?

There they were. Standing side by side, far from any harm. In the blink of an eye, Thomas knew they were safe. He understood what he had to do. He turned around and stared into the abyss of a bloody mess made of broken knuckles, gashes, and busted lips. Then he charged ahead.

There was only hell everywhere Thomas looked. It was as if an unnatural force compelled them to such ruthless actions. The wild look in the eyes of the protestors told a story that was impossible to understand by earthly rules. Dilated with hate, spraying in every direction, these were the eyes of enraged beasts. With gnashing teeth and flailing fists, the people fought ferociously with only a handful of Cassidy's supporters. Those who remained continued to form a barrier to protect their self-anointed leader.

Through it all, Thomas waded deeper to find his sister. She was beyond yanked in every direction, screaming and shoving to no end. Just as Thomas was able to reach out and grasp Kaya's shoulder, they were stopped in their tracks alongside everyone else at the sound of Cassidy's voice.

With the flip of a switch, from dark to light, from noise to silence, from chaos to civility, every person in downtown Jefferson remained still and watched the man standing above them all speak. His voice echoed throughout the age-old buildings and wrought iron fences, contained only by the cobblestones below and the blue sky above for all to hear. To Thomas, his words came as prophetic and even a little preachy, but to Kaya, the words were laced with poison.

"My dear city, and those who would invade it, this violence will not get us anywhere. It is a directionless refuge. It is a means to an undesirable end," he spoke with near-righteous intent. "There is a better way."

Thomas and Kaya were every bit as transfixed as everyone around them. The protestors and the ones who stood in their way were no different in this. Against a backdrop of the Big Cypress Bayou winding through the trees, the people watched a different kind of force of nature carve out its own path in the world. It was every bit as unpredictable, unstoppable, as the creek. But it was also terrifying.

Thomas and Kaya didn't see just a man leading a city into disarray—they saw Coyote. The beast stood upright on its hind legs, snarled through an evil grin, and looked out at its work with unnerving content. It was a towering menace covered in matted hair standing at the lectern, and it was holding a bloody eagle feather. The voice that reached the ears of both siblings was that of a man, though.

Before they could come to terms with what they were witnessing, the situation took yet another turn for the worse.

"Daniel, please show them the way."

A man rose up from somewhere behind Coyote, a stamped and sealed document in one hand and a black pistol in the other. He didn't say a word, he only looked out at the crowd without so much as an expression. A second man was lifted up next to him. This time, Kaya gasped.

"Adam! No!"

Daniel lifted his arm, extending the pistol out to meet the forehead of Adam, who had been forced to kneel and accept his damnation. There was nothing left to say or do. Only for a simple pull of a trigger to bring it all to a cataclysmic end.

Bam.

CHAPTER 15

The Wild Bunch of the 1800s wasn't known for their gentle-heartedness or willingness to roll over to accept a fate they did not intend. They were known all around for their exploits, but not everything that was told turned out to be true. Despite the legend's insistence, they were killers. It was money and riches they were after, of course. From what was locked away inside the biggest banks to the trove of wealth that was loaded onto every train through the West, they were only a gunshot away from calling it their own. Whether their back was against the wall, or their eyes were set on a fortune in gold, they too would call upon death's name.

With the return of the gang under Cassidy's watchful eye in Jefferson, they lived up to their name in every way imaginable.

When Adam's body collapsed to the ground, it should have signaled a panic. It should have caused emotional distress to take hold and for everyone in the vicinity to flee for their own lives. That is not what happened, though. Air as thick as the blood still filling the street hung over the crowd frozen in fear, the only believable explanation as to why no one who'd witnessed the gunshot was willing to even take a breath.

"We gotta go," Thomas insisted, his hand still gripping Kaya's shoulder. "Now."

"We can't," she said, refusing to look away.

"Kaya, it's now or never."

"We can't leave him! I won't leave him!"

Thomas wasn't begging anymore. He squeezed Kaya's shoulder hard enough to leave bruises where his fingers tightened and dragged her away from the bloodshed. They put one foot in front of the other, passing through a street full of people incapable of moving a muscle. This lasted for only seconds, but they felt like hours. When they had reached the sidewalk where Rose and Davy waited, the crowd snapped back to their senses, and like the turning of a tide, fled the streets of downtown Jefferson.

"Run!" they screamed almost in unison.

"Call the cops! Call 9-1-1!"

"They killed him!"

"He's gonna kill us all!"

The protestors were drowning in their own dismay. They couldn't sprint fast enough, leading to many tripping and falling to the ground. Skinned knees and cries in terror poured away from the lectern where Cassidy once stood. It was a brief appearance, but it was more than enough to accomplish what he, and his followers, deemed necessary. The uprising which had threatened Cassidy's rise ultimately cost Adam his life.

"He didn't deserve to die like that," Kaya said.

"There aren't many who do," Rose assured her. "It isn't safe here."

Thomas and Kaya locked eyes, both refusing to acknowledge out loud what they had just experienced. It wasn't something either of them could easily put into words, but they both knew what they'd seen was as real as the bullet that had taken Adam's life. They didn't need to say anything for Davy and Rose to know what they were going through.

Thomas turned away before he could be convinced otherwise. When he looked down, he was sprinting as fast as he could. It was like his own thoughts had to catch up to what his body had already decided. He was thirty feet away before he knew it, running right back in the direction he'd just come from. There was no Cassidy hovering over the crowd, no Daniel threatening them all with a gun, and no protestors raging on one another. By the time he'd even realized what he was doing, the adrenaline had carried him right back to a puddle of blood staining the gravel road.

He lifted his right arm without realizing his trusty .44 magnum was resting within his grasp. His eyes scanned the chaos, leaving them behind. There was no catching up to any of them. The out-of-town protestors were scattering to their crossover SUVs, electric cars, and rideshare vehicles, none of them giving so much as a glance back as they ran.

"He's good." Kaya's voice came from behind him.

"There's no way he got out that fast. He's here somewhere. He has to be."

"Don't make my mistake, Thomas. That isn't a man. It's Coyote who has come for our own land and everything we have. There is no winning this one."

"If that's what you really think, then you need to be hightailing it outta here with the rest of your hippie friends."

"How many times do we have to keep losing before we come to terms with it? How can you still not understand just how dangerous this whole situation is? I know you saw the literal coyote figure standing up on its hind legs, same as me."

"I don't know what I saw," said Thomas. "Other than the fact that one man shot another man in cold blood, killed him right in the street in front of everyone. That was enough for me."

Had they not been talking, they would've seen the three men clad in flannel and denim doing a downright horrible job at sneaking up on them. Their heavy boots and labored breathing would've given away their presence to anyone.

Thomas was the first to get sideswiped. One of the burly men speared him to the gravel, pushing his face into the rocks. Blood and dirt mixed into the skin being scraped off his face as he slid forward with the man on his back. His weight was unbearable. Hundreds of pounds crushed his ribcage and his spine, forcing Thomas to fight for every breath. A sharp pain on his left side told him a rib had been broken, but there was nothing he could do about that.

Kaya didn't last much longer, but it took two men

to bring her to the ground. With one on each arm, they dragged her kicking and screaming to the same gravel that her brother was pinned against.

"Tell him we got them," the one on top of Thomas said.

"You don't got shit! You hear me?" Kaya was enraged.

"Get the hell off me!"

One of the men sneered and laughed, pushing all of his weight onto Kaya and forced her cheek against the pavement. A single scratch made a red line across her face. No matter how hard she struggled, the men matched her efforts to keep her unable to move even a single limb.

"Where are we supposed to take them?"

"No one ever told us."

"Someone get a hold of him. We won't be able to hold them for too long. This whole thing has gone to shit."

There was an awkward silence interrupted only by the struggling of the siblings trying their damndest to get away.

"Are we sure these are the right people?" The voice of one of the men on Kaya betrayed the doubt in his gut.

"What do you mean? This one had a damn gun. A White guy and a Native woman. That's what he said."

"They're younger than I thought they'd be, that's all."

"Well, that just goes to show you don't need to be doin' any more thinkin'," the one lying on top of Thomas quipped.

These weren't just concerned citizens, they had been prepped and debriefed exactly for what had happened. One of them pulled out a wad of black commercial-grade zip ties, fumbling with trying to get situated while preventing Kaya from swinging her fist at random. She fought valiantly, but her efforts were in vain. With a quick jerk, the zip tie pulled tight and Kaya could only wiggle against the restraints. She sliced her wrists in a matter of seconds, staining her hands with a deep red before finally succumbing.

By the time she had the sense to check on Thomas, he was in the same situation as her. His wrists were tied behind his back, and his nose was flattened against the pavement. His entire face was soaked with blood, and his breathing was choppy. There was a worry in her gut for Thomas that she almost didn't recognize.

This time, when they made eye contact, it was only deep concern that could be found. There was no more animosity hidden behind reserved niceties. For siblings, this was the best they could ever hope for. A lifetime of competing and a few years of giving one another the cold shoulder had changed their dynamic.

The fight they'd both found themselves in changed all of that, though.

Downtown Jefferson looked different by the time Thomas and Kaya were dragged onto their knees with their arms still behind their back. The protestors had fled, and the outbreak had died down. All that remained was the despair of a town being hijacked from within.

"What just happened?" Thomas couldn't bring

himself to look at his sister. The feeling swirling in his stomach wasn't guilt, but it damn sure felt like it.

When Kaya didn't respond in time, one of their captors took the pleasure of answering for her.

"You don't care what's happening. You never cared when our town was dying. You never cared when our people couldn't eat, much less afford a place to sleep. Cassidy told us all about you. You people don't care about anything you can't get your greedy fingers wrapped around."

"Cassidy ain't what you think he is," said Thomas. "You are being lied to."

"He also said that's what you'd say," another man said, this one with a thick accent and an even thicker skull.

Kaya let out a sigh. She finally took the time to turn to Thomas and—ignoring all of their captors standing around like bored construction laborers—told her brother everything that she was feeling with just a glance.

He couldn't accept her resignation, however. He twisted and turned his wrists against the zip ties. On the verge of breaking loose, he moved like a madman against the razor blades, digging into his wrists. His bloody hands soon matched his sister's who was futile in her own attempts to free herself.

The three men who'd captured them soon turned to six, then a dozen. There were more than either of them could take, and they knew it. After listening to the confusion about who they were told to apprehend, both Thomas and Kaya had an unspoken understanding.

They were not the ones who were supposed to be taken.

At least one of the men had enough brains to bring a pair of canvas bags. When the sun was blotted out, and they were both forced to surrender to whatever may come, Thomas was the first to feel the fury of Cassidy's followers. The blow landed in the middle of his face, turning his nose to the side and splattering blood inside the bag. He coughed and doubled over but was held from falling to the ground. As soon as he recovered his breath, another blow landed, this time directly into his gut.

Kaya wasn't much luckier. A fist the size of her head slammed into her left cheek, then the right. Her brain rattled with every hit, and her vision went blurry. She refused to go down, though. She held herself upright, accepting whatever torture the men felt they could enact on her. The grunts that came out with every strike were reactionary, but that would be the only inch she'd ever give them. Anything else would come through blood alone.

When they were both sufficiently beaten down, one of the men they couldn't see gripped their shoulders and dragged them away, still on their knees. The gravel was rougher than Thomas remembered it being. Rocks scraped the skin off his knees, and the blood from his wrists left a trail no one should ever follow. If he had seen the writhing and squirming his sister was doing to challenge those who obeyed Cassidy's every wish, he might've been inspired to fight more himself.

There was no changing what was about to happen to them, though. A dozen of Cassidy's strongest, most loyal followers amounted to a lopsided confrontation with Thomas and Kaya. The best they could hope for was a distraction, but even they knew such a thing would never come easily.

"You still alive?" Thomas risked a question.

"Gonna take a lot more than these so-called men to put me under."

Her voice was reassuring. She was as headstrong as ever, even with a bag wrapped around her face while being carried off to some random location to likely be killed without drawing undue attention.

"What are we going to—"

"Shut up!" A gravelly voice boomed out over the top of them both, interrupting Thomas's next question. "Or I'll have to get to swinging again."

"Were those your fists? I thought a preteen girl obsessed with boy bands had found us. I'd be embarrassed if I were you," Kaya said, followed by a slight, condescending giggle.

"You don't need to make things harder on us," Thomas told her. He wanted to believe he knew what she was up to, but it was the furthest thing from the truth. He felt his body lift from the pavement, offering a little relief from the burning sensation of his kneecaps that had been torn to shreds in the process. "I'm sure these gentlemen train a heck of a lot more than they'd admit, or at least that's how they smell."

"I'm not so sure about that," said Kaya, turning her head to try and find where Thomas was through the canvas bag tied on her head. "I've been hit harder by a mosquito in the middle of winter."

This time, the blow from one of the men came to

the back of her head while she was being carried. It was disorientating, jarring. There was only a brief, guttural grunt that she couldn't refrain from letting out. Judging by the force of the impact just above her neck, Kaya knew she'd struck a nerve. Someone had the gall to use the butt of a rifle to try and knock her out cold.

"This bitch is so annoying." The words came as sweet justification for what she had been trying to do.

"She won't be running that mouth much longer."

"Not when that thing gets a hold of her."

"Y'all ever see it in person?"

"Nope, and I don't wanna either."

Kaya was starting to rethink her plans as she listened to the conversation taking place. She knew what they were talking about, even if they assumed she was in the dark. That wasn't what made her second guess herself. It was the fear that had been struck into the kind of men that weren't afraid of beasts in the night. These were the kind of men who'd carry a spotlight and a .30-06 rifle slung over their shoulder to trek across a few hundred acres at midnight only to find any four-legged creature unlucky enough to cross their path. It wasn't natural.

Thomas was practically begging his sister to not make matters worse. The only problem was he couldn't actually say that, and any facial expression he tried to convey was covered by the canvas bag tied shut over his face. He knew exactly what the men were afraid of. He was afraid, too. He knew Kaya wasn't the one to back down from any fight, but he needed her to think about this differently. If they had any chance of surviving what was to come, that would be their only hope.

"I heard he's actually a cannibal, that he ate the mayor and threw his body off the roof of his own home to hide how mangled the body was."

"I heard all the money he's promised is actually his," another man who hadn't spoken yet chimed in. "Rumors are that he's richer than any of us know. They say he made up all the companies he says are investing in our town. You can look it up online, there ain't a single trace of the guy. It's like he didn't exist before he showed up at that city meeting."

"Let me tell you something," the one holding on to Thomas started in. "If you need to tell everyone to go read whatever shit you found on your phone, it probably ain't as credible as you want it to be."

"Why you always gotta be a dick to me?"

"Billy," the man said, trying to fight back a sigh. "Everyone in town knows what you get up to when you're by yourself. It ain't no good. You been spreadin' the wildest shit around as long as I've known you. That's all good and well, but let me give you a piece of advice."

Everyone was interested now. Thomas and Kaya refused to interrupt the contemptuous conversation taking place.

"Don't push your luck with this guy," the man continued.

"You mean Cassidy? It ain't him I'm afraid of," said Billy.

"You should be."

"He don't have near as many teeth as what I seen

running around my woods. If you saw what I saw, you'd be right there with me."

"Even you just admitted he's got millions of dollars. Don't matter how he came about all that money. What matters is that he's got it. You really think someone with that much money has any problem putting down people like us?"

"Cassidy is going to save us," one of the men holding on to Kaya said, changing the mood immediately. "It ain't about the money. Why would someone with that much money care about any of us?"

"He's got a point there."

"He doesn't have to do anything for our forgettable town in the middle of East Texas. He's doing it because he cares."

"The words of a true believer right here," said Billy.

It was about this time that Thomas began to catch whiffs of something that he couldn't quite put his finger on. The bag that had been used to blind, or otherwise confuse them, carried with it a scent that lingered in every breath Thomas took. At first, he listened to the prattling of their captors and tried to imagine what they would do to escape when given the opportunity. His thoughts only drifted back to the metallic tinge in the air he was forced to suck down from inside the canvas cover.

"He's dangerous," one of the men said.

"There's worse out there," said Billy. "Trust me."

Was it rotted onions? Thomas cycled through anything he could think of that might match what he was smelling. Maybe it was some kind of fishing equipment storage.

"The only thing that could be worse is living like we have for another few years. I don't really give two shits whether he is a psychotic murderer or a real-life godsend straight from the heavens above. I am sick to death of putting in eighty-hour weeks making eight bucks an hour only to spend it all on that damn daycare because my wife can't stick around any longer than it takes to sort through the medicine cabinet."

"I'm telling you," the one holding Kaya reaffirmed. "He's here to save us. I know he is."

It might have taken longer for Kaya to catch wind of what Thomas had picked up on, but when she did, she put the pieces together in a matter of seconds. The bags tossed carelessly over their faces had been doused in blood. The thing about being forced to inhale rags soaked in blood that wasn't their own was the realization of what had to happen for them to get that way.

They had both only been dragged away from downtown Jefferson for what felt like minutes, but the slamming of heavy steel doors and twisting of bolted locks told them their situation hadn't gotten any better. The air was musty and hot, like there hadn't been any air conditioning pumped through the room in months.

"I'm going to do more than save you," a voice suddenly hissed through the room, chilling and depraved. It was familiar, deathly serious, the kind of voice that raised the hair on the back of Thomas and Kaya's neck. It was Cassidy.

"I am going to remake you."

CHAPTER 16

Steel bars extending down into the earth itself, reaching for the heavens above, have a funny way of stopping anything that dares to enter its path. They know nothing other than to be exactly as they are, unflinching no matter the will of those trapped on the wrong side. They can do nothing to help ease the burdens of those people. They can only remain steadfast. As is so often the case, the same steadfastness can be found in the ones who find themselves staring down these bars. Hard-headed and stubborn about it, these people tend to meet their match in such a place. It is as inevitable as the sun's light they cannot be warmed by, or the rain they cannot feel coming down.

The jail cell is where many things can happen, where all walks of life can find themselves, and where anyone can be forced to come to terms with who they really are. More importantly, it is where people are placed as recompense for what they have done.

Anything less than this can be summed up in a single word—unjust.

That is exactly the place where Thomas and Kaya found themselves. They were locked behind bars in a cell that was just barely large enough to hold both of them. It was too dark to see a hand in front of their face. There were no cicadas screeching in the distance or cars rushing by. There were no whispers of men nearby or shuffling of paperwork. There was only a deafening silence which threatened to swallow them up long before the darkness ever could.

"Kaya," muttered Thomas.

"What?"

It was as blunt of a response as he could expect, but at least it was confirmation that she was still alive. After what had happened to them, not even that was certain.

"You okay?"

"Don't know. My face hurts like a son of a bitch, though."

"Mine too."

Kaya reached up to feel her cheekbones and recoiled at what she discovered. Both of her cheeks had gashes that stung like a fiery brand piercing through her skin when she touched them. It was impossible to tell how much she had bled in the darkness, but her face and now her fingers were both sopping wet. She knew deep down what it was.

"What the hell happened to us back there?"

"We got our ass kicked. That so surprising for you?"

"What's that supposed to mean?"

"Exactly what I said. You ran off into a mess of shit and got both our asses kicked into the dirt. So, thank you for that."

"This ain't all my fault."

"That's news to me."

"Do we really need to talk about how you flew off the handle bringing in hundreds of fuckin' Austin hippies to deep East Texas like they would ever make a difference? On top of that, you did it without telling anyone, and you did it hours after we found out our family was being attacked by something that wasn't even a man."

"I'm not apologizing for taking the fight in our own hands and putting it on their doorstep instead of fending off gunhands in our front fuckin' yard."

"You didn't bring in an army, Kaya, you brought in a bunch of trust fund nepo babies who can afford not to have a job," said Thomas.

"So, that's what you think of me, huh?"

"I didn't say that."

"You might as well have," Kaya shot back.

Silence returned to the cell they were both locked inside of. They had done their best to

not shout at one another to not draw unwanted attention. Their voices rose to a loud, raspy whisper, doing everything possible to convey their own burning anger in their bellies. All of the pent-up frustration with each other that had built up through the years was starting to give way, and what remained was a relationship in name only. They were nothing alike, Thomas and Kaya. They walked different paths in life, and they did so for a reason.

The years were starting to catch up to them. When it came to the struggle of their family and their role in it, they almost never agreed. It should come as no surprise they would clash only days after returning to their home. Sucked into a fight that was theirs because of the lineage they were born into, there was only one opportunity to turn the momentum in their favor, and they had blown it spectacularly. Now, they could only sit and stew in their failure.

"When you left, Mom and Dad didn't know how to handle it." Thomas changed the subject. "They turned away from everything. I'd never seen them act like that before, and they never really got over it. Nothing ever went back to normal. They let every business they had, go to shit, and if I hadn't stopped them when I did, they would've sold every bit of land to their name and hid inside that damned house."

"Let me guess, that's my fault too."

"Shit, Kaya, can you just hear me out on this."

After an extended sigh through the dark, Thomas decided that was as good as it was going to get.

"They never wanted to push you away. Dad didn't take it half as hard as Mom, though. She didn't talk for weeks, and when she did, it wasn't the same. She would never admit the only thing bothering her was that she missed you, but that's what it was. I could tell."

"Since you want to pour your little ol' heart out, why didn't you stop me?"

"How could I? Nobody ever could tell you anything."

"You didn't even try."

"I did the only thing I knew," said Thomas. "I went to work. I started Coyote Crude to put our land to work the same way those who came before us did."

"By raping it?"

"By supporting our family."

"You can call it whatever you want, but there was no way you could catch me standing behind those businesses. I couldn't even sleep in that awful house, knowing what it was built on. Every time it so much as crossed my mind I would get sick to my stomach. I had no choice but to leave. The fact that no one could understand that only proved why I had to go."

"You really want to say it was just because you were better than all of us? We don't even do any drilling. Did you know that? We offer exploratory services, that's all. Mineral rights can't make any money if no one is using the minerals."

"Call it whatever you want. I had a spine at least. Still do, too. Y'all may be fine selling out to those who stole and pillaged our people before damn near wiping them from existence, but I just didn't have it in me."

"So, the answer is to forsake your family and run off with a bunch of strangers who don't give a shit about you? Do you even hear yourself? You didn't have a spine, you just ran from your problems just like everyone else."

The last sentence hit Kaya like a ton of bricks. The weight of the darkness enveloping them and the suffocating silence that threatened them between every breath was enough to set her off, but what Thomas had said cut deep. She relished the fact that it was too dark for him to see the tears splitting off into several streams down her swollen, bloody cheeks. If it didn't hurt so bad to wipe her face, she would have discarded those tears the moment they showed themselves. Stuck in a jail cell with the one who had made her cry to begin with, she could do nothing but wear every tear with pride.

Thomas's eyes had finally started to adjust to the blackness around them, allowing him to see shadows in the night, but not much else. He couldn't see the tears he'd caused his sister to shed or just how rough she'd been beaten just to stand by his side. He couldn't see the look in her eye as she listened to him coming at her. All he could see were the steel bars in front of him.

He was sitting with his back against a block wall that was colder than it ever should have been. He'd woken up on the floor right where he sat, and he assumed Kaya had done the same, only that she was lucky enough to have been placed on the lower bunk. It wasn't his first cell to be locked inside—something he never cared too much to admit—but this one felt different. They hadn't been read their rights or even told what charges they faced. They'd been scraped off the pavement, dragged to the closest jail, and dumped in a cell all alone. That meant two things for sure.

First, Cassidy was already too close to the local law enforcement. He had them doing his bidding, whether it was legal or not. That wasn't something he was expecting, but after what they'd learned back at the cave on their family's property, he wasn't surprised either.

Second, they were most likely too late to stop whatever Cassidy had planned to finally take out their family. It would be hard to do anything from behind bars, much less carry on the fight. There wasn't anything they could do to change that fact.

"You think he knows Mom and Dad are still out there?" Thomas asked, awkwardly trying to change the subject.

No response came from Kaya.

"Before they put us here, they said Cassidy had told them to look for a white guy and a Native woman," Thomas continued anyway. "I know I'm passing and all that, I just can't help but think that description was meant for Mom and Dad."

"He was here," she finally said. "He talked to us."

"With bags covering our faces. Anyone could make that mistake. And if any of the stories Mom told us growing up about Coyote are true, we can count on him to be just a little accident prone."

Kaya was starting to see his point. She sat on the bunk motionless, staring ahead at the bars slowly coming into focus as her own eyes adjusted. There was no way to know for certain if Cassidy knew exactly who they were, but if there was even the slightest chance that his dipshit followers got the wrong people, they still had a chance.

"Think about it. If Mom and Dad got away back at the rally, they should be here any minute to break us out. They aren't going to just let us sit in here."

Kaya didn't hold such certainty. "You think they're going to let them just walk in here and take us home? After all these years I just don't understand how you can still be so damn naive."

"If it helps, you haven't changed either. You are every bit as hateful and discouraging as you've always been. The glass is always half empty, right?"

"We don't have to talk, you know," said Kaya. "We can just sit here and wait for whatever they have planned for us."

"Like getting shot? No thanks. I'm going to fight them, literally, whether you want to or not," Thomas was dead serious, and his tone reflected every bit of it.

"If he wanted us dead, he would've killed us already."

She had a point, Thomas hadn't thought of that. If he did need them alive, he couldn't think of a single reason as to why. They had nothing to offer him.

"It's not like it matters anyway," Kaya continued, her voice sounding more and more defeated. "This whole thing is over. There's nothing we can do. We can't stop him, and even if we could, I'd rather see every bit of land taken from beneath our family's feet than help you pillage a single acre of it."

"Then why the hell did you even come back? Why not just stay in Austin with your ten-dollar coffees to complain about injustice to a bunch of people who couldn't care less? You came back, same as I did."

"I came back because I didn't want to see anyone get hurt. I know that's hard for someone like you to understand, but I still care. I'm still their daughter."

"If you ask me, it's about damn time you started acting like it then," said Thomas, instantly regretting the words as they escaped his lips. "All you're doing is trying to butter your bread on both sides and that's not how things work." He tried to dial down the temperature just a little.

"Oh, get real," she sighed.

"It's true. You want to walk around all high and mighty all the time like you're too damn good to be a part of this family, but you show up here pretendin' you got all the answers."

"You really want to do this? You keep pointing your finger at me like it was my fault the whole family fell apart. Let me ask you somethin', where you been at? Huh, Thomas? What have you been up to these last few years?"

"I've been keeping this family's bills paid. Is that not enough?"

"You think splitting up some of that mailbox money once a month is enough to pay for you never being around? You've been hiding out in West Texas for years, acting like cutting a check resolves you of any responsibility. I know exactly who you are."

"You don't know shit," said Thomas. "You been gone more than I have."

"You sure about that? You might say I ran from my problems, but you've been runnin' a heck of a lot longer than I have. If I had to guess, I'd say you're still runnin'. The only reason you came back was because your problems finally caught up to you. I'd even be willing to bet Mom and Dad's letter that showed up in the mailbox next to your livelihood just happened to be good timing."

This time it was Thomas's turn to answer with silence. He knew in his bones she was right. His thoughts turned to the man he'd shot down just for confronting him at his mailbox out in West Texas. He remembered the way he laid in the dirt, and the final breaths he took, refusing to break eye contact as his life faded away into a blackness that Thomas could only imagine matched what was inside the jail cell they lingered in. What stood out to him most in the few seconds he afforded himself to reflect on were the man's last words. That man's entire life boiled down to just three words he chose to impart on Thomas before he left this world.

You're gonna die.

It was enough to put a chill down his spine. There was no way Kaya knew about what he'd done to that man before coming back home, but she might as well have. She hit the nail on the head and it forced him to rethink everything.

"What if we stopped running?"

"Take a look around," Kaya said. "We can't run anywhere anymore."

"I mean from our family..." Thomas hesitated to say the words that were floating around in his head. He'd gone this far, though. Might as well finish it. "From each other."

"We can't change who we are, Thomas."

"Maybe we don't have to."

Kaya considered what her brother was trying to say. She could recognize the fact it was an olive branch being extended her way, even empathize with his sentiment, but she couldn't bring herself to agree. Their family was built on oil and gas money, generation after generation buying up any land they could get their hands on and using it to prop up the very machines of progress which tore their own people from the land they reclaimed. Her brother was yet another willing participant in the continuation of what she could only feel to be absolutely abhorrent. There was only one way to break the cycle in her mind, and that was to refuse becoming just another participant.

She threw herself back on the bunk she'd woken up in and exhaled all the air out of her lungs as dramatically as she could. Thomas was right, and she knew it, but that didn't mean she'd have to admit it right away. Even she couldn't bring herself to dislike the idea of being with her family again. It had been so long.

"Maybe we don't," she finally said, staring up into the darkness hovering over her.

For a few fleeting seconds, the two siblings basked in the simple idea of not having to carry a grudge they'd grown accustomed to for so many years. Their disdain for one another and the way it soured their relationship with their parents had, in a way, come to define who they were as adults. The simple concept that all of that could be wiped away was almost too difficult for either to come to terms with.

Despite their progress, the steel bars holding them back seemed to have only grown deeper roots to reach higher into the sky. They'd grown impossibly strong, and they threatened both Thomas and Kaya with the prospect of death before ever reaching the other side. What promise they kept hidden away, though. It was almost prophetic, as if they were guiding the siblings through their trauma.

Neither knew who was expected to move the

needle further after their heart-to-heart talk. They didn't even know what that was supposed to look like at this point. Surprisingly lucky for them, there was only so much they could do in their current predicament.

"What do you have in mind?"

"First, we gotta get out of this jail."

CHAPTER 17

"There has to be a weak spot somewhere here."

"When was this jail even built? I don't remember Jefferson having anything like this."

"It ain't new, but it ain't old either."

"That's helpful."

"Just keep looking, the sun is about to come up. We're already gettin' more light coming through. Soon, we'll be able to see enough to find where to start working on those bars. If we can work on getting just one loose, you could slip through the gap and get us out before anyone knows what hit them," Thomas explained.

"This ain't some old Western movie," Kaya told him. "We'll be lucky if they don't just leave us in here to die of dehydration or be forced to kill each other."

"What the hell, Kaya?"

"It's true. If law enforcement is getting in bed with Cassidy, we might be totally screwed here."

"Okay, you might have a point there."

With the slightest bit of gray light finding its way through the cracks and crevices of the cell impossible to fit through, Thomas and Kaya were struggling to find so much as a pinhole weakness in their captivity. They scoured every corner of the concrete block walls, searched beneath the steel bunks bolted to the floor, and yanked on every bar blocking their exit until their arms were too sore to move. There was no way out, but neither was willing to admit that just yet.

The two soon fell into a rhythm of circling the cell, desperately searching for anything they could exploit, all while keeping any words they could have let out to themselves. It was a fool's hope to think they had any way of escaping, but they held onto it with everything they had. After the sun's light had changed from orange to yellow and brought with it nearly unbearable heat, Thomas finally decided to voice what had been on his mind for the last few hours.

"Where do you think Mom and Dad went?"

"How am I supposed to know?"

"You saw them last," said Thomas.

"They were there to watch you run off like an idiot, headfirst into a fight you had no chance of winning."

"Then they weren't."

"I'd like to think they snuck off, that they're working on a way to get us out as we speak."

"Yeah, me too."

It wasn't much, but their shared hope was one of the first things they'd found common ground on after their discussion the night before. In ways neither could ever imagine, things were looking up for them.

Such a pivotal moment would have never made itself known if they hadn't been captured and beaten together, but it did, and they were doing their best to move forward with the understanding they'd reached.

The bars of the cell grew more problematic by the hour. They mocked Thomas and Kaya. Both of them allowed their thoughts to drift to what they would give to tear them from where they stood if given the chance. They knew better than to say anything so futile, though. There was nothing left for them to do but to return to the same positions they'd woken up to. Reflecting on what brought them to such a place would do no favors, but they didn't really have much else to think back on.

"Let's say we actually do get out of here," said Thomas, trying his best to change the mood. "For whatever reason, we walk our happy asses out of here, no harm, no foul. What is our next move?"

"You think now is the best time to daydream about that?"

"Unless you have something else to talk about," Thomas replied. "Yes. I do."

"I wish I knew," she admitted. "We need to get some help from people who aren't from Jefferson. He's got everyone here in his back pocket. It's useless to go against all of them."

"We can't bring more people into this. We can't trust them."

"Let me guess, you want to kill him."

Thomas didn't answer at first. He wasn't sure if that was what he wanted, but hearing the words outside of his own thoughts confirmed what he didn't want to admit. Cassidy would have to die. He was trying to take too much from them, and they couldn't allow him to get away with it.

Kaya already knew what he'd been thinking about. She would have never considered such a thing had she never returned home. It was one of the pieces of who she was that she could never escape. This place, her family, brought that out of her. At the end of the day, with their backs against the wall, she would do what she had to. What bothered her most was the fact that she wasn't completely against the idea.

"Doesn't do us any good to think about that," Kaya said.

"Sure it does. I don't buy for a second that we're gonna die here. I just want to be sure when we do get out, you're gonna be on the same page as I am."

"We're on the same page, all right?"

"That's good to hear."

The sun did what it always does throughout the day. It rose steadily in the east until it was high above their head at noon. By the time it started its descent in the west, Thomas and Kaya were starting to feel the rumbles in their stomach and the scratchiness in their throat. The cell became an oven in the process. The temperature climbed over the course of the day and refused to drop even when the sun gave way. It was miserable. Yet, still no one came.

Thomas and Kaya swapped where they sat, the only thing they could do, just as the night's shadows started to creep back over them. The bunk was as uncomfortable as the concrete floor, moreso even, but just a change of any kind, even momentarily, was more than welcome. Kaya had no feelings on the matter. All they could do was stare at those same steel bars, waiting for something to happen on the other side.

In the light of the sun, the room revealed itself to be just as mundane as the cell they were in. A desk with manilla folders, a chair worn beyond its own use, and a windowless door which promised freedom with the turn of a knob. But in the shrouded darkness hiding even a soft glow of the moon, the room might as well have been the mouth of a cavern into the depths of the earth. The cell held a particularly uneasy ability to disassociate from the world and carry with it anyone trapped inside.

They felt alone.

Staring into a void, running out of spit to wet their lips, much less any crises to reflect on. An idea would come, as sure as the sun would rise. It was only an issue of figuring out the puzzle of their escape. Thomas and Kaya had finally fallen into a worthwhile partnership in this mission. Aside from the fact that their lives surely depended on stepping foot on the other side of the bars, it was a moment to realize their own potential shunned through the years, now finally being given an honest chance.

Just as soon as they had found common ground, they ran into a brick wall, though. There was no way out of jail. Kaya was right, this wasn't some cliché old-Hollywood Western where you could just lift the bar right out or bribe a scruffy mutt with a key ring in its teeth. This was the kind of cell where you were forced to wait until a meeting with the county judge before even thinking about leaving.

Still, the darkness behind the bars both welcomed and threatened Thomas and Kaya. The night lingered on without end for what felt like weeks. Each minute dragged by and the two did everything they could not to think about the taste of cool water. It would be just after midnight when anything of interest happened on the other side of their enclosure.

It was a single light, impossibly far in the distance, coming for the middle of the mouth of

the cavern opening up beyond their cell. Too steady to be a candle and too bright to be a lightbulb, the glowing white light seemed to shine brighter by the minute, reflecting in every direction, yet somehow swallowed by the night's shadows around them all the same. It grew and grew, starting out as a negligible nuisance before becoming something else entirely. It demanded their attention. It blinded them both, yet refused to illuminate anything around them. It was unnatural.

"Is this real?"

"Shut up," said Kaya.

"What is—"

"Shut up!"

Thomas wasn't happy about it, but he went back to staring without saying anything, more confused than ever about what was happening right in front of their faces. Kaya was doing everything she could to keep from trembling. They waited together for the unknown, side by side.

Just as quick as the light filled the opening of the cell ahead of them, the blackness they had become all too familiar with swallowed it whole. It faded into oblivion, leaving something behind that had not been there before. Rotting meat and sulfur mixed with whiffs of a wet dog followed shortly behind the dwindling light. There was just enough time to let both Thomas and Kaya's hearts fall into their stomachs before they heard the growls.

"Kaya...Thomas..."

Their names came between snarls before they could see the fangs in the night. They were whispers in the distance, inhuman despite their language. Thomas and Kaya remained frozen in their cell, waiting without moving a muscle.

What approached them came first on all fours. It was surrounded by fleeting shadows that threatened to envelop them all. There were first fangs, drooling to the floor below, smeared by the paws of a beast not of this world with claws that made themselves known. *Tick. Tick. Tick.* The claws crept closer. The moving swirl of shadows soon revealed what both Thomas and Kaya feared most.

It was Coyote, with eyes as sharp as daggers and matted fur as dark as the night surrounding the cell. Coyote came closer, locking unblinking eyes on each of them. There was no room to move and no time to think. Coyote was staggeringly sized. Every movement was decisive, calculated. For a beast born of oral storytelling told to children and adults alike,

Coyote was a force to be reckoned with in stature alone.

"What do you want with us?"

It was Kaya who had the nerve to question the presence of Coyote. She never did quite grasp the concept of self-preservation like her brother.

"You are not them." Coyote's voice was a cold wisp against the night air. "They lied."

"We're gonna be more than you can handle, you son of a bitch," Kaya spewed.

Coyote was inches from the bars separating Thomas and Kaya, who could see as plain as day the deadly fangs waiting for flesh to tear into. This didn't stop either of the siblings from playing the only hand they had—the bluff.

Thomas was the first to slam against the bars holding them prisoner. His body weight hitting the steel was enough to echo throughout the jail. "You think you're going to stop us, you hideous creature? I've gunned down man and beast in cold blood without a second thought, now I've got a bullet with your name on it."

Kaya was next to follow suit. She threw her hands into the air, let out a shriek that could be heard for miles, and leaped into the bars. "Get out! Get out! Get out!" she screeched over and over again.

Coyote would not budge. Seconds burned away like ash disintegrating in the air, leaving the three in a wild standoff with no end. Before Thomas or Kaya could make the next move, they realized the fangs threatening them in the shadows had started to rise. Their eyes followed the beast's drooling teeth into the air just as they realized what was happening. Coyote was standing up on its hind legs.

It was a sight torn from the nightmares of children whose parents knew to warn about what lurked in the woods when the sun went down. Tall enough to force Thomas and Kaya's eyes up into the ceiling, Coyote stared down through a curled snout with a yellow glow softly beginning to emanate behind empty, blown out pupils.

Thomas and Kaya refused to stop fighting. They thrashed and screamed and threatened, all to no avail. There never really stood much of a chance for them to rattle what stood in front of them. The only other option, to surrender and relinquish control of their own lives, was unacceptable.

Amid their frantic outburst, Coyote did not act, but instead came to an understanding. A plan was hatched in that moment, notwithstanding the one that was already in motion, to allow nature to take its course with the two locked inside the cell. Believing the two needed no more of Coyote's time to be eaten from within, one of the hind paws slowly began to move backward, then another, and another. The same blinding light which ushered Coyote into the room began to grow once more in the darkness, reaching every corner without end. Coyote became lost in the contrast. A silhouette turned into a figment of Thomas and Kaya's imagination within an instant. Just as soon as the legend of their childhood was born before their very eyes, it was gone without a trace.

"That Coyote talked to us," said Thomas, never

one to waste a moment to state the obvious. "What in Sam Hill just happened?"

Once again, it was lonely inside the cell. While Thomas questioned everything from what they just saw to his own existence, Kaya had already come to a not-so-welcome conclusion. It was there from the moment they'd woken up in the jail, only becoming more apparent by the hour.

"Are you even hearing me? The Coyote fuckin' spoke. It stood up like a man. Is that thing wearing Cassidy's skin? What could a thing like that want with our family's land, much less an entire damn town?"

Kaya touched the cool steel bars in the night with one hand. Rarely is anyone able to recognize a life-changing moment when it is happening. That wasn't Kaya's problem, as she allowed her mind to enter a fog. The darkness she'd been thrust into became her. Her thoughts were swept away. Her focus drifted anywhere but where she stood. The indecipherable rumbling that was Thomas's voice echoed to and fro on a wave of her consciousness she wasn't sure she should be in. Her problem wasn't what was happening to her, her problem was what she was going to do about it.

"If we don't get outta here, we're gonna die," she admitted.

CHAPTER 18

A man's study is his kingdom. A refuge away from the world, which gives him a place to rest his mind when no one else ever could. There is an unspeakable yearning for this, and when earned, it can, in a sense, provide the foundation for how a man's entire life may unfold. By sheer circumstance alone, this place also becomes the most personal environment to be found through his remaining years of existence. More than a bed shared with a spouse of five decades, more than a room devoted to an entire childhood, the study is a reflection of the man which resides inside.

The flame dancing off the walls, casting a presentation made of shadow across every corner of the study, told a story of the man who hid in his place of refuge. Fitting and remorseless, the fire was a signal of what was underway, a purging and cleansing, with a hint of entertainment for good measure.

Cassidy's boots were propped up on the only oak-built desk in the study. Crackling and hissing from the Franklin stove smoking to his right was a soundtrack to the many problems that dominated his every thought. Life inside Mayor Walker's old home had once been warm, comfortable, and inviting. Since Cassidy had called it his own, there was something cold and unsavory about the closest place the town of Jefferson could call a mansion.

Knock. Knock.

"Just come in already." His voice was exhausted. "It's too early in the morning for pleasantries."

The door complained with an unnecessary amount of creaks as it swung open to reveal the face of Daniel Coleman. His eyes were bloodshot and carried dark bags beneath. Daniel looked as though he hadn't gotten a good night's sleep in weeks. Yet, even then, he walked inside the study of Cassidy's straight-backed and alert, unwilling to show even the slightest bit of weakness.

"How goes it?"

"It's goin', sir," said Daniel. "The guys thought those two matched the description you gave. I should have checked it myself. Won't happen again."

"Do you realize those two put up in the county jail were their children?"

"I sure didn't, sir."

"Well, they are. Rowdy little shits, always have been. I never thought they'd show their faces around here again. It was a stroke of luck we put them behind bars when we did."

Daniel's mood got a bit more chipper at this news. He was expecting an ass-chewing and had even braced for it for a few minutes before knocking. Cassidy had seen his shadow flickering across the bottom of the door.

"Why are you here?"

"We had a few people call in saying a truck was seen driving through town," Daniel reported. "Texas tags, unknown drivers. We've got the sheriff's department running the plates. Gonna have more information within the hour, just wanted you to be up to speed in case we find out it's someone who don't need to be here."

"You be sure they don't get anywhere near my land. Two squatters on my land is already two too many. You already screwed up once, don't you dare let it happen again. You hear me, Daniel?"

"Yes sir," he said.

Cassidy pulled one boot down from the table, dragging it slower than he had any right to do. Just before it fell off the table, the man dressed in black toppled over backward, slipping out from under an office chair leaned further back than it could handle. His boots went over his head and he tumbled over onto the hard wooden floors. Without missing a beat, Cassidy popped right back up and picked right back up on his train of thought. "I've never really talked much about what brought me into town. Come to think of it, no one even really asked me either."

"Why did you?" Daniel was only playing nice at this point, but it was enough for Cassidy to continue.

"People don't really know much about where they live these days. They are lost in their phones, living lives that have nothing to do with what is around them. That is every bit as true right here in a town of less than two thousand people as it is in a town of more than two million people like Houston. They just don't care anymore. Is that really my fault?"

"I'm not exactly following you, sir," said Daniel, letting his eyes dart around for a place to sit. He was just too tired to stand up throughout the entire story that was sure to come.

"What I mean is, if anyone knew what the town of Jefferson was built on, they would also know the reason that brought me strolling through your streets. The fine people here know all about the port on the Red River and the Big Cypress Bayou, about the boomtown era that made the town one of the largest in the state. But do you think they know about the Great Red River Raft and its eventual destruction?"

"I'd be willing to bet most people know what brought their town down, or at least they did."

"I wouldn't be so sure," said Cassidy. "Well, as history would have it, the Great Red River Raft was the logjam that built the town. It was known to have always existed, from before man found the more than hundred-mile stretch of the Red River. The Caddo people, escaping oppression, found what they so desperately sought to flee at the foot of what they called the Great Red River Raft."

Cassidy walked around to the other side of the simple oak desk surrounded by old bookshelves filled with even older leather-bound books, covered in dust and cracking from age. The clicking of his boot heels against the floors were hypnotic, carrying Cassidy across the room to stand face-to-face with Daniel.

"I always liked you," said Cassidy. "From the moment you pulled a gun on that old man at a town meeting no one cared about enough to show up for. You cared when others didn't, and that alone caught my attention."

Daniel turned his head to the side, trying his best to understand the sporadic conversation unfolding between them. His face betrayed his thoughts, his eyes gave away what he truly felt—terror.

"People who care tend to be more understanding. It's just human nature. That being said I'm going to need you to understand what I'm about to tell you. It won't be easy."

"All right…" Daniel's voice trailed off.

"Jefferson was built on land stolen from the Caddo. History may claim to use the word ceded, giving it a legal precedent based on a system that did not recognize the rights of those being stolen from. It is a word that carries no meaning. If the governmental system carries no weight, why should their actions?"

"Yeah, no, that makes sense."

"You may think of me as retribution, arriving at long last."

"If you don't mind me asking, sir," interrupted Daniel. "What you just said was fine and all, but what does any of that have to do with all the jobs we're bringing to Jefferson? You know, the fifty-million-dollar investment, all those companies moving in, beginning Jefferson back to its heyday."

"You're a good man, Daniel," said Cassidy.

"I sure appreciate you saying—"

"But you're as dumb as the day is long. Not a single bit of that is gonna happen."

Daniel took a step back. It was the only reaction that made sense. Cassidy's words were a gut punch. There was nothing left to say after such an admission. The tension hung over them both like a saddle blanket in the night air.

"Don't act so surprised. You know what they say about things that are too good to be true. Just do your best to forget all that nonsense. You aren't here to save the city at my side and get rich in the process. You aren't gonna spend millions of someone else's money on pipe dreams of achieving what the modern world calls success. You aren't even alive to do a single damn thing other than what I say."

Daniel looked over his left shoulder to double-check if he left the door open behind him. Cassidy was watching him closely and knew the dismay that was making itself right at home after what he'd just said.

"If you walk out that door, you won't live to see the next sunrise," said Cassidy. "I just need you to know that."

"I ain't leavin'," Daniel's voice couldn't mask his trembling. "Just trying to figure out what my place is in all this. If you was just putting us all on, and you really just want us all dead, what's in all this for me?"

"Well, Daniel," Cassidy took a step closer, "I didn't bring you in here to have my last conversation with you, I'll tell you that. Personally, I'd say your life should be reason enough, but now that I'm looking you in the eye, I'm not so sure that's the case."

"You asked me why I was here, only fair I ask the

same," Daniel said, forcing himself to speak when every bone in his body told him to shut up. "Why are you here?"

"To take back the land that was stolen."

"What the hell does that even mean?"

"You're losing sight of what is happening here, Daniel. You keep up those kinds of questions and I'll have to find someone else to participate in my quandaries."

"What happens then?"

"You won't care. You'll be dead. Along with the rest of the Wild Bunch, if only for the fact they follow your every lead."

Cassidy watched the man who'd already gone to the furthest ends of sanity for him. Daniel had killed for what Cassidy proposed for the city, and he had no problems doing far worse than that. For what would come next, Cassidy needed to look him right in the eye and see that dream die inside. He needed loyalty to him, not an idea. This was the only way to know for sure who he could ask to undertake the unthinkable.

Cassidy set his Wild Bunch gang loose on the town to cause a specific brand of chaos. As he stared down a future where the keys of the city were practically already in his hand, he knew the loyalty of those willing to kill in his name would certainly come in handy.

Standing in the musty room built of lumber from another time, the fire continued to dance until the oxygen itself began to feel exhaustion set in. Every flicker of a flame was a struggle against the inevitable suffocation of its own existence. Hissing when crackling came only as desperate pleas for help. An orange glow from a well-fed fire soon turned an ominous red to foreshadow a coming death.

"So, we're all settled then?"

Daniel hesitated to respond. He wasn't in the state of mind to question what he'd put himself through for what was turning out to be a pipe dream. Cassidy could see that much. He could see the delay in Daniel's head as he contemplated the path in life he'd set himself on. Then, like the flip of a switch, a light-bulb went off in Damiel's eyes, and everything fell into its rightful place.

"Good to hear," Cassidy affirmed the decision by Daniel to remain silent. "Because there are more important matters than your loyalty to tend to. In case you've been under a rock the last few days, this whole thing is moving quicker than I could've anticipated. If we don't get every single person in the city onboard, we're gonna lose it all. And by we, I mean *you*. The city, and everything it was built on, lies at our doorstep. Even the slightest inconvenience could bring it all tumbling down."

Punctuating Cassidy's final sentence, a man came barreling up the stairs, hollering gibberish and slamming heavy boots onto the wooden steps. The closer he got, the clearer they could hear the man's frantic cursing. "Shit! Shit! Shit!" He kept yelling, stumbling his way closer to the room where Cassidy and Daniel both waited with dumbfounded looks plastered across their faces.

By the time the man finally showed his flushed, sweaty face at the top of the steps, he realized the mistake he'd made barging into the house unannounced. When he made eye contact with Cassidy, there were only two words he could mutter. "I'm sorry."

Cassidy stood with his hands on his hips, refusing to so much as blink until the intruder spoke. There was an awkward pause, hanging heavy in the humid air that filled the old house. After a few seconds, the man finally decided to get on with it, if only to hasten the time it would take to see him out the way he came.

"Did you tell him yet?"

"Tell me what?" Cassidy wasted no time.

"Yes, I told him. I swear to God if that's the reason you broke into this house, I'll do everything in my power to make sure it's the last time that ever happens to you." Daniel was all too ready to take his frustration out on anyone other than the man he'd promised his life to.

"If I don't know what's going on in about two seconds, I'm gonna start slappin' this hammer," said Cassidy, patting the trusty revolver hanging on the usual spot on his hip.

"The truck that was seen drivin' through town," the man started, trying to speak as quickly as he could. "When we tried to stop it, shit hit the fan."

"Go on."

"The sheriff's office just called. They said there were gunshots fired, a couple of guys got tagged, and the truck just sped off. They're sending a couple of cars to chase it down now."

"Who in the hell are these people?"

"Jefferson sits right off Highway 59, criminals flying through town isn't really all that uncommon."

"No," said Cassidy. "This isn't just a coincidence. Those people are up to something. Don't you dare let them further than the city limits."

"We got guys going after them as we speak."

"Did they get a description of who was inside? Any way we can get an idea of who we're dealing with?"

"Sheriff's office said there were three of them inside the truck. Two males, one female. All of them armed and dangerous."

"That ring a bell?" Daniel turned to Cassidy, only to realize their boss had turned his back to them both.

Cassidy was staring into the fire that graced the room with its presence. Flickering off his black eyes, the flame lulled Cassidy into a trance where he could envision how the next steps of his takeover would play out. Convincing the people of Jefferson to throw away their future in the name of a quick buck was the easy part. He knew, deep down, getting the Hunter family to give up their fortune locked away in the land surrounding the town would be almost impossible, but he was prepared for the fight.

Now, as luck would have it, he knew exactly who he'd be fighting against.

CHAPTER 19

oom.

The explosion came long before anything else. Dust particles and steel bars flew through the air at impossible speeds, destroying anything unfortunate enough to be found in their path. Fragments of cinder block peppered the air, making it unbreathable and worse, impossible to see through. The reverberations of the explosion rocked the inside of the eight-foot-wide cell. It was disorientating, chaotic, miserable, and deafening all at once.

Even worse, Thomas and Kaya had only just fallen asleep.

A blinding flash of light came next. With everything flying in every direction, the light from the explosion struggled to reveal the extent of the damage underway. It was over in a second, ending quicker than it had made itself seen, and it left behind an unthinkable reality. The air was thick with spent gunpowder and debris. Darkness immediately returned to the cell, and with no bars to separate them from the rest of the building, it did more than threaten to swallow up anyone inside, it finally followed through.

"Kaya!" It was the first thing Thomas could think of. Before even realizing if he was hurt or bleeding, before even considering what had actually just happened, he was feeling through the blackness around them for his sister. "Kaya! Kaya!" No matter how much he yelled, or how loud he pushed his voice, there was no response.

"I'm not deaf, I just can't see anything," she finally said.

"Are you okay?"

"I don't know. Are you?"

"I don't know," said Thomas.

"Y'all better be," Another man's voice pierced through the night and floating dust in the air.

"Who the—"

"This way," a woman cut Kaya off.

"Hurry the hell up, you two! We ain't got all fuckin' night." This time, it was yet another man. "Let's go!"

Thomas and Kaya finally grabbed each other's hand. Neither of them could see, could barely breathe, but they pushed forward together through the night together. They didn't have to go far, either. After a few unsure steps, a hand reached out through the night to grasp Thomas's, leading them through a hole where the steel bars of the cell once stood.

Stepping out of the cell was pure vindication. Thomas and Kaya didn't have to say a word to know they shared the same feeling. It was as if nothing else mattered in their life other than to be free of the jail's confinement. It didn't matter who had broken them out, or even if they might find their way back into a new cell after what they had schemed together, it only mattered that they had rid themselves of that unjust imprisonment.

"Who did this?"

"Where are you?"

It took a few seconds for their eyes to adjust. The hand grasping Thomas led them through the room on the other side of the cell they were being held in, through a single door and into a long hallway every bit as dark as where they had just come from.

"I swear to God, if someone doesn't tell me what is happening right now…" Thomas was starting to lose his patience.

It wasn't until they were on the other side of the hallway that a simple yellow light became their saving grace. As their eyes finally began to adjust, Thomas was surprised to see Kaya's smiling face before anything else.

"You came," she said, her grin stretching from ear to ear and adorning her grime-covered face with a bewildering look. "I didn't think you'd actually show up."

That's when Thomas turned his attention to who was standing in front of them. He couldn't believe his eyes, but there they were, as real as the daylight he yearned to feel as his face again.

Cannon Hunter was staring back at him, with his partners Jim Bob and Cathay standing next to him.

"Half brother or not, we're still family," said Cannon. "Even if I ain't around all that much."

"I couldn't be happier to see anyone else, Cannon," said Thomas.

"What in the hell took you so long, you asshole?"

"Kind of hard to get a letter when you don't have a mailbox or a PO box," Cannon said. "We've been out of pocket for weeks now. You do remember the Nations Heritage & Culture Preservation, right? We haven't stopped."

"My turn," Thomas cut in. "How exactly did you just get us out of here?"

"That was me," said Jim Bob, holding a cylindrical package in one hand for everyone to see. "Dynamite. Old school."

"I like that guy." Kaya pointed at Jim Bob, keeping the smile on her face.

"The whole damn town of Jefferson just heard you blow the door off of that jail cell. Now that I think of it, how are we even alone? Did they not have anyone here to guard the place, or make sure we didn't try to bust out ourselves?"

"That part was easy," Cannon said, patting a revolver slung haphazardly onto his hip.

"Shit."

"You didn't kill them, right?"

"Well…" Cannon tried his best to find a different way of saying exactly what both Thomas and Kaya didn't want him to say.

"Speaking of getting the hell out of Dodge." Cathay picked up where she knew Cannon had dropped the ball. "We should leave. Now."

"She keeps us all in line."

"Is that what it is?" Jim Bob couldn't help himself.

While their rescuers turned to lead them out of the old Marion County jail, Thomas gripped Kaya's arm and pulled her to the side. He spoke in a harsh, raspy whisper, his concern betrayed by a grip that would undoubtedly leave bruises.

"Where the hell are Mom and Dad?"

"They ain't here," she said with a glare. "What else do you want from me? I know about as much as you do."

"Shouldn't we go find them? What if they got locked up somewhere here, too?"

"Just keep an eye out, this place can't be that big."

"They aren't here," said Cannon from several feet ahead, already becoming lost in the shadows filling the corners of every room. "How do you think we knew where to find you?"

"Because we're that good?" Jim Bob was deadly serious.

"Please," Cathay cut him off.

"Are you gonna take us to them?"

Cannon stopped walking, paused momentarily, then turned to make eye contact with Thomas. "Mom and Davy are waiting for us, yes. But I need to be honest with you."

"Here we go," said Thomas. "I knew something was up."

"Would you just shut up," Kaya shot back.

"Listen," Cannon continued. "We shot our way in here."

"You what?"

Bam. Bam. Bam.

"Oh shit!"

Bam. Bam.

"Get down!"

Bam. Bam. Bam.

In a split second, flashes of muzzle blasts lit up the darkness in front of the group as bullets ripped by and slammed into the block walls of the old Marion County jail. Thomas and Kaya were the last to duck and sprint for cover, running in the opposite direction as Cannon, Jim Bob, and Cathay. They were split by a lane of gunfire from the hallway separating them from the side exit used for officers.

The gunfire was sustained without any periods to reload. There were enough to rotate laying down cover, enough men to immediately overwhelm and outgun the group trying their damndest to break out of the jail. Every bullet tore through the air with a whizzing whistle before lodging into the wall at the other end of the room. Combined with the cry of every gun firing at them, it was enough to go deaf in a matter of seconds.

"You good?"

Kaya patted herself all over. She pushed on her chest, stomach, and legs before finally looking at Thomas and nodding.

"We need a gun," he said to her before realizing he needed to be telling the three who weren't at his side. "We need a damn gun!" he shouted before even turning to look at Cannon on the other side of the hallway.

Just as the words came out of his mouth, a polymer

9mm handgun came sliding across the floor before bumping against Thomas's knees. It had been a long time since he shot anything other than his .44 magnum revolver, but he knew as well as anyone in times like this, beggars can't be choosers.

He grabbed the stippled grip and trained his eye on the night sights that he'd never admit to anyone were actually helpful. With a punch of both hands, he extended the pistol out and went to work.

With no lighting and under heavy fire, Thomas could only get off a couple of rounds before being forced to duck back behind cover. By the time he had gained his composure again, he popped back out and fired two more. The best he could do under this kind of duress was to fire his shots at the muzzle blasts and hope they put a stop to them.

The first time he heard a man grunt before letting out an all too familiar scream, he knew his bullet had struck home, and he was on the right track. It was his fifth bullet, leaving his pistol with at least a dozen more, judging by the size of the double-stack magazine. As he listened to the wounded man being dragged away, he knew right then and there this was a fight they could win.

Kaya was much less certain. Unarmed and unable to see how many they were facing down, the only thing Kaya could focus on was the amount of bullets flying right beside them. She watched as her brother fought back before Cannon and Cathay both joined in on the fun.

It was impossible to distinguish who was shooting at who, but the situation was getting worse in a hurry.

They weren't making as much headway as they needed, and they didn't have the ammunition to keep up the fight for much longer.

"Need a mag!" Thomas hollered.

Just like before, without another word, a black magazine with hollow points sticking out of the top came sliding across the floor. He dropped the empty magazine from the bottom of the grip and jammed the next one in. With a flick of this thumb, the slide shot forward to chamber a new round, and he got back to it.

Kaya watched as they all popped in and out of cover, shooting for a brief few seconds at a time. It wasn't enough to save them. Somebody would have to do something drastic.

"We gotta do something!" It was all she could think to call out in the chaos.

"Already on it, ma'am," Jim Bob yelled.

He was holding two six-shooters, pointed up at the ceiling, his fingers itching to find the trigger. There was a grin that no man should ever have across his face. Against the flickering light of the flame from every bullet being fired at them, those who dared make eye contact with Jim Bob saw only a crazed stare without so much as a blink.

"You sure you wanna do that?" Cannon asked as the bullets paused just long enough to speak.

Another volley of rounds came, chipping away at the block wall behind them with deadly force. All any of them could do was look at Jim Bob, though. He was preparing himself to do something crazy, to face death without any guarantees. Luckily for everyone else he was with, Jim Bob was the kind of man who would do so with a smile on his face any day of the week.

"Ain't much else to do," he answered Cannon. "Besides, I've lived through a lot worse."

Thomas and Kaya watched a man they'd just met mentally prepare himself to risk his own life for them. With only the deathly flashes of light spewing gunpowder and lead in their direction to see Jim Bob getting ready, what they saw was a man who had lived by the gun for most of his life. This was nothing new to him, like a rodeo roper staring down a calf, his whole life had a funny way of boiling down to just a few fateful seconds. There was plenty of grit and a bit of stupid involved, but Jim Bob understood more than anyone, this kind of life required something else entirely. There wasn't a particular word to describe what it was, however. Strangely enough, putting it into words was exactly what Cannon requested of him.

"Got any final words?"

Jim Bob lifted the dual six-shooters gripped in his hands. With both barrels pointed up into the air, bullets continuing to just barely miss them, and not nearly enough ammunition to get them out of the mess they'd found themselves in, Jim Bob did the only thing he knew.

"Yeeeeeee!"

He hollered at a dead sprint. He charged head first, both revolvers blasting rounds off matching his stride, right into the hallway ahead shrouded in darkness where only surefire misery waited. The only question was at whose hands.

"Haaaaaaw!"

His voice echoed throughout the entire jail. It was proud and came from down in his belly, and it was broken up only by the wailing of every bullet he fired.

Bam. Bam. Bam.

Each second that ticked by seemed to deliver yet another gunshot. It was pure agony to wait, but they had no other choice. The gunshots refused to obey any sense of a rhythm, instead firing off sporadically, sometimes in rapid succession and sometimes with dreadful pauses in between. This continued for no more than thirty seconds, but it felt like hours.

When the bullets finally came to an end. Cannon was the first one to break and walked into the hallway leading them to freedom. Thomas and Kaya followed, with Cathay opting to bring up the rear. It was Kaya who first noticed the puddles splashing gently against her boots as she walked. Thomas could hear it, but he never acknowledged what they all knew it was. Their walk in a single file line was short-lived. Even though the inside of the jail had once again fallen into a blackness where no one could see what was directly in front of them, it didn't take much to make their way into the next room, where a glowing white light waited for them.

Sitting with his back against the wall and one knee propped up, Jim Bob was breathing heavily, still gripping one of his revolvers in his right hand. There was a flashlight resting upright on the floor, pointing toward the ceiling. In its soft light, they could see the carnage one man had wrought upon so many.

"They get you?" Cannon asked as soon as he saw Jim Bob.

"Not for lack of trying."

"The hell did you do to them?" Cathay was still scanning the room full of a dozen dead men, most still clutching their firearms.

"What they were tryin' to do to us. I shot 'em."

"You sure did," said Thomas. "Need a second to catch your breath?"

"Don't think we have time for a nap," Cannon cut in. "We need to get going. There are only gonna be more of them showing up soon enough."

As if to punctuate his point, two cell phones tucked inside the pants pockets of a couple of the men lying face down in a pool of red. The vibrations against the floor were an eerie presence that sent a chill down the spine of both Thomas and Kaya. They'd underestimated the fight they were in, that much was becoming painfully clear right in front of their eyes.

It was Cathay who grabbed Jim Bob's hand to lift him back to his feet. "How many times has running blindly headfirst into bullets actually worked for you?"

"More times than I'd like to admit."

"Are we supposed to just kill everyone in town?" Kaya couldn't wait any longer. There were too many questions and too much death hanging over her head not to ask them. "It's Cassidy we're after. He's doing something to these people. They're all out of their minds, it ain't natural."

"We know who is doing this," said Cannon. "This isn't just about our family. This is what the NHCP does. Sometimes, the stories we pass on to one another get loose. It's our job to track them down and keep them from getting out of control."

"You know it's Coyote?"

"Of course we do," said Cathay. "Cannon has already caught us up to speed on the tricks he's played so far. They don't usually go so well, we've been on Coyote's trial before. It usually turns out to be a dead end, though."

Thomas and Kaya made eye contact. Not knowing what else to say, Kaya asked one more question she couldn't hold on to any longer.

"Are we really going to kill a legend?"

"We're gonna put a stop to all of this," said Cannon. "We're gonna do exactly what the NHCP set out to do and get this under control. Just like we've done time and time again. It don't matter if this one hits a little closer to home."

"We don't show up just to kill everyone and leave," Cathay admitted.

"We do get shot at *a lot*, though," said Jim Bob.

"Before we do anything, we have to get our asses out of this jail." Thomas pushed forward, being intentional about making eye contact with everyone as he spoke. "If we don't, none of this is gonna mean anything. I'd say, if we're planning to make a move to protect our family and prevent Coyote from taking this town, and everything we own, we need."

"Great speech," said Cannon. He reached behind his back and yanked out another pistol, this time a snub nose .38 special revolver, and handed it to Kaya.

"I'm serious. It's now or never."

"We need to scrounge up some ammo and maybe borrow some of the guns these fine folks won't be needing anymore," Cannon continued, not paying any attention to Thomas's pressing.

"Are you even listening to me? I know you just got here and think because you decided to go off and run Mom's hobby at the NHCP you can do whatever you want, but that ain't what this is."

"Thomas, dial it down a bit," Kaya told him, trying to defuse the situation.

"No. He needs to know. It's time we took the fight to that son of a bitch."

A .308 hunting rifle with wooden furniture and an oversized matte black scope fastened on top came flying through the air. Thomas reached quickly, preventing it from smacking him in the face as he talked. He stood there, holding the rifle, searching for the words that would convince Cannon of what he knew had to happen.

"In case you missed it, the fight is already here," said Cannon. "Get ready."

CHAPTER 20

"**A**re we really going through with this?"

"Seems like an awful lot for a damn paycheck."

"It ain't just a paycheck, he promised us lives we couldn't even dream of. Most of us done already spent most of our lives here, no different than our parents. How much further along did we get? In twenty years, and correct me if I'm wrong y'all, but all we got was a freakin' gas station."

"It's got that place that makes the footlong sandwiches in it too."

"Exactly my point."

"You make it seem like we've all just been sittin' on our hands doing nothing our whole lives. We all worked our asses off to get to where we are. It ain't like we chose to let this town die. Jefferson is more than just where we all wound up, it's our home. It's a place worth saving.

"I agree. But if we don't take the opportunities that

come our way, nothing will ever change for any of us, much less our kids."

"If I can play devil's advocate, do we really want this place to change so much? Jefferson is a small town, and my family has always loved it just how it is. Are we willing to sacrifice what makes this place so special just so our kids can stay home a few more years?"

"We don't want them to grow up and run off to the city or move to some other state, right?"

"The only thing I really want is for our home to still be here in the next five years. At the rate it's going, we'll *all* have to move off to some city. There ain't no other options."

"You may not like it, but Cassidy is our best chance at survival."

"So, that settles it, we all agree to kill the Hunter family?"

The room fell to a somber silence. Cassidy's Wild Bunch had steered the conversation right where they all knew it needed to be. They were surrounded by anyone who was anyone in Jefferson. Sitting around a table older than anyone there, Daniel was stoic, motionless. His eyes were sunken and bloodshot, his lips dry and cracked, and his gaze was hollow. There was a discussion playing out in front of him, but none of that mattered.

They were at the local historical museum, a dedication to the golden age of the once-great city of East Texas built by commerce and trade brought by water and by rail. The building was erected in the dying days of the Wild West in 1890. The ornate, high-ceilinged rooms were adorned with era-specific portraits and furniture too delicate to use as originally intended. Track lighting and roped-off areas turned the once Federal-held building into a true museum for any random passerby. It harkened a time long gone, a time of delicacy and civility that could never find a home on the frontier. After the coming of the industrial age and the pursuit of progress that ushered it into existence, the museum was a place frozen in time.

It also just so happened to be a place where Cassidy felt most at home. After growing tired of the old mayor's home in downtown, he had started to spend more and more time in the museum. An authentic vision of the high life long gone, all within historic Jefferson, it was a place that Cassidy knew could withstand the fight ahead, just as it had withstood time itself for generations.

The building was built of a pristine red brick that looked as though it hadn't aged a single day. There was a tower several stories high with vertically ascending windows at its front, standing tall above a creaky wooden door beset by arched glass on either side, all tucked behind an iron spiked fence. It was designed for a time long gone, but stood every bit as brilliant as the day it was completed.

Cassidy had brought with him the darkest days of the building, though. Having survived the Great Depression, every modern war, and the onslaught of decay as people and resources alike, abandoned the historic town, it was now a home to grim conspiracy.

His exotic books clicked against the hardwood floors as he paced around the ornate table surrounded by men and women who could only be described as the most prominent wielders of power and influence in Jefferson. Cassidy kept his focus on Daniel, who was deadpan through it all. His right-hand man was far from lost, but he was falling from grace. If his plans were to be followed through to the bitter end, they would have to be done through the entire town, no matter the cost.

Maybe Daniel had come to realize that he would, in fact, sacrifice every single person willing to step foot in the town if it meant he could take what was right-fully his. Maybe Daniel had finally reached the under-standing that he was a pawn in a game he never even understood the rules of. No matter what, Cassidy knew his hooks were lodged in too deep to ever lose their grip on the man's sanity.

"Where are they?" Ed was eager to get down to brass tacks. "We can't take them out until we know what happened to them."

"Ben took a couple of trucks full of guys down to the jail around the corner and not a damn one of them came back," the response came from Tonya. She had fallen in line after the protest brought all the wrong people to their backyard. "We get anymore of these flare-ups, we're gonna draw the attention of a bunch of people we don't want snooping around here."

"Well, I'm sure open to ideas," said Ed.

"Daniel?"

Daniel didn't respond. His stare was endless. What lay behind his eyes was the furthest thing from humanity. He was no longer in control, operating almost exclusively by forces that were not of this world. It was in these eyes that each person sitting at the table could find the answer no one wanted to believe. There were no simple solutions, only those which required them to risk life and limb. In Daniel's eyes, they witnessed the depravity they would have to sink to in order to achieve such a goal.

Finally, his answer came. It was cold and uncaring, and his stare into oblivion, even then, was unbroken. "We need guns."

"Finally, a man with some sense!" Cassidy's interjection was neither warranted or wanted, but he was there, and they were going to listen to him.

"Guns?" Tonya couldn't hide the shock in her voice. "You expect us to do it ourselves?"

"Would it be the first thing you've ever done yourself in your life? Is it so shocking?" Ed never faulted in his loyalty, even with his own life being decided for him. "It ain't that hard, just point it and squeeze the trigger."

"It's not the gun I'm worried about," said Tonya. "It's shooting someone down in cold blood."

"That ain't so hard either."

"We need more men." Daniel spoke again.

"Already on their way," Ed answered. "We got the Higgins boys coming in with a few of their cousins and God knows who else. They'll do what we say, no questions asked."

"If I didn't know any better," Billy started to make himself known at the table. "I'd say you need to sit this one out, Daniel. Maybe get some sleep?"

Daniel once again refused to answer, or even so much as glance in Billy's direction. There was an inexplicable tension hanging in the air. No matter how many times Cassidy circled the table overlooking his handiwork, there wasn't a single soul who felt increasingly comforted by what was happening at the meeting—except for him. It was the culmination of everything he'd wanted. Watching the people who carried on a legacy stolen from his people fight to the bitter end, only to leave him with the key to it all, just felt right.

As is so often the case when everything is going better than ever expected, a wrench came flying in at the worst time imaginable. The group had only just started to formulate a plan to put an end to the fight when the front door to the historical museum slammed open and smashed against the wall. Heads turned, and the room fell silent.

It was the local feed store owner, Mark Anderson, who just put his worn leather boot right through the door to make his sudden entrance. His face was red and sweaty, and he had a slight stumble with each step. He was drunk. Tequila always had been his poison of choice, and it was noticeably heavy on his breath, even from a few dozen feet away. He didn't look angry, he looked pissed off.

"I knew I'd find you lowlifes loitering around a place you had no business being in," said Mark. "You people are drinkin' the Kool-Aid. You don't even care, do you? That asshole ain't got no right to do what he's doin'. That man is *not* our mayor. He was not elected by anyone."

Mark took a few steps forward. Ed and Tonya

stood up instinctively, but Daniel didn't even look in his direction.

"If there ain't no one else in this town with the balls to put a stop to all this, I'll have to do it myself."

"Mark, you're drunk." Ed held his hands out, trying to calm down the raging man. "You need to turn around and take your ass home before you get into something you can't handle."

"You think I can't handle you?"

"You should listen to him," said Tonya. "None of this has anything to do with you."

"Jefferson is my home! That son of a bitch wants to burn it all down! Don't you see that?"

A round of laughter burst out. As the unnatural howls from those in the historical museum rang out, there were three who refused to so much as crack a smile. Mark was stone-faced and on the verge of taking his rage out on each and every one of the people in front of him. Cassidy watched with strange curiosity at what was unfolding, continuing to pace around the room even during the conflict. Daniel, however, had seemingly not even noticed the old man's intrusion.

"I'm giving you a warning because I've known you a long time, Mark," said Ed. "Now, I was there at your wife's funeral back when that damn cancer got her. I was the one who kept gettin' my chicken scratch from you even when no one had any money. Remember? Well, what you're doin' here is wrong."

"Shut the hell up, Ed." Mark's face was only getting redder by the second.

"If we don't take this opportunity now, it might not ever make its way back in our lifetime."

"An opportunity to tear down the whole town? You must be thick in the head, Ed."

"Cassidy is going to do more than bring us jobs. He's going to make us one of the greatest towns in Texas, bring us back to a glory not yet seen by anyone in our lifetime. You should hear his plans for Jefferson, it's unbelievable."

"You best not believe it," said Mark. "Because ain't a single bit of it is ever going to happen."

"I'm only gonna tell you one more time."

"Mark," Tonya interjected again. "There is a time and a place. Trust me, this isn't it. You need to turn around and leave."

"I ain't leavin' until that man right there is lying dead on the floor."

Bam.

A single gunshot rang out, echoing off the original hardwood floors and throughout the tall ceilings. It was loud enough to leave every person inside with ringing ears, except for the one struck by the bullet.

Mark stood upright—with rigid knees locked—for a few seconds. Then his lifeless body collapsed to the floor.

A trail of smoke lifted into the air from the end of a barrel. Gunpowder remnants filled the air, followed by a metallic trace that filled the nostrils. Blood poured into the floorboards, creating a pool of red where Mark was lying face down. It was a gruesome death, not anything like the movies made it out to be. His body spasmed and jerked against the floor, his boots bouncing with clicks reminiscent of someone walking, until a final exhale sending the last breath of air he ever took back out into the world brought it all to an end.

Daniel gently pushed his pistol back into a holster tucked into his waistband. He never made eye contact, or said a word, he just took the life of the old man and didn't even think twice about it.

No one else in the room had the nerve to talk about what had just happened. Everyone just stared at the dead body bleeding out into the floor as if Mark would suddenly get back up and pretend nothing ever happened. Amid the hesitation, clapping came from a corner in the back. It was slow at first but picked up speed with each clap. The noise was foreign and unwanted, but for the man in black in the corner, it was a time to celebrate.

"Now *that* is how you put a stop to a problem." Cassidy finally spoke. "Daniel once again shows the leadership that has so often been missing from this community. That old man was a relic of a time we're all putting to rest. He simply was not needed."

"He was warned," said Tonya.

"You are exactly correct," Cassidy pointed a finger at the woman as he shouted. "He made his choice. Our good man, Daniel, was simply the one who delivered. For any of you who remained on the fence, you have just witnessed firsthand the consequences of standing in the way of progress. If history has taught us one thing, it's that progress will catch up to us all—one way or another."

"So, you're saying that's what we should do to that

family?" Ed commented before turning his attention to the dead body lying on the floor. "Seems awfully obvious."

"I'm saying Mark, in his current state, won't be a problem we have to worry about anymore. Isn't that much better than constantly looking over our shoulders? I would have to say so. If we are going to take control of the land that rightfully belongs to us, it really is the only solution that makes sense." Cassidy produced a deed to all the land he'd promised with those last words. It unfolded in his hand to showcase an official stamp on a letterhead directly from the state.

"We need guns," Daniel finally spoke again, barely even acknowledging what he'd just done. "We need more men."

"A man who knows what he wants is a man who gets what he wants," said Cassidy from the other side of the room this time. "As your newly installed emergency mayor, or whatever you want to call it, I lend my own endorsement to those two very prudent requests."

"I ain't afraid to do it myself," said Ed.

This time, a round of nods and agreement followed. Cassidy was eager to see his Wild Bunch grow, to see those who had no influence use what they had just been given to carry out even the most violent commands. All he had to do was ask.

There was only one problem. The people who filled the room, or at least those who were still alive in it, did not yet offer the numbers needed to commandeer an entire town. The population of Jefferson was pushing two thousand people. The handful standing before him were powerful enough to enact certain changes, but to take the land from beneath their feet, he needed every able mind.

"It can't be any single person," Daniel seemed to come back to life. "If the trigger is pulled by any of us, we'll all take the fall. The local sheriff's office is only gonna get us so far. If we go and gun some family down in the street, it's going national."

"I'm not following," this time, a man who had not spoken up before tried to make his voice heard. His name was Randy Tillman, he was an entrepreneur who owned several businesses in the downtown area. Typically soft-spoken and none too eager to put himself before his work, Randy was the kind of man who chose to wear blue-collar clothing like a canvas jacket and steel-toed boots, even though he'd never had so much as a callous on his hands. He was also the kind of man who stood to benefit a little more than the average person in Cassidy's proposal. "If you are asking all of us to kill these people, there ain't no sense in dragging it out. Let's do what's gotta be done and get on with what's been promised."

"You want to grab a pitchfork while you're at it?"

"We need a distraction," said Tonya.

"I just so happen to have an idea of my own. Well, less of an idea, more of a declaration." Cassidy stepped slowly toward the table surrounded by his followers.

He placed his palms on the cracked and weathered tabletop, leaned forward to place his weight on his hands, and focused his convincing gaze on each individual who dared bring their eyes to meet his own. There was both an inspiring and belittling air about him.

"I am going to give my acceptance speech, and I want the entire town to spectate. Men, women, and children, all arriving downtown to celebrate their new mayor and their new future," exclaimed Cassidy with his hands in the air before pointing his right index finger at each and every one of the people sitting at the table.

"And it will be *your* job to make it the talk of the town."

CHAPTER 21

The first bullet that almost took Thomas's life left a red line across his face as a warning of what could have been. His blood was thick, it swelled out of the gash like a sausage casing being squeezed out. Its trickle down his neck was a constant reminder of everything he'd ever lived for, everything he'd ever ran from, all coming to an end in the blink of an eye. The searing pain on his face was a physical manifestation of the screaming he was doing on the inside.

They'd been fighting for what felt like hours. His muscles burned, his legs were threatening to quit on him, and his lungs had already thrown in the towel. Their escape was short-lived. After leaving a trail of bodies on their way out of the gym, Cannon had taken Thomas and his sister to a pickup that looked like it had gone from one coast to the other, one time too many.

He never would have guessed the last thing he

could potentially do in life was hang out of a diesel truck window, firing a pistol at another vehicle while his sister did the same. The burning feeling across his cheek only fueled his fight, though.

Kaya had no close call, no unwanted opportunity to cross paths with her own fate in the world, and no blood of her own spilled in the fight so far. That wasn't to say that she didn't have her own problems. In fact, she was staring down a life-threatening problem that had to be dealt with. It forced her to consider her actions just the same, and it begged her attention with every squeeze of the trigger on her snub nose revolver.

She was running out of ammunition.

The pickup Tomas and Kaya rode in raced around the farm to market roads, darting around Jefferson going toward Caddo Lake. They were being followed by anyone who spotted them and fired at by every willing man who could squeeze a trigger. It was as if the entire town had come alive only to find a way to put them down.

"If we don't get to wherever you are trying to take us soon, there won't be any reason for all this fighting." Thomas was trying to reload his revolver as he spoke, dropping one bullet after another with trembling fingers, trying not to burn them any more than he had to on the burning cylinder.

"We need to get home," said Cannon.

"You know damn well we can't run from this."

"When did I say we were running? What we can't do is keep up the fight much longer without more ammo."

The cackle that came from Jim Bob sitting in the

middle of the back seat was frightening to Thomas and Kaya, only because they didn't truly know who the man was. This kind of fight was right up his alley, and he was waiting on pins and needles to get back into the fray.

"Are Mom and Dad waiting for us?" Kaya traded with her brother, giving him a chance to hang out the window to fire off more rounds while she reloaded.

"Haven't heard from them since I got into town."

She shot a glance over to Thomas who had heard the comment in between gunshots. She didn't expect to see he was more worried than her, but it was all over his face. A gush of emotion rushed to her face, and she fought with everything she had to push it back down. Her cheeks flushed, and her eyes glossed over. All she could do was focus on the indention in her thumb, where she pushed each new bullet down into the magazine, forcing the spring inside to compress further and further.

As the pines and oaks and yaupons gave way to bald cypress trees covered in the all-too-familiar sweeping Spanish moss, the truck began to pick up speed again. It was riddled with bullet holes but far from being on its last leg.

"Got another one!" Thomas shouted before blasting off another round.

"My turn!"

Jim Bob leaned over Kaya, disregarding her attempts to reload, and stuck a revolver out of the window. Without even looking back, he squeezed the trigger over and over, hollering something indistinguishable in a high-pitched voice. With five shots fired, he finally stopped, pushed his head out, squinted his eyes against the wind, and laughed once more.

"I forgot to count for windage!" he hollered to no one in particular.

The SUV creeping closer in the mirror swerved back and forth in the road, doing its best to avoid taking any bullets. Cannon kept the pickup racing in a straight line, though. If anyone in the back seat stood a chance at putting a bullet through anyone trying to stop them, he'd have to give them every advantage he could.

Bam.

"Got him!"

The SUV suddenly stopped swerving around and faded back away from the truck before rolling into a ditch. The last thing anyone inside the truck could see of the SUV was a trail of smoke rising from the crumpled hood.

Before anyone could take a breath, another car replaced the SUV, this time a maroon sedan, with an overly eager bearded man hanging out of the passenger side window holding an AR-15.

"Go! Go! Go!" Cathay shouted. It was too late, though.

Bullets rained down from the assault rifle, shattering the back glass and forcing everyone inside to duck for cover. A single bullet slammed into the touchscreen display on the dash, rendering it useless. This was the final straw for Cannon.

He slammed on the brakes and turned the steering wheel to the left almost hard enough to roll the truck in the process. Thomas and Kaya did everything they could just to stay inside the cabin, clawing for any handle or grip that promised to keep them alive. Jim Bob and Cathay had no reaction but instead used the few seconds of sliding on the road to flash a smile at one another. When the truck came to a stop, Cannon had his arm out the driver-side window and a look on his face that could stop a charging boar right in its tracks.

Bam.

The first shot spiderwebbed the windshield and sent a splatter of red across the inside of the sedan.

Bam.

The next shot slammed into the front end of the sedan, causing a domino effect that resulted in not just the car coming to a sudden stop but also causing the rear end to flip right over the top. When the car landed back on the pavement, all four tires were up in the air, and a sea of sparks enveloped anything that remained. Anyone who was once alive inside the vehicle was no longer sucking oxygen.

"Damn," said Tomas.

The diesel was left idling as everyone inside stared at the carnage they had left in their wake. The fight they found themselves in seemed to never end, but with no more ammunition to feed through their pistols, it was about to come to a screeching halt whether they wanted it to or not. They all listened to the motor whir beneath the hood for a moment longer before the urgency at hand hit them again.

Once again, they were not allowed to catch their breath. Before the truck could get turned in the right direction, another vehicle popped out from behind the overturned SUV and raced toward them. It was a blacked-out, early 2000s, three-quarter-ton truck, and it didn't take long to see whoever was driving it meant to bring their bodies in—just like all the rest.

"Anyone got anything in the chamber?" Cannon looked in the rearview mirror as he steered the truck back down the road.

"I'm out."

"I got nothing."

"You gave my gun away," Cathay quipped.

Before anyone had a chance to respond, their heads slammed into the back of the seats as the diesel engine roared to life. If they couldn't shoot their way out of the fight, it seemed Cannon was hell-bent on getting out of Dodge, even if it meant a high-speed chase. The screeching tires against the pavement lasted only a brief second before the speedometer hit fifty miles an hour, then seventy, then ninety. The curves were sharp, but the truck hugged every one of them with a satisfying surety.

The truck behind them didn't miss a beat. As they wound their way down back roads and hauled ass through a couple of stop signs that even drivers whose lives weren't on the line didn't bother to stop for, the distance between the trucks grew closer and closer. It was hardly an ideal route to outmaneuver another vehicle, but the drastic turns helped to stave off the occasional potshot from a gunhand in the truck behind them.

"We ain't gonna lose 'em like this," said Cathay, trying to get Cannon's attention.

"I'm open to ideas if y'all want to speak up."

"You could break-check them," suggested Thomas from the back seat.

Their truck banked left hard, and everyone inside slid in their seats. The trees rushed by their windows faster and faster, becoming blurs of brown and green mixed into an orange glow cast down from the sun, beginning its daily descent in the west. Any other day, it would have been a serene, picturesque portrait of a natural escape, but the chase they had found themselves in turned it into a hectic nightmare impossible to escape from.

In the rearview mirror, encroaching closer with every passing second, the men sent by Cassidy promised their demise by either bullet or wreckage. It was only a matter of time before the decision would be made for them. There was little else that could be done. The chase turned down a single lane paved decades ago, overtaken by the earth itself. The diesel thrived in such terrain, however. It howled in response to Cannon flooring the acceleration. A scream came from just behind them, followed by the clatter of more gunshots barely missing the cabin.

"What's the plan here?" Kaya asked anyone willing to speak up.

"I'm still working on it," said Cannon, white-knuckling the steering wheel as he fought to keep the truck on the dirt road.

"There's an old oilfield location coming up on the right, we could try to put their truck through something it can't make it out of."

"No chance at this speed. This is gonna come down to whoever makes the first mistake."

"Just slam on the brakes. See what happens."

"If we could get back on a highway, there's no way that ratty piece of shit could keep up."

The truck was devolving into a flurry of suggestions with none holding so much as a promise to get them out of their mess. Everyone inside knew their way around a gun well enough to get out of most situations, but with none left to spend, it was time to get creative. Their options were limited. Eventually, someone would have to make the decision on what to do, or else it would be made for them.

There was no turning back, and even the blazing sun in the distance told them it was now or never. Its flickering hues danced across the truck, desperately coming to end their fight, begging for an end that no one could prevent. It was a natural progression. Everyone inside listening to the diesel engine continue to roar could feel it in their bones.

One more hard turn to the right caught everyone but Cannon off guard, sending them scattering throughout the cabin. As everyone went scattering across the inside of the cabin, it wasn't until the passenger side tires began to lift off the dirt road that Cannon finally figured out not even he was in control of the truck anymore. Gravity had taken hold, and there was no stopping what was about to happen to all of them. Back roads had taken the lives of drunks and the absent-minded plenty of times before, but rarely had they ever put a stop to a high-speed chase. There was a first time for everything, though.

Glass shattering was the first thing Thomas felt on his side of the crash. An explosion of metal and broken glass rang out in his ears before he realized he had been thrown upside down. Jim Bob and Kaya tumbled on top of him, and he felt a crack in one of his fingers as their weight came down. Breathtaking pain became the least of his worries as the truck continued to thrash its way into the woods, far from the road.

The last thing Kaya remembered seeing was the sun in her passenger side window. She knew it wasn't supposed to be there, though. It was gone in the blink of an eye as the truck rolled, smashing into the ground and sending her body helplessly flying into anything bolted down. When she saw the sun once again shining its light down onto her, only to be immediately gone again, she realized there was nothing left to do but relinquish any hope of control of her own body.

When the truck finally came to a sudden stop, it miraculously landed once more on all four tires, but it stood no chance of driving again. The diesel engine no longer roared with life. Instead, a sputter of smoke and grinding of unknown metal told everyone left conscious all they needed to know about what had happened.

Grunts and groans were met with a single yelp from Cathay, who had just discovered a broken rib or two preventing her from taking a deep breath. Jim Bob was the only one who had yet to move a muscle. Cannon, meanwhile, still had both hands on the steering wheel, his knuckles bleeding from the impact of the glass.

"Son of a—"

An unexpected collision sent everyone inside flailing once again as the truck behind them rammed into the rear end of the diesel. It hit with enough force to cause Cannon's head to smack into the steering wheel right between his own two hands and send a steady stream of blood pouring down his face.

Thomas and Kaya had enough wits to brace themself against the seats in front of them, but poor Jim Bob went floundering right into the front windshield that had somehow remained intact. His back cracked against the glass, and he fell back into the laps of Cannon and Cathay, still unconscious.

"We gotta go!"

"Thomas! Now!"

Cannon's voice was muffled in Thomas's ears, but he could see Kaya's lips move and her hands motioning for him to get out of the truck as fast as he could. Without thinking, he followed her lead and fell out of the back seat into the grass and mud. Dirt still swirled into the air from their wreck.

Kaya had just enough time to drag Cathay by her arm to the other side of the truck to find Cannon and Thomas still struggling to pick themselves up. There was no time to collect Jim Bob who was still lying inside the cabin motionless. With mere seconds to regroup, they only managed to gather themselves into an easier target for the men who had chased them down.

The creaking of the vehicle door swinging open behind them should have been a call to arms. It only made their stomachs turn in knots, however, because they all knew there wasn't much of a fight to be had.

Thomas and Kaya had no quit in them, though. They stood to their feet, still dazed from the crash they'd just barely survived, and lifted their fists as if they stood a chance. Cannon did the same, with Cathay still fighting to get back to her feet, clutching her chest and taking short, rapid breaths.

The first man to step out of the truck behind them planted one worn work boot into the mud before falling out of the driver's seat and slamming the door behind them. He had a bottom lip packed full of snuff and a bewildered look in his eyes. When he raised his right hand to reveal the stainless-steel Beretta, his lips turned into a wicked smile.

Boom.

A red splatter painted the side of the truck that the man had been standing next to. His eyes rolled around before his knees trembled and gave way. When he collapsed to the ground, he released his grip on the pistol and face-planted into the dirt. Blood streamed down the black paint of the vehicle as Thomas, Kaya, Cannon, and Cathay watched in awe.

The passenger side door swung open next. Before anyone could come barreling out and finish what the driver had started. Another crack of a gunshot echoed through the woods surrounding them, and the inside of the cabin burst into a violent, bloody mist torn from the most gratuitous of Hollywood movies.

"I wasn't sure if they'd ever make it," said Cannon, nudging Thomas with his elbow.

"You knew?"

"You *didn't*?"

Kaya glanced over and let out a begrudging smirk. "We sure should've."

The back passenger side door clicked, hinting that someone was hiding inside after watching what had just happened to their buddies. It was as if the shooter watching over their confrontation already knew the third gunhand was inside, though. A rifle in the distance cried out once again. The gunshot echoed through the woods around them, warning anyone nearby of the fate that awaited them.

"Now he's just showing off," said Thomas, nudging Kaya with his elbow.

"You got 'em, Dad!" she screamed with her hands cupped around either side of her mouth. "You can come on out now!"

Davy popped his head up from behind the brush with a grin as big as Texas itself when he heard Kaya. The hunting rifle with worn wooden furniture and a 50mm scope mounted on top was slung over his shoulder, pointing at the sky. He raised a hand into the air like he was waving down a friend.

"Look at this guy," said Cathay, finally standing on her own two feet, speaking between shallow breaths.

Davy was sprinting through the woods, knees rising as high as his chest and the smile never leaving his face. It had been some time since he'd seen his whole family together, and the excitement was palpable even from a hundred yards away through the dense woods. It was an awkward few seconds watching him dart back and forth through the brush, trying to make his way to everyone, but it was well worth watching.

Kaya was searching the trees in their horizon, letting her eyes scan back and forth before she finally spoke up. "Where's Mom at?"

"I'm already here."

Rose was already standing behind them. Her words were soft and caring, but that didn't stop Thomas and Cannon from jumping in fright at her presence.

"What the—"

"How long have you been standing there, Mom?"

"Long enough," she answered.

Standing beneath swaths of sweeping moss blotting out orange rays of light, the family's reunion was far from something out of a storybook, but it was every bit as meaningful. Although Cathay had never met them, even she couldn't help but to fight back the tears forming either from the pain of her ribs or the sight of a family set to embrace one another for the first time in far too long.

Davy was just in time to hop in the group hug that had taken shape. He thrust himself onto them, stirring a much-needed laugh from the group and wrapping his arms around anyone he could get close enough to. The rifle was still slung over his shoulder, the men still lay lifeless in the dirt, and even though he had not been mentioned yet, Jim Bob still remained unconscious in the floorboard of the totaled diesel truck.

Rose was the first to break free of the group. She stepped back with a solemn look on her face and ensured she made eye contact with everyone standing in front of her. The team that had assembled before her, the family that had come back together, warmed her heart more than anything in the world she had experienced before. That feeling would not last long, though.

"Cassidy is preparing to accept the position of mayor as we speak," she said. "You all know what he has planned for us. His goal is not to build, but to destroy, and to return the land taken from the Caddo people back to what it once was. When that happens, it won't be Cassidy who comes for everything our family owns—it will be Coyote."

"No sense in standing around then," said Kaya.

"She's right," Thomas agreed. "Let's go kick his ass."

CHAPTER 22

There ain't much else in the world to be had that is more worthwhile than family. Arguments and grudges be damned, to have a family to stand beside and to fight for is the one thing in this world that will never fail to withstand even the harshest of storms bearing down. It is a gift too few are able to experience and even fewer are able to hold on to with all their being. When it comes down to it, family is the foundation in which we all take on the world head-on, for better or worse.

For the Hunter family, the fight always lurked behind every corner, waiting to catch them off guard, to crumble their already fragile foundation, and to turn them against one another by any means necessary. Not this time, though. This time, they were bringing the fight with them.

There were seven of them, of blood and not, banded together to put a stop to what most couldn't even bring themselves to believe was real. Thomas and Kaya led the way, with their parents Rose and Davy beside them, backed by the strength of the NHCP in Cannon, Cathay, and Jim Bob. When they finally made it to downtown Jefferson, they had only one goal—to crash the celebration of Cassidy.

It was a dull roar coming from more people than anyone expected to actually show up to the acceptance speech rushed together by Cassidy. There were posters scattered throughout town, clung to business doors and light posts, spreading word about the arrival of a new era of not just the beloved historic town, but of East Texas itself. Cassidy promised wealth and opportunity for even those who knew nothing of his existence, and he promised to deliver it on a silver platter sooner than anyone could imagine. Such extravagant ideas had attracted the attention of every class and creed, drawing them into the streets to hear what he had to say to kick off his new position of power.

"Sure glad y'all brought enough ammo for this mess," Jim Bob commented at the first sign of the crowd beginning to take shape. "Wish my headache would go away, though." He held up his right hand and gently touched a knot in the middle of his forehead the size of a baseball, casting a shadow over two black eyes that had formed since the crash.

"You are clearly still not thinkin' right," Cathay told him.

"Has he ever?" Cannon was alone in chuckling at his own joke.

"We aren't here to shoot up the whole town," said Kaya. "We just need to put a stop to Cassidy."

"Remember, that is no man," Thomas cut in. "We

are not dealing with anything of this world. We would be fools to think lead and gunpowder could stop it."

"First, we have to get to him," said Rose, always the realist.

"When we do find him, we have to find a way to protect the people who don't even know what they are involved in." Davy followed up without missing a beat. "If we don't, we're no better than those who have been trying to gun us down since Cassidy got here."

"And if we are able to do that, we have to figure out how to actually send Coyote out of this world and back to legend," said Cannon.

The group stood in silence, trying their best to come to terms with the task ahead of them. They knew what waited for them, what Cassidy had done to those closest to him, and the lengths they would go to in order to give their newfound leader not just the town of Jefferson but every acre owned by the Hunter family as well. They had already faced dozens of gunmen willing to do his deadly bidding, and there was more than likely plenty more that would stand in their way.

Although no one wanted to admit it, the likelihood of everyone coming out alive in the end wasn't in their favor. It was a reality they were unwilling to speak into existence but knew they would be forced to confront sooner or later. No matter how many guns were strapped to their hip, there was always one bullet destined to do the unthinkable.

"Well, are we gonna stand around and talk about doing it, or are we just gonna go out there and get it done?" Jim Bob was getting anxious to start the fight.

"You two go ahead, just like we talked," said Rose.

Thomas and Kaya glanced at each other, then took a step forward simultaneously without a word said between them. They had met in a patch of woods just off Canal Street, headed toward the downtown area. There were still a few blocks they would have to make their way through, but they knew it would be easier with just the two of them as opposed to the entire group.

"Y'all don't forget about us," said Thomas.

"What was the sign again?" Jim Bob asked.

"You'll know it when it happens."

With those words, Thomas and Kaya broke off from the group and made their way toward the crowd noise breaking through the trees. A single voice carried on the gentle breeze sweeping through, powered by a megaphone with static that followed every indecipherable sentence. As they trudged through the brush, keeping just out of line of the few houses dotted around the area, they had nothing left to talk about.

Thomas walked with his hand on his hip. His trusty .44 magnum revolver was right at home on his hip. There wasn't a single spot on his belt that hadn't been taken up by a circular speedloader filled with hollow point brass. Even if he had a dozen reloads, he knew even that wouldn't be enough to get him through what was to come, so he had taken the extra precaution to stuff each of his pockets with loose bullets just in case shit really hit the fan.

Kaya had become partial to the micro pistol she'd been given before. She kept it tucked away in her waistband, alongside two other polymer 9mm handguns with extra magazines hidden in her jeans and canvas jacket she borrowed from her mom.

Together, they probably carried a few hundred rounds, but that didn't stop the doubt from creeping in with every step closer to the downtown event they took. It took half an hour to get close enough to the crowd to hear the megaphone voice with enough clarity to make out the speech itself. When that happened, it took only a matter of seconds to know that it was Cassidy who was doing the talking.

"That man will no longer be with us," said Cassidy. "But his dying words to me were to push for a new era of prosperity for the people of Jefferson. My final words to the man who once served as your mayor were a promise, a promise to single-handedly usher in that vision, to deliver what has been taken from you."

"Do you hear this guy?" Kaya whispered.

"He'll say anything at this point," Thomas whispered back, keeping his voice low. "We need to get in there before whatever poison he gave to the people who chased us finds its way into the rest of the community. If he goes on too long, we'll never stand a chance."

"For too long, the people of East Texas have been overlooked, have been taken advantage of," Cassidy continued. "I alone will ensure that those elites down in Austin, those billionaires in their high rises in Houston, and those megalomaniacs out in Dallas no longer forsake your interests for their own. They will come crawling, and they will beg for even a sliver of the opportunity that is being laid at your feet."

The swell of the crowd at Cassidy's words sent

shivers down Thomas and Kaya's spines. There was no doubt Cassidy held sway with his words, but that was all he had. There were too few who could see what was truly happening, who could feel the rug being tugged at beneath their very feet. There were even fewer who knew the truth behind the land they stood upon, however. It was a simple fact, repeated all throughout the state of Texas and the greater nation. A constant struggle for what was not theirs to begin with was the basis for a tug-of-war where most had the luxury of becoming complacent in what they felt they were owed.

Cassidy had arrived at a moment of weakness for a community. They were willing to accept his lies, blinded by misled ambition, and he was all too eager to lead them astray. Thomas and Kaya would never be recognized for what had to be done, they would in fact be belittled and shunned if they were ever discovered. Taking away a promise believed by most is oftentimes worse than the lie that was sold to them.

Applause continued to drown out the words coming through Cassidy's megaphone. It was both a welcome and a disheartening moment for both of the siblings, who suddenly found themselves entering the back of the crowd just off Austin Street near the Big Cypress Bayou boat launch. There were hundreds of people lining the street and sidewalks, some with children propped up on their shoulders, most with cell phones lifted into the air, all capturing the same moments to stream online or simply to record what they believed to be a historic event.

"He's done something to those closest to him,"

Thomas said, keeping his eyes locked on the crowd ahead. "If all he's done is talk, then this might be the worst-case scenario for us. I think the whole damn county showed up."

"We need to get through this crowd," said Kaya. "If we don't stop him from speaking, we might find ourselves facing down the entire community here."

"Better get to it then."

Thomas took the first step, pushing aside two men who couldn't even be bothered to pay attention to them. It was the first of many, and with Kaya following closely behind, they wasted no time in shoving their way deeper and deeper into the fray. Cheers and laughter and applause surrounded them, contrasting the darkness laced into every word spoken by Cassidy.

Although they were unable to see the man speaking from his stage, his voice carried through the area with a curiously foul stench that neither Thomas nor Kaya could pinpoint. As they moved forward, they each grew more cautious of what they were about to do. For all they knew, Cassidy could have assumed they were already dead. They saw no security, no armed men hovering beside the crowd. They saw only the palpable excitement from the lives promised to be changed forever. It was a trap for more than just themselves, and Cassidy had laid it perfectly.

The walk down West Austin Street for several blocks took longer than they would have ever wanted. Pushing their way through the swarms of people caused only slight annoyance in those trying to pay attention to Cassidy's speech. It dragged on regardless, as the newly inducted mayor continued to make impossible promises made of the millions of dollars he would sink into their town. He claimed industry-wide revelations, from tourism to energy, and along with the new jobs, he promised new homes, new entertainment venues, and even groundbreaking infrastructure.

"I can't believe these people are buying all of this," Kaya remarked as she was shouldered by a man who refused to give up his spot in the crowd. "This whole thing is like a fever dream."

"They wouldn't if they were in their right minds. We have to remember that."

"I don't see how we can break everyone free of this."

"They won't like it, that's for damn sure."

A red brick tower topped with a green-colored roof soon rose in the distance, overlooking the people still fighting to get closer to the stage set up just in front of the building. It was the Jefferson Historical Museum, once utilized as a simple post office for the people of the county, but now distorted into a home to deliver the message of Cassidy's grand schemes to take what he believed was always his to begin with.

Thomas and Kaya both stopped dead in their tracks at the exact same time. They had finally come into view of the stage from which the voice amplified through the megaphone originated. It was lined with familiar faces, standing stoically with their arms behind their backs. There was a single flag, ten feet long, stretched across the front of the stage. It was not Old Glory or the Lone Star, it was something else entirely, not seen since the town was known as the fifth largest in the state. None of that was what caught their attention, though. It was what was standing behind the podium that froze them both.

There was not a man giving the speech. It was Coyote with snarling teeth and matted fur, standing up on its hind legs. Its eyes were hellish, its posture hunched, and its claws placed on either side of the podium.

"What the hell is going on here?" Kaya tried to make sense of what she was seeing. "Are we the only ones who are seeing this?"

"They are blinded. They can't see the truth behind what is speaking to them."

"How could they not?" She shook her head in disbelief.

"Jefferson will return to its former glory under my leadership." Coyote spoke with a voice that could never match the nightmarish creature standing at the megaphone. "Jefferson will stand as a testament to what was taken from you all, and I will be the one to ensure it is never stolen by such evil ever again."

Cheers broke out once again. A deafening roar threatened to swallow Thomas and Kaya whole as everyone standing in the street clapped and hollered and screamed for a man they didn't even know.

Coyote suddenly lifted a document high into the air and let it unfold three times to showcase an official stamp and signature to the crowd. It was the manufactured deed to the Hunter family land. "I will give you back what was taken, starting with hundreds of acres right in our own backyard to build our future upon. Grass will no longer grow in our streets!"

Somehow, the crowd managed to get even louder. They responded to Coyote's unfounded claim with a boisterous ovation.

"I've seen enough," said Thomas.

"You think everyone is in position?"

"They better be. We ain't waiting any longer for this to get worse."

"I'm ready when you are."

Thomas looked over at Kaya and gave her a grateful smile. They'd come a long way to be at this moment, standing side by side together in the middle of a fight for what neither of them had ever been so eager to claim as their own. There was so much they had to say to each other, so much that deserved to be said to each other, but there was no time for even a single word to be spoken.

Thomas raised his right hand into the air, gripping the same trusted .44 magnum revolver that had saved him from countless dire situations in the past and squeezed the trigger.

Bam.

The revolver spewed flame and a deafening blast that made every ear in a ten-foot radius ring. Their response was delayed, but when the shock of what had just happened settled in, their focus on the man they came to know as Cassidy was broken, and they did exactly what any sane, rational person would do in such a situation.

They ran.

It was chaos, plain and simple. Only a handful of people knew where the gunshot had even come from. Those that did sprinted in the opposite direction, but the rest could only scatter like ants facing a boot coming down on top of them. The scene unfolded just as Thomas and Kaya had figured it would, leaving Cassidy's acceptance speech in ruin and exposing Coyote for what he truly was.

The trickster knew when it had lost the advantage, however. Amid the panic of people fleeing for their lives, screaming, climbing over one another, and desperately clamoring for an escape they feared would never come, Coyote slipped away from the stage without uttering another sentence.

"Where did he go? Where is he?" Kaya was hollering as she moved closer and closer to where he had been. "We can't lose him, Thomas!"

"This isn't good. We need to find him—before he finds us."

"We need to tell everybody to start looking."

"How?" Thomas scanned the mayhem they had unleashed upon downtown Jefferson. He had shot his gun to save the lives of those unaware of what they were being roped into, but he had fully expected to kick off a firefight where he could easily put down the one who had caused it all to begin with. He was now learning that things would not be so simple.

Kaya had already pushed her cell phone to the side of her head and started running. It was difficult to make out what she was saying, but her face was red and her eyes were wild.

"He's gone! He's gone!" she shouted over and over into the phone.

Thomas was right behind her. By the time they made it to the stage, there was no one left. The flag hanging above, adorned with a riverboat against a backdrop of pines, was the only thing which remained unscathed. They both immediately searched the area, shoving their way through scared attendees still trying to find their escape, finding not even a trace of where Coyote had gone.

Thomas and Kaya met again behind the stage, only to share a concerned look. Their gaze drifted to either side of one another, where they saw one armed man after another make themselves visible at nearly every vantage point in downtown Jefferson. They all held rifles, some with scopes already trained on them, aiming down from rooftops, balconies, and even from behind alleyways of the historic buildings.

They had hoped to ambush Coyote when he least expected it, but from the way things had just played out, they realized they had only sprung a deadly trap set just for them.

CHAPTER 23

To the untrained bystander, it was only firecrackers popping off in downtown Jefferson, complete with sporadic bright flashes of light and unplanned crackles of sparks and debris. By all rights, it should have been a joyous celebration filled with colorful explosions from shells fired into the air with black powder. The lingering smoke should have been broken only by the cheers of a picture-perfect show taking place in the sky above. The people should have been able to come together beneath a brilliant display in recognition of a brighter future filled with prosperity and untapped potential.

They were not fireworks, though. Thomas and Kaya had been thrust directly into the firefight they had hoped to gain the upper hand in only a few fleeting moments before. They were not watching beautiful presentations of blues, greens, yellows, reds, and white light dancing in the sky above. They were faced with muzzle flashes and bullets ricocheting only a few feet from their heads.

Pop. Pop. Pop.

"Gotta find cover!" Thomas yelled between bullets striking the pavement all around him.

Pop. Pop. Pop.

"Just go, dammit! I'm right behind you!"

Without looking, Thomas ran toward the closest building he could find. He didn't know if there were more gunhands hidden away inside or if he was leading Kaya to a fate worse than what they were running from, but he went anyway. The double doors burst open, nearly shattering the glass as they slammed into the walls. Despite the gunshots still ringing out all outside, they couldn't help but find the humor in the business they had broken into for temporary safety.

Ceramic statues, aging books, and furniture as old as the grandparents Thomas and Kaya never met filled the inside of the antique store. It was musty inside, and the floors creaked and groaned with every step. As the bullets popped off just outside at random, Thomas and Kaya both shook their heads in disbelief. They knew help was on the way, it would only be a matter of time before the cavalry would arrive and they could push back.

They had to do something while they waited, though. From the top floor of the antique store, Thomas and Kaya found a few beat-up wooden desks to flip over and tuck themselves behind. It wasn't much, but it was enough to allow them both to get to work.

Thomas popped his head up first. Across the street, on a balcony looking right into where they were hiding, were three men, two with rifles aimed in their direction and one already firing off rounds at random from a pistol he didn't have the sense to even hold properly. Thomas gripped the revolver in two hands, finding the sweet spot with indentions worn into the handle, and lined up the sights. The first squeeze of the trigger sent shockwaves inside the store and left his ears humming, but one of the men across from them was already having a much worse time.

As Thomas watched him grab at his chest and fail miserably to stop the bleeding from the bullet hole that had just torn through him, Kaya wasted no time in taking advantage of the lull in the gunshots that came as a result. Three rounds popped off in an instant, their blasts broken only by her own screams to fuel the fight. Two bullets sunk into another man holding a rifle, and he collapsed immediately.

With one man already dead and another well on his way, the third decided to make a break for it. He'd abandoned any hope of cover fire, much less landing a lucky shot on either of the siblings, but his retreat only provided an opportunity for Thomas to ensure he could never come back to put a bullet in their back.

"Time to move," he called out to Kaya.

"On it."

They broke their cover and made their way back downstairs, hoping to find their family in the middle of the firefight to save their ass. Unfortunately, they only made it a few steps out onto the sidewalk before bullets started raining down all around them again.

After an unexpected shriek, Kaya took off running, just barely getting ahead of a trail of lead bouncing off the pavement. Thomas knew better than to follow this time. Instead, he lifted his revolver and cycled through the rest of the cylinder to give cover to his sister.

Whenever the hammer came down with an empty *thunk*, he knew it was his turn to move. He could see Kaya posted behind a brick column with dust flying all around her from bullets striking only inches away from her. It looked like she had even been nice enough to save him a spot next to her. When he took the first step out into the open, the cover she'd found seemed a whole lot further away, though.

Pop. Pop.

"Keep running!" Kaya shouted.

Pop. Pop. Pop.

"Where the *hell* are they?"

"Doesn't matter! Just go!"

The chaos in downtown Jefferson seemed to only get worse. Around every corner, on top of every roof, was yet another man holding a gun, ready to put them down. Cassidy had enlisted more people than either of them could have anticipated. As much as they didn't want to shoot their way through the misled followers, it was apparent the situation they'd found themselves in was kill or be killed.

Sweat started to drip into Thomas's eyes by the time he threw himself against the column next to Kaya. He wiped furiously at his brow, already feeling the effects of exhaustion setting in. He had no choice but to keep fighting, though.

Kaya may not have been as well equipped as her brother, but from the cover she had hidden herself behind, she was doing most of the dirty work already. Every squeeze of the trigger put her one step closer to finding Coyote and putting a stop to their family's onslaught. She'd tagged three gunhands by the time her brother joined her side. Even still, she was nowhere near done.

As the bullets continued to fly between Cassidy's men and the siblings, there was a

rhythm that began to take shape. Thomas and Kaya would pop their heads out, unleash a few rounds, and draw the fire of more men then they could stave off in the process. Every couple of minutes, they would crouch deeper into cover and go through the motions of a reload.

For Thomas, it meant dropping the cylinder to his .44 magnum and letting the thumb-sized brass fall to the pavement. They clinked against the ground as they bounced, like bits of spent gold dropping at his feet. The speed loaders he brought allowed him to drop all six new rounds in with just a single motion, and with a flick of his wrist, he was back in the fight.

Kaya, however, only possessed a couple of magazines for her polymer striker-fired pistols. After she'd burned through the spares tucked away inside her pockets, she was forced to drop a magazine individually, fumble for spare rounds and jam them into the magazine. It was slower, more tedious, but the capacity kept her in the fight longer.

When they were both reloaded, downtown

Jefferson once again turned into a warzone filled with gunfire and frantic screams of the wounded trying their best to escape with their lives. Thomas and Kaya had no time to speak. They fired off round after round, only aiming when given the time. They had downed several men, but for every one that fell lifeless to the ground, two more seemed to take their place.

Once more stuck reloading her magazines, Kaya was given the chance to get her bearings to see if their family had yet arrived. She was disheartened to see only those out to kill them and none there to save them. She jammed bullet after bullet down into the magazine, compressing the spring harder and harder each time.

It was an inexplicable feeling that made her turn around to check the antique store they had just come from. Something inside her felt an undeniable urge to simply turn her head, and when she did, she saw two gangly-looking men clutching a pistol in their hands aimed right at them.

There were only fifty feet separating them. Thomas was already in a fight for his life with his booming .44 magnum making its presence felt every few seconds. There was no time to call for help, so she did the only thing her body knew to do. Kaya jammed the half-loaded magazine into the grip of the pistol, flicked the slide release and punched her fists out.

The first bullet she fired missed, splitting the two men charging right at her. They didn't hesitate to keep moving, firing two rounds that sunk into the brick column just beside her. It was the last volley of gunfire they would exchange. Kaya took the opportunity to steady her sights, exhale, and squeeze the trigger twice.

Their bodies fell almost simultaneously, thrown backward as if smacked in the chest with a sledgehammer. Their boots went up into the air as the back of their heads collided with the pavement. They were lifeless, betrayed by the twitching of their hands, no longer able to grasp the guns they sought to kill her and her brother with moments before.

"Time to move!" she hollered, never breaking her concentration on the two men lying on the sidewalk in front of her.

"Where?" Thomas shouted back between gunshots.

"Anywhere but here!"

Thomas turned his head, just barely avoiding another bullet chipping away at the brick he was hiding behind. Dust and debris blew into the air, giving him only a few seconds to make a break for it. This time, Kaya was right behind him.

Just as they started to run, what was once sporadic gunfire coming across the street turned into a dizzying spray of blasts from what seemed like every caliber imaginable. The .300 Win Mag rifle could be recognized from anywhere in the downtown area, releasing a force that Thomas and Kaya felt in their chest with every shot that trailed just behind them. Hitting a moving target was nothing like putting a hesitant shot placed just behind the shoulder of a whitetail standing still, staring at the shooter.

Just when they thought it couldn't get any worse, they heard a cacophony of firearms rise up in every direction around them. It was deafening and disorientating. Yet, despite downtown Jefferson turning into the worst depiction of the Wild West, none of the bullets came anywhere near Thomas and Kaya.

They both stopped in their tracks, their eyes wide and alert, searching for who was responsible, hoping more than anything, the tide had finally turned in their favor. Thomas was the first to spot Cannon, and his face lit up. By the time Kaya noticed Cathay at his side, they were cheering like they'd just won the lottery.

Cannon moved like a gunslinger torn from the silver screen of the 1960s spaghetti era. With a revolver in each hand, he fired a round with each step forward, moving right through the middle of the street from where they had just come from. His cowboy hat was pulled down low over his eyes and his worn boots firm in his stride. Cathay was right at his back, slamming down a lever action to chamber a new round in between each shot from Cannon's dual pistols. Her tight, curly hair formed a glorious halo around her head and her shoulder was sturdy enough to not so much as flinch against the kick of the rifle. They were in sync, moved in rhythm, and never missed a shot.

Armed followers of Cassidy fell left and right to their bullets, but they were only the decoys. Davy had taken to the high ground of a rooftop directly above where Thomas and Kaya had stopped, and his trusted hunting rifle, the same .30-30 that had been used long ago to save his wife, Rose, was hard at work.

"About damn time!" Thomas screamed at the top of his lungs.

"We better not let them have all the fun," Kaya said before returning fire at a man brave enough to show his face from the balcony across the street. "If we don't find Coyote, this whole mess will be for nothing. We need to keep pushing."

"He's hiding somewhere, we just gotta figure out where."

"There." Kaya used the barrel of her pistol to point out the Jefferson Historical Museum towering over them in the distance.

"It's as good as any place."

"He's there. I know it."

With Cannon and Cathay at their back and Davy on top of the building, Thomas and Kaya felt more confident than ever to keep charging ahead. The streets were clear enough to finally step foot onto, as Cassidy's men had felt the momentum shift and started to show themselves for who they truly were—cowards.

"We're missing Mom and the crazy one," Kaya commented as they walked without firing a single shot for the first time in what felt like hours, even though it had only been minutes since the hectic fight had broken out.

"They're here," said Thomas. "Just a matter of time."

The Jefferson Historical Museum stood like a castle at the end of the street. Thomas and Kaya may not have had an army to storm its gates, but they had family. What was once a raucous commotion of gunfire and death had now dwindled to only sparing shots aimed at the few men with enough backbone to face an untimely end for no gain.

Cannon had broken off to chase down a man twice his size attempting to get the jump on them. Thomas could see the two running down an alley out of the corner of his eye. Just as the follower of Cassidy turned to fire a shot, Cannon let one of his revolvers cry out, and the would-be killer buckled to the ground.

Kaya walked alongside her brother toward the tower, refusing to stop even when a man popped his head up on top of the hotel building separated by a small open lot from the old post office they were walking toward. The hotel was built in the 1850s, and this was far from the first shootout it had been caught in the middle of, but the man hoping to gain the upper hand would soon become just another victim lost in time, fated to become another ghoulish presence in the downtown area's famous ghost tour. The camouflage cap on his head offered no protection from the deadly aim by Cathay and her lever action.

The gunshots continued to echo throughout the downtown area as Thomas and Cathay walked along a red-paved brick road lined with lush trees and a white picket fence. Its scenic appearance contrasted the grim atmosphere their violent outburst had created.

"We need to make this quick," said Thomas.

"I actually agree with you there."

"Got enough ammo? I doubt he's alone in there."

"I got enough," said Kaya, patting her hip where the pistol was tucked inside a nearly hidden holster.

"I wish you'd listen to me for once," a familiar voice came from behind them. "You aren't going to shoot your way out of this one."

"Mom?" Kaya turned around as quickly as her body would allow and threw herself onto Rose, surprising even herself.

"We can't forget what we are dealing with," she said without so much as raising her hands. Kaya took a step back and joined Thomas in an awkward silence as they waited for her to continue. "Legend cannot be put down by bullets or by any force born of this world. It cannot be reasoned with, nor can it be rid of its intention. It is the one thing we have that simply is."

"You always solved your problems with a bullet," said Thomas. "Why can't we?"

"It's not the same. Coyote cannot be killed."

"Only one way to find out." Thomas put his hand on his hip, just above the revolver tucked into the leather holster he'd carried for most of his life. "You can come with us, but I won't guarantee anything."

Thomas turned to continue walking toward the red brick building with a tower at its center, as if beckoned beyond his own control.

Kaya made a face at her mom, showing her split feelings between Thomas's ambition and Rose's intuition with contorted lips and a nod of her head. Before she turned to follow her brother into the building, she gave her mom a slight wink which proved an unspoken understanding between them.

"Wait up," Kaya called out. "You ain't going in there alone."

"Hurry up. This all ends today, one way or another."

The sun had reached the highest point in the sky for the day, shrouded in rolling clouds threatening a storm yet to make itself known. It was an inevitable reckoning promised on the horizon, one that could never be overcome, only withstood. Surrounded by nature's own means of washing away the past, Thomas and Kaya faced the winds of change blowing against their every step.

The glass door leading into the building, once known as a post office, was a reminder that it had been turned into a museum for out-of-town tourists, people who would not call Jefferson home but wanted to experience the feeling regardless. It was Thomas and Kaya who stood in front of the door first, but when it came down to it, neither could make the first move to enter.

As luck would have it, that wasn't a choice they would be forced to make. Just as Rose stepped up behind them and placed her hands on either of the shoulders, the glass on the door shattered into a thousand pieces through a hail of bullets being fired from inside the building. All three ducked to the ground to avoid the incoming fire, hoping not to catch a stray bullet on their way down.

With each of their faces planted firmly into the red brick-paved road, a high-pitched call came out from behind them, answering the spray of gunshots with an unforgettable battle cry. It was filled with misplaced confidence, a sort of unadulterated bravado achieved only through years of sustaining consecutive traumatic brain injuries with little to no medical attention. It was Jim Bob, and he was at a dead sprint.

"Yeeeeeee haaaaaaw!"

CHAPTER 24

A life running toward danger is more often than not, a life well spent. At the very least, it's more eventful. Boredom is a feeling reserved only for those without the nerve to face down the worst of their fears, to lay claim to what belongs to them. It is a feeling meant for those content watching their own lives pass them by without so much as lifting a finger. Risk isn't something most become familiar with, but for those who know the feeling of a life well lived, it has a way of becoming second nature.

Jim Bob always was one who was willing to meet danger head on. He had been his whole life. From being the first to cling to the backside of a sheep to go mutton busting as a child to being the first one let out of a chute on the back of a bull too rank to ride, Jim Bob fought the urge to be placated by empty ventures as long as he could remember. If there was an opportunity to haul ass headfirst with guns blazing—he'd damn sure be the man to take it on.

Such an opportunity had presented itself to get inside the Jefferson Historical Museum, where Cassidy and whoever was left alive had holed up inside. Their promises to bring back the former glory days of the old town had resulted in one of the largest shootouts East Texas had ever been home to, but it wasn't over yet.

Jim Bob knew who was behind him. He had grown to become family members with Cannon and Cathay on their exploits with the NHCP, and he knew what it meant for their line of work to continue. Sometimes, running right at a hailstorm of bullets was just in the job description. When he went charging by Rose and her kids, Thomas and Kaya, he knew it was better for him to go in first. With the same revolvers clutched in either fist that had gotten him out of plenty of worse situations before already firing inside the building, he was as sure-footed as he ever was.

It was this headstrong willingness to do what most would be too afraid of that both Thomas and Kaya took notice of. It would also be what they remembered Jim Bob most for. As Cannon and Cathay continued the fight at their backs, ensuring a stray shot never snuck by, Jim Bob left them all behind.

Thomas and Kaya could only stand by and watch while the old bullfighter most would call stupid, but they would call brave, made a last stand at the doorway and emptied a dozen rounds from his matching revolvers while catching half as many bullets in his own chest. Both barrels were still smoking by the time he hit his knees, and not a single bullet was left to be fired from inside the building. The crunching of the glass as his body collapsed to the ground would be something neither of them would ever forget. Before they could push forward to see the fight to its bitter end, they could hear the frantic calls from those who weren't there to stand by his side in the final moments.

"Jim Bob!" Cannon's voice echoed through the downtown area.

"You stupid son of a bitch!" Cathay screeched. "You weren't supposed to die like that! I told you!"

Rose didn't pay them any attention. She took a step forward, urging Thomas and Kaya to do the same. "He won't die for nothing," she said.

"Wait," Thomas answered. He grabbed Kaya by the arm and leaned closer to his sister. "This has to be us. No one else needs to be dyin' on our behalf."

Without saying anything else, Kaya planted her right boot and took off toward the front door of the building. It was all the agreement Thomas needed. Instinctively, he ran right beside her, letting tunnel vision set in as they climbed less than ten concrete steps to reach the shattered front glass door still swinging on a green frame filled with bullet holes.

They had to step over the body of a man they had only just started to consider their friend before he saved their lives. When they saw just the seven dead men he'd gunned down in his final few seconds, their perspective on him was forever changed. There was no choice but to put an end to everything right then and there. Anything less would be disrespectful to Jim Bob's sacrifice.

Thomas held his .44 magnum six-shooter all too

ready to dispense the only brand of justice it knew. Every step over a lifeless body was harder than the last. His tunnel vision had set fire to his concentration. It was impossible to steady his breathing, much less his thoughts about what he'd do when he laid eyes on Coyote. The sheer thought of the deadly tricks that were wielded against the city, only to turn them on his family, was all the fuel he needed to squeeze the trigger one more time.

Kaya knew exactly what had to be done. She knew Coyote was a trickster, and she knew they had fallen prey to a tale as old as time. Her pistol was gripped every bit as tight in her fist, but it was aimed low, unable to fire at a moment's notice. Her thoughts drifted to what her mom had said back at the cave, about the winds of death that had blown against their faces for so very long.

They were on the same path their ancestors had been on, that much they both understood. Only one of the siblings understood that they were also on the same path of the ones their ancestors fought against, though. They were trapped in a vicious cycle of death where the only thing that ever mattered was what the family owned, what land they stood on—not who was standing on it.

The inside of the Jefferson Historical Museum was packed with antiquities and artifacts from a time long ago. There were paintings and sculptures, dioramas and instruments, and a guided walkway for tourists to follow a predesigned route through the history protected by the old post office. Despite so many areas to explore where Coyote could be hiding from them, it was inside the Moseley Gallery, named from the highest bidder who led to the museum's opening, that a single voice beckoned them.

"Are you ready to accept what you could never change?" Cassidy asked of them before anyone could lay eyes on him. "Have you at long last come to your senses to do what none of these people ever could?"

"I'll show you what you can accept, you piece of —" Thomas rushed around the corner, his revolver aiming for a man he knew was standing just inside the room. When his jaw fell slack, Kaya joined him by his side.

Although it was his voice, standing in front of them was not the man who came to be known as Cassidy—it was Coyote. Snarling fangs protruded from a cloud of shadows in the corner with eyes that could cut right through any bullet fired in their direction. Coyote stood on all fours, with claws digging into the hardwood floors.

"I should kill you right here," said Thomas. "You'd thank me for doing it, too, compared to what the people coming in behind us are gonna do to you."

Coyote did not respond.

"I should kill you for what you've done to this town, and what you had planned to do to our damn family. You'd deserve the bullet. Even if you aren't worth the lead it would cost me."

Coyote only snarled, baring fangs that hung down far enough to pierce through each of them in an instant. There was a screech that echoed in the room, caused by Coyote's claws digging deeper into the boards of the floor. As each talon-sized claw scraped against the wood, the voice of Cassidy once again entered the room.

"Do you not do what you will with what is yours?"

"The hell is that supposed to mean?" Thomas was wagging his revolver with every word.

"You and I are no different."

Just then, Thomas noticed the bloody eagle feather separating the two from Coyote. It dripped red, lying in a puddle twice the size of the feather itself. It was spinning in circles at random, like the needle of a compass unable to find the magnetic field needed to point the way. With so much death caused by their own hands, she knew the eagle feather in its current state was not an indicator of what was to come, but an indictment on what they had just done.

He turned to look at his sister. When their eyes met and he realized what had become of their family, he could see the understanding pouring from Kaya.

She knew at that very moment her brother had reached the same conclusion she had. It was one that their mom had likely always known but could never bring herself to confront. The world of fighting back the forces of time and nature alongside her all-too-eager husband, Davy, and of protecting what she cared about most through its rewards, was everything. There was no room for what needed to happen.

Rose and Davy were the first to enter the Moseley Gallery. Cannon and Cathay were only seconds behind them. Each one stopped dead in their tracks when they saw what was happening. Their eyes were wide. No words came to mind. Thomas and Kaya had dropped their pistols to the ground and were holding their hands up with empty palms facing out. It wasn't a fight they had walked into—it was an agreement.

"You can have all of it. It's yours," said Kaya. "Every acre."

"We won't fight you anymore," said Thomas.

They took a step closer to Coyote. Against snarling fangs dripping with saliva, a dull, rumbling growl emanating from the depths of unfiltered blackness, they approached without any trace of fear to be found.

"That's what you wanted, right? You wanted the land taken from your people, the land Jefferson itself was built on. You wanted ours, too, right?" Kaya urged.

"We all know that is exactly what this was all about. Damn near every generation of our family has fought for what is ours," Thomas said. "We're tired."

"We won't kill for your games."

"You're gonna have to find something else to fill your crooked time."

They each walked closer with each sentence, backing Coyote farther and farther back into the corner of the room as they approached. Shadows crept back as Coyote gently placed one paw after another backward, refusing to let out so much as a whisper. Crazed eyes darted back and forth between Thomas and Kaya before a heavy panting set in. Coyote was out of moves, out of tricks to be pulled.

The Hunter family had long stood as a fabled message for anyone who dared to cross their paths. But as with any story worth telling, there was always a lesson to be learned. The winds of death made permanent in this world by the creature standing before the family had chapped their lips and burned their faces for too long. Such a force of nature could not be put to rest. You can either take cover from its impact or change your direction, put the wind at your back and let it carry you onto an entirely new path.

Thomas and Kaya were the ones to change. They had fought every bit as hard as those who came before them, but they had dedicated their lives to a different kind of future.

"The entire city of Jefferson plus the thousand and more acres we own surrounding it, from Caddo Lake to Ore City, from Lodi to Darco, and even more around the country. It's all yours."

Kaya pushed ahead, coming within inches of Coyote, who had no more room to retreat from.

"We'll have the deed written, signed, and stamped before the week is through."

Thomas followed his sister's lead, closing the distance between him and Coyote to only inches.

"The fight is over."

"We won't spill more blood for you."

The deranged look in Coyote's eyes would be keeping them up at night for years to come. A putrid scent stung their nostrils. The creature's back hunched over, and a horrid cough exposed its rib cage, first only briefly, then again and again and again. Thomas and Kaya stood firm. They watched Coyote hack and choke on something they could not quite make out, lodged deep in its throat.

With a sudden splatter of saliva mixed with blood, Coyote spat out a folded piece of parchment, still soaking wet. It sat alone in a pool of spit only a few inches away from the siblings, but both refused to take the time to bend down and find out what it was for themselves.

Only a few seconds ticked by before Coyote's strange display continued. This time, the creature reared its head back and pushed itself up into the air. It stood on spindly hind legs, making Coyote no less than seven feet in height, even with a hunched back, as if the creature would double over at any moment.

Thomas and Kaya moved together, as if they had shared unspoken words not only with each other, but with Coyote as well. They stepped aside, eyes locked on Coyote's, and watched as the creature hesitantly walked right by the two of them.

Rose and Davy followed their lead, with Cannon and Cathay forcing themselves to do the same, doing their best to keep their fingers as far from the trigger of their firearms that they still clung to so tightly.

It was an odd moment they each found themselves in. Watching a legend come to life leave their presence without a word, after so much had been said and so much blood had been spilled, it almost seemed unfathomable. But it happened. Coyote walked out of Jefferson Historical Museum, out of the fight to take over everything they'd known, and in doing so, walked right out of their lives.

"How did you know that would work?" Thomas stared at the empty door leaving the bullet-riddled building they'd found themselves in as he spoke.

"Coyote may be a trickster, but we were the ones fooling ourselves," said Kaya.

Rose was the first to walk up to them. She didn't

say anything, but the faintest trace of a smile washed over her face, and she gently leaned in to hug them both.

"For generations, we've all believed the only thing to be done was to win the fight, only so that we could finally stop all the killing, all the struggling. It just so happened that would become the one thing all of us were incapable of doing. If the fight ever came to a stop, we would seek one out. I believe we were being given an opportunity to finally do something different in the world."

"We just didn't know how to accept it," Thomas finished for her.

"We shouldn't be destroying towns only to protect the land we exploit by the truckload for our own gain," said Kaya.

"You do realize the Nations Heritage & Preservation organization is funded entirely by this family, right? What we do isn't destruction, and that ain't what Jim Bob gave his whole life for," Cannon interjected, still unable to grasp the last few minutes.

"It's not enough," said Rose.

"It is a start, though," Thomas placed his hand on his mom's shoulder. "Coyote was just showing the way. There ain't much in this world we haven't had to be dragged kicking and screaming into. Why should this be any different?"

Davy was practically beaming with pride. Despite knowing damn well no one still standing inside the Moseley Gallery beneath dozens of paintings and surrounded by dozens more antiquities was in the mood for a group hug, he made it happen anyway. Not even Cathay could escape his embrace.

As the family huddled together amid the chaos, doing their best to wrap their heads around what had just happened, as well as all the work that still had to be done, Thomas was the first to break free. He walked slowly to the folded paper still lying in a puddle of saliva and picked it up.

Kaya was right behind him before he could finish unfolding it. His hands were wet with spit and stuck to the corners of the paper pinched between his fingers. Together, they read the handwritten document as it continued to unfold.

"It's the deed to our land," said Thomas as his eyes scanned the handwriting that came from a time he didn't recognize. "It's signed by Henry Hunter."

"It was never going to be taken from us," Kaya said.

CHAPTER 25

"Y ou think it's really over?"

"As much as anything could be, I guess. No guarantees in this world."

"Things do have a way of coming back when they are least expected. Especially when it comes to this family."

"You have a point there."

"It's over for now. That's all that really matters."

There was a pause in the conversation unfolding at the dinner table. It was made of oak, as heavy as everyone's weight at the table combined, and had stood through time as a testament of what it meant to bring the family together. There was enough seating for ten people, but only six were there to pull up a seat.

Thomas and Kaya were a chair apart on one side. Cannon and Cathay had taken the other side, sitting closer together than they ever had. Rose and Davy took their assumed seats at the heads of the table.

They were talking easily over a homemade meal that looked more like a buffet than a dinner. There was Salisbury steak for Thomas, frybread and fixings for Kaya, burgers for Cannon and Cathay, and enough fried fish for Rose and Davy to share with everyone there. It wasn't a celebration, though.

For the first time in as long as Rose and Davy could remember, the family was together, but it was bittersweet. There was an empty seat at the table where there shouldn't be one. The loss of their friend Jim Bob hung heavy over the table. They were grieving, doing their best to eat their feelings after what they had just experienced.

The Hunter family was never known to waste much time either, however. They had already started planning for the future they knew was up to them to create. Spread out in the middle of the table was a map filled with architectural drawings and price tags labeled over everything. The map was as long as the table and filled with red lines, notes, and scribbles from an all-nighter of planning.

"You sure this is gonna work?" Cathay said between bites of a burger smashed between her fingers. "Looks expensive."

"This is just downtown Jefferson," said Kaya. "It's a blueprint we can tailor to every town who truly wants our help."

"Jefferson is just the start. This revitalization plan is economically sustainable and its impact will be felt by every person. We're gonna take this plan to as many forgotten towns of Texas as possible," explained Thomas.

"With enough money to pull it off for years to come," said Rose with a smirk.

"I have to ask one more time," Davy interjected.

"Yes, Davy," Rose cut him off. "We have plenty to spare."

"It's gonna double the size of the Caddo Lake State Park."

"It's a small tract," Thomas answered. "It won't hurt us none."

"If we're gonna pull this off, it has to be bigger than anyone expects," Kaya said. "People are gonna come after us, but we're gonna know how they work, because we were them for too long. We sat back and let the world pass us by, hoarding whatever we could get our hands on and killing anyone who got in our way."

"No more hiding," Thomas agreed in his own way.

"I can think of a few people at the NHCP who are gonna love this," said Cannon, glancing over at Cathay. "There's a lot we can do with ten times the budget we're used to."

Davy was the first to put his napkin over his plate. He pushed back from the table and let the screeching of the chair against the hardwood floors signal his intent. Before he could turn away, the clattering of everyone else following his lead filled the dining room of the old Hunter home. Silverware hitting the table and sighs from overeating took the place of any conversation. Thomas and Kaya stood next, as Cannon gave Cathay a hand to help her from her seat. Rose watched stoically, unable to find the right words for what she was feeling.

As was so often the case, it was Davy who knew what to say at just the right time. He took the words she was desperately looking for and uttered a single sentence to capture exactly what she was feeling. It was a simple phrase, a common sentiment they'd stuck to quite often in their time together. He'd been a man of action since they met so many years ago and helped to secure the very future they were planning together. He'd instilled this same sentiment in their children and helped to inspire Cannon in the process. It was only four words, but it was exactly what they all needed to hear.

"Let's get to work," he said.

A LOOK AT RIDIN' WITH THE PACK VOLUME TWO

A WESTERN SHORT STORY COLLECTION

Saddle up and venture into the wild frontier of the American West with *Ridin' with the Pack: Volume Two*, a gripping anthology that celebrates the timeless allure of Western storytelling.

From rodeo circuits to deadly secrets buried in Montana grasslands, each story unravels a vivid tale of survival, justice, and redemption.

Readers will navigate the trials of a young veteran fighting to keep his family's ranch, a man haunted by his past on a quest for vengeance, a former outlaw struggling to leave behind his crooked life, and a Norse adventurer facing his fate on the shores of a newly established colony. Alongside these gripping tales, the search for a legendary pirate treasure tears apart a man's life, a family legacy built on grit and fortitude is threatened by an old frontier rivalry, and the desperate choices of a woman stranded in Dodge City lead to unexpected salvation.

In every tale, the spirit of the West shines through, each story unraveling like a chapter in the epic saga of the untamed frontier—where freedom, grit, and the unyielding quest for justice resonate like the timeless strains of a cowboy's humble heart.

Written by a talented crew of seasoned veterans and rising stars, Ridin' with the Pack: Volume Two *showcases the enduring spirit of the classic Western tale.*

AVAILABLE NOW

ABOUT THE AUTHOR

Nicholas Osborn is a second-generation ranch owner and storyteller from the heart of deep East Texas. With a career encompassing everything from entertainment marketing to news journalism over the last decade, he has studied the craft of authentic storytelling and honed his writing throughout the years.

Nicholas's debut series aims to mythologize the pineywoods he grew up in and welcome readers to a new chapter of modern Westerns, born of the tall tales that helped shape the genre. His writing is inspired by the history of the Lone Star State, the greater United States, and the larger-than-life heroes, gunslingers, and "black hats" that gave us the myth of the west we know and love today.

Nicholas is an owner at his family's limousin cattle ranch and first-time father with his wife of over ten years. As one of multiple generations of his family working on the Red Rock Limousin Ranch, Nicholas has put his experience into words as an author with a passion to keep timeless Western culture alive and thriving for today's readers.